DRAGON REDEEMER

WORLD OF ALUVIA, BOOK THREE

DRAGON REDEEMER

WORLD OF ALUVIA, BOOK THREE

AMY BEARCE

SECOND EDITION

Snowy Wings
PUBLISHING

This is a work of fiction. All of the characters, organizations, and events portrayed in this novel are products of the author's imagination or used fictitiously.

DRAGON REDEEMER

World of Aluvia, Book 3
Published by Snowy Wings Publishing
www.snowywingspublishing.com
© 2017 **Amy Bearce**
http://www.amybearce.com
Cover Art and interior art by **Amalia Chitulescu**
http://ameliethe.deviantart.com
Map by Ricky Gunawan
Licensed from Whampa LLC

The Library of Congress has cataloged the 2017 original editions as follows:
ISBN 978-1-62007-975-1 (ebook)
ISBN 978-1-62007-976-8 (paperback)
Second Edition 2019
ISBN 978-1-948661-18-8 (ebook)
ISBN 978-1-948661-19-5 (paperback)

To Mom and Dad

SAOL SEA
Twilight Realm
Midnight Realm
KEEPER HANNON'S COTTAGE
SIERRA'S JOURNEY
SKYCLAD MOUNTAINS
THE ABYSS
PORT BELTANE
PORT MABON
COVENSTEAD
CAILETTE DESERT
MORGANCE MERFOLK VILLAGE
Shallow Realm
PORT OSTARA
LYR ANCIENT CITY OF THE MERFOLK
PORT IONA
TUATHAIL
LITHA FISHING VILLAGE
OBAN FISHING VILLAGE
THE ICE-LOCKED LANDS
SOUTHERN SEA
ALUVIA
N

Nellwyn Brennan's tremendous skill with a sword was matched only by her love for it. The sword never lied. Its justice was clear and sharp. It cleaved through tangled knots of conflict and could most often solve any problem—but not these days, which really got under Nell's skin.

The late afternoon sun slanted through the forest glade as she hacked and swung her longsword at an invisible, unknown opponent. In years past, she envisioned Jack while training, sometimes Donovan, and often Jasper, all members of the old Flight crew she used to work with. These days, there were no real fights and the sword was no longer her future, but training still soothed her. Corbin, her beloved, didn't understand, so Nell practiced alone, just her and the lilting song of a woodlark among the towering red oaks and bristly pine trees.

She spun, ducked, and twirled. A stranger would see a lethal dance, but one beautiful in its stark strength. People might not describe Nell as pretty, with her white-blonde hair pulled back in a plain braid and her intimidating blue-eyed stare, but when she moved, she was *arresting*.

Her sides heaving, Nell finally lowered her blade. The sun dropped below the treetops, vanquished like her imaginary foes.

By all the stars, she missed a good sword fight. But life went on.

As if to drive that fact home, her mother called out, "Time for dinner!"

With a sigh, Nell sheathed her sword and went to clean up, thankful it hadn't been her turn to cook. She might be nineteen now, but unlike most girls her age, running a household wasn't one of her ambitions.

After a quiet dinner with her family, Nell kissed her sisters goodnight—though they were almost too old for such things—and then curled upon the cot in the living room where she stayed these days. Her sword lay within easy reach on the floor. Old habits died hard.

She traced the dagger stashed under her pillow with one fingertip before she flipped onto her back and closed her eyes. Even though her hands twitched to hold the dagger—more comforting to Nell than any worn baby blanket had ever been—she left it alone. She took some deep breaths to calm herself instead. Despite the late afternoon training session, sleep danced in and out of reach until slumber finally carried her away.

Sometime in the blackness of the night, the front door creaked. Nell's eyes flashed open. The noise made the barest whisper of sound, but that was enough. A sliver of moonlight fell on the floor, and a tall shadow, a man's, stretched across it. An invader. In her home. She hadn't even heard the person pick the lock, which suggested someone with skill—and practice.

It had been at least a year since the last intruder threatened her, trying to silence the message of Aluvia's continued need for healing. Tonight, the shadow of a knife extended from the intruder's hand. That was new.

She slid her own sharp dagger out from under the pillow.

Nell might not be an enforcer anymore, but that didn't mean she could relax her guard. Jack's death hadn't destroyed the dark alchemist's crew entirely. It only meant a new ringleader had moved to the top, like fat rising in a broth.

The leather-bound hilt felt comfortable in her hand, an old friend. Nell tensed her muscles.

The door inched open another crack. The toes of a pair of dark green boots poked through the shadows.

Fury burst through her. She knew those boots. Jasper. He was the worst, skulking around Nell when she worked for the crew, like a rat sniffing for its next meal.

One of Jasper's untied boot strings coiled along the floor. Her lips curled with disgust. Always sloppy. Nell focused her anger into a fine point, the intensity that gave her such skill with a blade for one so young.

He took one step closer and crossed firmly into the home. That was enough.

Instinct and training kicked in hard. Nell whirled out of bed as silent as an owl swooping on its quarry. She snatched up the long blade on the floor along the way. By the time her spin ended half a heartbeat later, she'd knocked his weapon to the floor. In one quick motion, she pressed her sword tip to his throat and her dagger at his chest. His pulse throbbed in the hollow of his neck, right next to the steel threatening to cut it.

"Nell!" Jasper gasped, voice strangled. Trembling, he threw his hands up in surrender.

She didn't care that she stood in her nightclothes, soft linen pants and a baggy shirt. It didn't matter that her hair hung loose down her back. She might look like a young, vulnerable girl, but appearances could be deceiving. She prayed the prophetic voice wouldn't take over her body now. Whenever the mysterious voice issued another warning for Aluvia, it spoke through Nell without any apparent concern over what she was doing in that moment. It had led to some awkward situations, but this time, it could be deadly. "Come to kill me this time, Jasper? You couldn't take me then. You can't beat me now."

"I came with a message. That's all. I swear."

"As if I care what you have to say."

"You'll care about this. There's a new boss in town. He either wants you on his side or out of the way. You and your devoted followers."

"Never going to happen."

His voice went softer, wheedling. "Nell, listen. Come with me, tonight. I'll convince him to assign you to my crew. You're too good to waste."

She snorted.

His expression darkened. "You never knew a good thing when you saw it." He lowered his arms, and Nell let him, though her own weapons remained ready.

"My life's full of good things now," she said.

"You mean your little fairy keeper? I reckon there's a reason you aren't even hand-fasted yet. He's not enough for someone like you." Jasper side stepped and tilted his head as if examining her.

She moved slightly to block him. "Like me?"

"Someone born with a sword in her hand."

The hands in question suddenly felt icy. "You're just jealous." Her tangled reasons for not formally committing to Corbin were nothing she'd talk about to this scum.

He glared. "Don't flatter yourself. Just saying it's a waste, you running around like some messenger of peace. War's coming soon. It'll be too late for you then. The new boss is gonna tame the dragons, stop 'em from setting the mountains afire. He's promised they'll carry us into battle to conquer Aluvia. Can you imagine anything better? You're a fighter, not some fairy fanatic."

"Your new boss sounds like a madman, and I haven't been with Jack's crew in a long, long time." She kept her voice low in hopes of not waking her family.

"You mean *my* crew."

She paused. "I'd say congratulations, but I wouldn't mean it. Why even offer me a spot on your crew? You said your new leader wants me gone."

"Or a part of the action. Whichever works. All the crews have a bigger purpose now, Nell. You could too."

"There's nothing bigger than saving Aluvia's future. You need to leave me alone. I've got a new life now."

"That new life's about to come crashing down around your shoulders." He licked his lips and gave a ghost of a smile.

"Is that so?"

She scanned Jasper more closely, alarms going off inside her.

He looked older than his thirty years—life in a crew aged a body faster than most—but his eyes had a new confidence to them. His shoulders were low and relaxed, his hands no longer trembled. His pose hinted at something. Something he thought would win him this fight.

He laughed, low. The hair on the back of Nell's neck stood on end.

Jasper said, "Things are about to get real exciting 'round these parts, girl. You don't want to come? Fine, but at least hand over some nectar. Then I'll do my best to keep everything peaceful, just between friends. I'll tell the Dragon you're on our side after all. I'm in tight with him."

"The Dragon?"

"That's the name he's taken, our new boss. Down in the Ice-Locked Lands. You've never seen someone with such power."

"Are you threatening me?"

"I'm warning you. You'll regret leaving the crew when you're not seen as a savior anymore. The people won't love you forever. The Dragon will rule Aluvia, and you'll have nothing." He snickered.

She pressed the sword harder against his skin, until a thin line of blood welled up along the base of his neck. "Who are you kidding? The people don't want a ruler. We have no kings."

"We might not have a king—yet—but you're practically a queen, ain't you? Always so above everyone, so high and mighty is our little Nellwyn, people always chanting your name. Not good enough for the likes of us, eh? But you'll see. We'll have magic like you can't imagine, and we'll use it as we see fit."

She scowled and delivered a swift kick to his shin

without lowering her weapons. Being barefoot reduced the impact, though, and she gritted her teeth when he laughed. She said, "Without the fairies, without Flight, you're nothing. Haven't you gotten the message?"

"Just biding our time. The new boss promised us all the nectar we want once he takes over the ports and controls the keepers. Until then, there's always poisons to sell, lovie. And there's bigger things than that yet to come, much bigger. But oh yes..." Jasper hissed and leaned harder into the sword point.

Blood flowed thicker, black in the dim light, dripping down his neck. He switched to a falsetto voice and fluttered his stubby eyelashes at her. "The fancy prophetess gets to tell us what to do and not do, take and not take. Stop taking nectar! Stop making Flight! Save the world!"

Nell's hands didn't waver, despite the heat that rushed across her cheeks. Luckily, the darkness of the room concealed her flush. She kept the sword steady but pushed the dagger harder against his chest.

"I'm not the one saying it." She still didn't know who was using her body as a messenger, but she sure wished it would let her in on the secret—or get out.

"That's not what I hear. Never saw you for a fairy fanatic, Nell. Now you're courted by one and best friends with another."

"Flight was death in a vial. You know it; we all knew

it. But the crew still sold it. You can't get any lower than that."

Jasper ran a finger along the dagger at his chest. "If people were stupid enough to take it, they got what they deserved."

"Ah, such compassion." Nell sneered at him. "Really, your kindness is heartwarming. Just shut up and keep your hands down, Jasper."

He dropped his hands but whispered, "Don't you miss being an enforcer? I bet you do. The power. The fear. The rush."

"No." Her voice was flat.

"Liar. You can take the girl out of the fight, but you can't take the fight out of the girl."

"The job was just a means to an end."

"What end, little girl?"

Her lips tightened. So did her throat, but she kept her voice steady. "Survival."

"The Dragon's coming. You want to survive, you'd better prepare to bow. It'll be too late to fight."

"It's never too late to fight."

Nell reversed her hold on the sword and knocked Jasper hard on the head with its pommel. He went down with a thump. She sighed at the unconscious slob of a man at her feet.

Her unwanted gift of prophecy might have brought her instant fame and gifts of food and supplies from fervent believers, but it couldn't deliver her from her past. It was a good thing she'd kept her fighting skills in practice. It sounded like she might need her sword yet, if this man named the Dragon was even drawing rats like Jasper to him. Rats only went where there was something to feed on.

She'd heard nothing of this man, though. Jasper could be exaggerating.

That was a real possibility, liar that he was. She discounted the bit about dragons immediately. Those weren't the kind of beasts that submitted to being ridden like donkeys. Either Jasper was trying to intimidate her, or the so-called Dragon was making impossible promises to impress people. But even so, some kind of battle could be coming. Sounded like it.

A battle. One she'd have every right to fight, in self-defense, prophetic voice or no prophetic voice. For a woman now sworn to bring healing and peace, such a battle was a rare opportunity. Her heart sped up, and she allowed herself a small smile.

She didn't miss the pain or the fear of the fight. But the sheer physical beauty of battle, the competitive nature of two forces clashing, oh yes. The singing slice of a sword was like nothing else. Almost perfection. A duel meant the best person won, fair and clear.

And the best was usually her.

There was none of that for her now. There were few honorable ways to earn coin as a fighter in Aluvia, almost none for a woman. And for someone touched by magic? Exactly zero. The voice that spoke through her needed to be heard; the people wanted a prophetess, not a warrior. She understood, even if she didn't like it.

She hoped for things to settle down one of these days: for the voice to move on and for a chance at... normal. Whatever that would be. But normal young women didn't have unconscious dark alchemists in their living room in the middle of the night.

Nell sighed again, tucked her dagger and his into the waistband of her pants, and got to work dragging Jasper out of the living room by his heels. His head bumped along the worn wood floor and clunked over the short ledge of the door to the ground outside. She didn't try to be gentle.

The grass made pulling him easier, but even with muscles kept strong from her workouts, she grunted with the effort of maneuvering his heavy weight. Propping him up like an oversized doll, she quickly tied Jasper to the last fence post along the edge of their land, making sure to knot the rope extra tight. Considering his rise to leadership, she added a chain around him and secured it with a padlock, the key kept on her belt loop. Then she tossed a sign around his neck that read: Never threaten Nell Brennan. Forty gold coins for his release.

Smirking, she backed up to admire her work. His cronies would find him in the morning. Just like the others over the years. By all of Aluvia, would they never learn?

A broken bone or two would send a stronger message, of course. Maybe even a simple dislocation would be enough to deter future break-ins. But she shook her head. She could hardly redeem her past violence by striking out against all who opposed her now.

Even if it would be incredibly satisfying.

A hard gust of wind whipped her loose hair across her face. She shivered, her smirk fading. It had been a mild summer, but tonight felt different. Colder than it should be. The sky held a deep darkness, despite the tiny pinpricks of stars glittering as if chipped from ice. Trees moaned in the wind, shaking their arms full of green leaves that looked black in the shadows.

Nell curled her bare toes against the chill of the damp grass and took a step back. A thin branch cracked beneath her foot, and a loud flapping among the trees had her reaching for her dagger. Wings flashed briefly, silhouetted against the glow of the moon, only to be lost in the blackness above.

Just a bird. She rolled her eyes at her own fancies. She'd let Jasper play with her mind. He was just trying to scare her. She'd never admit it may have worked. A little.

With one last look at the unconscious man in her yard, Nell went inside, rubbing her arms. Goose bumps crawled down her legs. She told herself it was just the chill of the air. But inside, a small part of her, a part she ruthlessly ignored, knew the truth. Change was coming.

CHAPTER TWO

Sleep was now further away than the Skyclad Mountains, with sunrise at least two hours off, Nell guessed. If Corbin were here, he'd be able to distract her with funny stories or tales of mystical creatures of legend. But alone, her mind spun endlessly. With a sigh, Nell flipped her legs over the side of her cot and stretched. She might as well get some work done.

She dressed for the day, tucked her dagger into its sheath at her waist, and headed off to the work cabin. She'd put off making more poultices for too long. When she had a spare second in her busy days, Nell tended to reach for a sword, not a pestle and mortar. Weapons work had always come easily to her, remarkably so. It had been her family's saving grace.

Before his death, Nell's father had worked for the crew, despite his distaste for it. After he was gone, Nell and her mother had struggled for a full year to make ends meet, but they were failing miserably. Her three baby sisters were fading away faster than shadows at dusk. Nell looked at her options and had seen only one.

She'd been all of nine when she'd first become a runner for Jack. Sierra Quinn, Jack's fairy keeper daughter, loathed Nell from the moment she'd sworn her oath to him. It wasn't like Nell had wanted to be a criminal, but business was business, and life went on. She'd learned how to fight, how to survive. She'd hated parts of the job, loved others, but she did all of it well.

Her life now had little in common with those days. On her way to the cabin, Nell passed by the unconscious Jasper and clunked him on the head one more time with her dagger's hilt. Just to be safe. He wouldn't be waking up any time soon. When he did, he'd have a headache meaner than a manticore.

Her work cabin, just inside the woods at the edge of their yard, held all the supplies given to her by Corbin's mother, a healer. Nell didn't plan on only being a conduit for a prophetic voice all her life. Healing was at least a steady and sure profession that offered a balance to the pain and hurt she'd caused in her previous profession as an enforcer. The work didn't hold the same sizzle and spark as a sword duel, but honestly, what did?

Nell had already moved herself and her family from Tuathail to Covenstead to live among Corbin's family and the other healers. They were some of the few people the alchemist crews didn't like to antagonize, so she felt safe leaving her family behind while she traveled.

Tonight, bright moonlight guided her to the door. Inside, a simple wooden table with two stools filled the center of the little room. Jars of dark liquids, glistening powders, and fragrant spices filled a tall shelf along the back wall, with empty bowls and vials along the bottom.

She took a deep breath of the potent scent of herbs hanging from the ceiling—rosemary, basil, thyme, even stinging nettle. Every herb had a purpose, as long as one had the knowledge to use it properly. No sense trying to heal a cut by slathering stinging nettle in it, but when mixed into a good broth, stinging nettle could cure a stomachache in a hurry. Just as she wouldn't use her longsword to pick a lock, she wouldn't use just any herb for a potion. In all situations, effectiveness was a matter of using the right tool for the right job.

She often felt like the magic of Aluvia had picked the wrong tool when it had chosen her to speak with the voice of prophecy.

What did she know of magic? Or healing?

She was the girl who mastered edged weapons faster than anyone their village had ever seen. So fast, in fact, she was chosen to study with a renowned sword master in Port Iona when she was just fourteen. Shane McConnel had been one of the few men in her life who seemed to believe she could do anything she put her mind to.

Admittedly, it had stung at first that her new trainer turned out to be a mere ten years older than she was, but Nell worked hard. By the time she'd left Port Iona, Shane had been the only one there to avoid defeat at her hands, with his own signature move she could never deflect or duplicate. She'd returned to Jack with her already impressive skills sharpened to a fine point. Now those skills had been left to rust like a dagger left in the rain.

Frustration begged to be let out. She grabbed a batch of rosemary. The pestle and mortar would get a good work out.

Braiding her hair out of the way, she stood at the sturdy table, too restless to sit. She slammed the stone pestle against the plant, and its piney scent blossomed from the mortar. She pounded and scraped the rosemary's firm needles and woodsy stalks until nothing remained but a green paste in the bowl. Her muscles burned pleasantly, but she had more frustration to spare.

Jasper. That troll of a man. Coming into her home, sneaking around the healing homestead. And this ridiculous Dragon person. What kind of a name was that, anyway?

As she stewed, she grabbed a palmful of wild dandelions and pulled out her boline knife and a cutting board. *Whack, whack, whack*, she chopped off the heads of the dandelions with gruesome gusto and sliced the stalks as finely as the hairs of a unicorn's mane.

In theory, Nell could sell this burn salve for a decent amount in the ports. The reality was people would swarm her as usual—not for her poultices, but for a message from the mysterious voice that used her as a prophetess. She preached messages of equality with magical creatures and proper stewardship of their world. No one saw her as a healer. They didn't even see her as a fighter anymore. She was more like... entertainment.

She gritted her teeth and sliced harder, leaving rows cut into the wood board. She hissed. Now she'd have to sand down the whole board. She lightened her pressure but kept cutting.

By the time she finished, pale morning light streamed through the window. She gently placed the jar on the shelf. Her gaze traced the large collection of empty containers waiting for her, and guilt prickled.

She was simply on the road too often to focus on healing skills. Everyone looked to her to provide answers on thorny questions about the ethics of magic because the voice lived within her. No wonder she'd put off returning to the ports, even while knowing she should be out among the people with messages for them. Sensing the troubles of Aluvia could send Nell into a trance faster than a dagger could drop a thief. She didn't want to lead a magical revolution. She didn't want to hold this voice anymore. She'd done enough, given up enough.

When would her future begin? She scowled.

It already has...

The words were so soft, almost like she'd heard them only in her mind.

Sweat sprung on her brow, and Nell turned to face the empty room. The whisper sounded familiar, but the prophetic voice always took her over to speak to a specific audience. Always. Yet she knew nothing had come from her lips.

She was alone in the cabin. Wasn't she? She took a steadying breath, looking for anywhere someone could hide. She yanked her dagger from its sheath. It didn't feel like enough. Her boline knife lay out of reach on the other side of the table, but she snatched up the heavy pestle with her free hand. She'd protected herself with less in times past.

A knock at the door made her jump, and she gave a disgusted snort at her unease. Enemies didn't knock. *Get a hold of yourself, Nell.* Exhaustion had played a trick on her.

"Nell, are you in there?"

There was no mistaking that voice, at least.

"Corbin!" She set down the pestle, feeling foolish for her fear. Returning her dagger to its sheath, she swung open the door and smiled with relief. "Good morning!"

His dark eyes twinkled with cheer even in the low morning light as he held out her favorite treat.

She laughed. "Chocolate truffles for breakfast?"

"You work plenty hard to enjoy a treat now and then."

"Thank you." She gently laid one hand along the warm brown skin of his cheek. She'd never get over how thoughtful he was.

Corbin leaned against the doorframe and said, "I saw your guest. He's going to wake your family if you don't make him hush soon. Why don't you let us help you when they do this? Or tell the elders?"

Good thing he'd brought her chocolate. It would keep her mood sweeter. She turned to give her work table a quick wipe down. "I can handle the crew by myself just fine, Corbin."

"Of course you can, but that doesn't mean you should have to. These days, you're living a life of peace. Why are you still so hard on yourself?"

"I'm not." She rolled her eyes.

"Then why do you look so tired? Couldn't sleep?" He stepped close and ran his hand down her braid.

She gave a noncommittal shrug, carefully storing each tool where it belonged.

"Maybe give yourself a break, and skip a day of sword practice or two while you're at it. I know you enjoy it, but you have little enough time to study healing as it is. You need to rest more."

She frowned. "I've got to be able to defend myself, and besides, yes, I do enjoy it."

She'd said so a hundred times before. He was proud of her for her skill and strength, but as time had passed, his desire for her to stop working with the sword had grown—in the name of peace and her own safety. His increasing concern made Nell secretly glad they had agreed to delay hand-fasting until life was more settled. What if he got worse in his judgment over the years?

His jaw set in a way that screamed stubbornness. "There's got to be a better way to protect yourself. Maybe the port elders would intervene if you told them. The sword brings division and danger. You're a healer now."

She huffed through her nose like a bull.

A sword can be a bearer of peace... came that voice again, floating through her mind like a cloud on a breeze.

She startled, and a shiver ran down her back. "Did you hear anything?"

"Only Jasper moaning over there like he's been bit by a naga. The big baby."

She must just be imagining things from lack of sleep. Corbin's disdain made her smile. It was strangely cute when the kindest boy on Aluvia was irritated.

"Well, I did give him a hard knock on the head. Or two. I'm surprised he's already waking up. Just goes to show his head must be made of wood."

He laughed. Good. She didn't want to fight. Not with Corbin anyway. Satisfied with the cabin's condition, she closed the door behind them.

"Have a truffle," she said, closing the conversation just as firmly.

He rolled his eyes at her before gulping the chocolate in a single bite. That boy was a walking stomach.

They set off in companionable silence to the house, though Nell was still thinking through their conversation. At least Sierra understood the situation. She was a powerful fairy keeper, but a realist, the one who'd led the quest that brought Corbin and Nell together.

Nell had thought after four years, she and Corbin would understand each other seamlessly. Instead, as time passed and the sense of crisis lessened, their differences loomed larger. They still shared the same love of music and stories. He'd taught her to dance; she'd taught him to cook, a sorely needed skill on his part. They laughed together and cared deeply for each other. But he was so happy she was training as a healer that he seemed to forget she was many other things, too. Or could be, if the voice inside her would let her go.

"We should go check on Jasper, don't you think?" Corbin angled his face to the sun. "Ought to be breakfast time soon. Truffles will only carry me so far."

She lifted one eyebrow. "His face may put off your appetite."

"Nothing puts off this appetite." He patted his flat stomach.

She laughed. On impulse, she added, "Please, don't worry. I have to show the crew I haven't lost my edge. A message from the elders' clerks won't get through to them. But their leader humiliated? They'll remember that."

They crossed the small yard, keeping a close eye on the slowly waking crew leader. A redbird called from a tree nearby, its cheerful whistle at odds with talk of threats and danger.

"Exactly. Don't you see? It's like baiting a dragon."

Nell shook her head. "I can handle it. But Jasper did say something strange, about dragons, actually. He said there's a new man leading the crews, called the Dragon, out in the Ice-Locked Lands. He supposedly wants to tame the dragons and use them to take over the ports somehow."

Corbin snorted. "Good luck with that. Not even fauns can control adult dragons anymore."

"Jasper seems to believe it's true. He said this Dragon sent him to recruit or kill me."

"Jasper tried to kill you?" Corbin's voice rose.

Nell clenched her hands. She hadn't meant to let that news out. "And failed."

Corbin visibly swallowed down more objections. "I understand self-defense is important for you. But why invite more violence in your life than you have to? I worry for you."

"And I am thankful for that. I am. But I chose the crew and got myself into their mess, and now I'll have to get myself out of it."

"You're not alone anymore, Nell. Don't forget that, okay?"

Corbin entwined their fingers, and a bloom of pleasure rushed through her. It still seemed like a dream that they could be a couple. But here he was, handsome fairy keeper Corbin, holding her hand and not one of the ribbon-bedecked girls who used to follow him everywhere.

Jasper's moans shifted to curses. He was definitely awake.

"His men will be around soon to pay his ransom, I think," Corbin said, eyeing Jasper. "Maybe we can get more information about this Dragon person."

"He's probably lying, just trying to scare me into working for him again. As if I'd ever."

"He doesn't know you at all if he thought he'd catch you napping." Corbin winked at her.

She smiled back, but then frowned as Jasper's curses became more creative, practically coloring the sky purple.

"You want the girls to hear that kind of talk?" Corbin asked.

Her mother's singing lilted from the open kitchen window. The girls would be up soon.

Nell said, "Let me grab my bow. Then we'll deal with him."

Inside, the scent of oats and cinnamon filled the air. Nell's mother had already set the table for breakfast.

"Morning, Ms. Brennan."

Her mother smiled back. "Staying for breakfast, I hope, Corbin? Fairy keepers need their strength, don't they now?"

"Thank you, ma'am. No one makes breakfast like you."

The clatter of the dishes barely covered the threats issuing from Jasper's mouth.

Nell hoped Jasper's men would come soon. It wasn't the first time she'd left someone trussed up. They no doubt knew what his errand was last night, and when he didn't return with morning's light, they would draw the correct conclusion.

From the corner of the living room, she grabbed her bow and tossed her quiver across her back. She added her sword to her belt, though an attack in broad daylight was unlikely. As Jasper had grumpily pointed out, Nell was still seen as a savior by most people in the region—she, Sierra, and Corbin were heroes who had started the process of healing the weary land. Even their friends Micah, Phoebe, and Tristan were well-known and respected.

Other fairy keepers had taken up the message throughout the ports, and the last earthquake had been over two years ago. Dragons and firebirds were awake again after their long hibernation, and though the dragons were admittedly creating some chaos, it was contained mostly to the mountains. The merfolk were finally healed, too, and they were trading once more with humans on a small scale, which helped both groups. Only the dark alchemists loudly protested the restrictions on magical supplies, but they'd been furious since the voice made its first appearance through Nell anyway.

She needed to hurry and get rid of Jasper before her mother noticed—

"Is that what I think it is, out there tied to a post? I thought we were past all that non-sense." Nell's mother stood in the doorway, hands on her hips, worry creasing her brow.

Too late.

"Nothing for you to fret over." Nell kissed her mother on the cheek, wishing she could remove the worry lines from her face. The older woman's hands were reddened and calloused from the lye used in her laundry business. She'd endured a hard life.

Nell squared her shoulders. "I can deal with it. Don't worry."

She and Corbin sauntered across the front lawn to

Jasper, who continued to name-call and issue vile threats.

"Shut up, you," Corbin said, pointing his finger at Jasper.

Nell barely suppressed a grin. Corbin didn't do threatening very well, but that was part of his charm.

She waited until Jasper paused for breath. "If you wake my sisters, your price goes up to fifty. And I might not unlock you until evening. You really want people to see you like this?"

"You'll regret this, girly. You should have changed your mind while you could. Traitors don't last, not even ones with special 'voices.' You won't stand against the Dragon."

Something stirred within her. No. Not now. Not in front of *him*.

CHAPTER THREE

Nell tried to walk away, but she was rooted to the ground as if she'd turned into a statue. She had just a moment to hope Jasper's men didn't arrive in time to see her like this. Then the voice took over.

The arrival of the prophetic voice was like being shoved underwater. The world grew softened and muted, like through a watery veil. The feeling was familiar, one she used to even enjoy but now sometimes hated. The low, resonate woman's voice filled her mind just before the words slipped from her lips.

"Aluvia's healing nears completion but could be thwarted still. The land has spoken. The sea has risen. But a new threat comes to destroy. This enemy has a heart encased in ice and plans to spread his frozen wasteland across all the world. Go

to the Ice-Locked Lands, where the fiery sword of Aluvia can be awakened to bring full healing to all. Balance must be restored before his strength reaches the sky."

"Where in the Ice-Locked Lands?" Corbin asked, his words rushed.

Sometimes the voice would respond, sometimes it wouldn't. Nell didn't have the presence of mind to wonder which it would be.

"The fiery sword waits at the tallest mountain peak for the hand that can claim it. It's held by the Tree of Life. You know the stories, fairy keeper. Listen to them." Nell's throat relaxed, and she gasped.

Jasper's olive complexion had turned sallow. "What on Aluvia did that mean?"

"It means we're in trouble," Corbin muttered, steadying Nell with a firm grasp under her elbows.

"H-h-her eyes..." Jasper's own eyes bugged out of his head.

Corbin had a rather smug smile on his face. "Beautiful, aren't they?"

Nell's eyes went black as night when she prophesied, or so she'd been told. People also said she all but glowed when the magic overtook her, thanks to the many fairy queen stings she received four years ago. Given reactions like Jasper's, she was glad she couldn't see the changes.

With another deep breath, Nell came fully back to

herself. She felt alone in her mind again—but the voice could arrive to steal her body and drop life-changing messages on them at any moment. She never forgot.

"That's one big reason why you don't want me back, even if I wanted to come. Which I don't. So leave me alone." She backed away from Jasper. The voice left her weakened, empty like a washed out shell on the beach. Vulnerable. But it felt good, too, like stretching after being cramped in a too-small space.

The voice had been quiet for a few months now, thanks to Nell's careful avoidance of crowds. And now the threat of this Dragon made it awaken? The thought made her testy.

Loud crunching in the woods warned of unwanted guests. Silently cursing, she aimed her bow toward the forest that ran along the edge of the open yard. They were far too exposed.

"Come on out. We know you're there." Nell hoped she sounded tougher than she felt.

Two men stepped out. One of them held a bulging cloth sack. "We've come to take him back."

She knew that man. Donovan.

Nell bared her teeth at him. Rumor said he'd been kicked out of Port Iona's dark alchemy crew when he failed to grab Phoebe. Looked like rumor was truth for once, and now he'd signed up with Jasper. Donovan only wanted to work where he could smash heads.

He once nearly broke Phoebe's knee and traumatized her when she was traded to their crew. He'd come after Phoebe again a few months back, too, scaring her so much she ran into the ocean and almost died from that sea beast. She growled and sighted down the arrow shaft at his face. Maybe if she just sliced off an ear…

Corbin put a hand on her arm, and she relaxed the string.

Donovan laughed at the gesture and threw the bag of coins at her feet. They jingled harshly in the quiet morning air.

She handed her bow and arrow to Corbin. After many lessons from her, he was a decent shot these days. Stepping forward to unlock Jasper, she said, "Don't try anything or Corbin will shoot."

Corbin furrowed his brow with a look of concentration, and within seconds, his fairy queen arrived to hover near his shoulder, her daffodil yellow wings a blur. Soft golden light shone from her, visible even in the morning sun. She was the size of a butterfly, shaped like a tiny human with elongated arms and legs. Long, silvery hair hung over her like a gossamer dress, and a delicate stinger protruded from the end of her torso.

"Grace, meet Jasper," he said with a grim smile. "Jasper, meet Grace."

The other men exchanged uneasy glances.

"Hey now, no need to threaten anyone like that,"

Donovan said.

Fairy swarms had killed before. Nell's father was a victim of one, years ago. Keepers had a powerful weapon for self-defense now that their queens obeyed them so well. One sting from a queen usually did the trick.

"Grace just likes to be near me," Corbin replied, smiling at his queen.

Nell snickered at the men's obvious discomfort.

With a quick caress to his face, Grace sat on Corbin's shoulder. His keeper mark—a birthmark of fairy wings on the back of the neck—had not changed into a tangible, jewel-like tattoo as Sierra's had. Even so, he said he could sense his fairy queen much clearer now, even without suffering a sting like Sierra had. Nell was glad. Few would have survived what Sierra did, and Nell had already lost enough to the fairies.

She turned back to focus on Jasper. A chill raced down her back at the intensity in his eyes. He'd never seen her be taken over by the voice, much less heard a warning like this one. The experience seemed to have changed his opinion of her potential value. She hadn't survived this long without heeding warnings like the one that hummed in her blood now.

"Tell me about 'the Dragon.'" Nell dangled the key from one finger.

"I already did. Let me go."

"No, you told me his name: the Dragon. Not even a real name. Why is he called that?"

Jasper looked at the other men. They grinned and took a step forward. Corbin whispered to Grace, who flew in lazy loops over to Jasper and hovered right above the back of his neck. He went sheet-white.

Nell pursed her lips in appreciation of Corbin's strategy. He'd never let Grace kill anyone, but Jasper didn't know that.

Donovan said, "Now, you just wait a minute—"

"Stop," Jasper commanded with a hoarse voice. "Do nothing. Say nothing."

Sweat dripped from his nose, and he glared at the men until they backed up, hands lifted in the air. They stopped at the edge of the clearing.

"It doesn't matter. They'll see him soon enough anyway." Resentment laced Jasper's words like acid. "He wears a dragon mask over his face and never takes it off. No one knows why, and no one asks. He's made such elixirs that you can't imagine. His very touch holds magic. He says he'll control all magical creatures, even the fiercest. I've seen it, too. His dragons, they aren't like the others. You should fear him like you've never feared anything."

"Why? What does he want?"

"What does any man want? Power. Unlike you, he has ambition. You may have kept the alchemists from taking our ports back for a time, but you didn't step up to lead when you had the chance. Your loss, stupid girl."

His words stung with the bite of truth she couldn't deny. Oh, she prophesied. She'd had no choice in that. But when people had asked her to become their teacher, to ordain them as acolytes in her mission, she hadn't. Her, with disciples learning at her feet? She shuddered at the thought. Sierra, the schemer, would be a better leader. Or Corbin the dreamer.

But the people had wanted Nell and the magical other-worldly voice. Every time she walked into town, crowds gazed at her with faces full of hope that made her feel guilty about her past and fearful of her future. She'd only let them down. She was no priestess.

Jasper continued, as if he sensed he'd hit a sore spot, "You think I don't hear things? How you cringe when people kiss your robes? The Dragon has plans to lead us. He demands respect and seizes it. And then we'll take back the magic that's ours. No more bending over backward for magical creatures that aren't even *human*. We won't be second-class citizens no more. He's promised. We'll be back in charge."

"We?"

"Humans. But not you, little girl. He's only sharing with those who kneel to him. You missed your chance. Besides, you're not really human anymore anyway, are you, sweet thing?"

She narrowed her eyes. This conversation was over.

She made quick work of the lock and the ropes, and Jasper stumbled to his feet. Without taking his eyes off her, he backed up to where his men waited at the forest's edge.

"You'll pay for this." Jasper tugged his sleeves over the red marks left by the ropes. "The Dragon will make you suffer, and I'll be sure I'm there to watch."

Fury rising fast, Nell grabbed her bow back from Corbin and shot two arrows in a row, blurring with speed. Two thunks sounded as the arrows pinned Jasper to the tree, one arrow in each shirt sleeve.

Corbin sucked in a breath but didn't say a word.

The same could not be said of Jasper, who shrieked, "You've cut me, stupid girl! I'm bleeding!"

"Barely, but I'll fix that if you show your face here again. And keep your so-called Dragon away from me. Dragons are wild but noble creatures. This man's just a scavenger who wants to prey on our world's magic."

"He's going to be a new kind of leader, a strong one," Jasper wheezed as the other two men pulled the arrows from the tree.

Nell stood straight and tall. She held her bow high, letting the sunlight flash against its polished surface, knowing the image she created was one of strength. "He's going to be dead if he comes this way. I'll shoot him down as easy as any other vulture."

Jasper paled further, and with a last glare, he darted off into the woods, accompanied by his men. It was just as well the voice had a mission to send her on. She really needed to get out of the area for a while. But while she might secretly welcome a good, fierce battle, she didn't want to put anyone else at risk. Especially not Corbin.

"We've got to talk to Sierra and the others right away. At least the voice gave us lots of information to work with this time," Corbin said. As always when the voice spoke, his eyes sparkled with excitement and awe, but his frown showed concern about the message itself. It didn't sound good. Then again, messages from the voice rarely did.

It was one thing for Jasper to make noises about this new threat. When the voice gave a warning, though, she had to take it seriously. Change and more hard choices. A journey to the Ice-Locked Land would test all who went. And with or without a bunch of dragons, the Dragon himself sounded like no easy foe, even for Nell.

But who else would fight him? Sierra? Corbin? Phoebe? The thought made Nell snort. None of them were warriors. There was no shame in that, yet the voice said the sword of Aluvia could defeat the Dragon. A sword—and Nell would be the one who would fight him with it. She knew the stakes, and she had the ability.

For Nell, battle brought a ferocious joy—and victory, almost always. But to others, it could mean death, far too easily. She could lose the ones she loved in the blink of an eye, a truth she learned young and had never forgotten.

When Nell and Corbin set off to Tuathail, her mother and sisters promised to stay with Corbin's parents once again if they had any problems. It helped Nell to know her family was as safe as possible when the voice called her away. The girls were big enough now to handle her frequent absences. In fact, they wouldn't need Nell to care for them much longer. The thought left an empty pang in her belly.

With the immediate crisis of Jasper averted and no thoughts required for the hike, her mind returned to the strange voice she'd heard twice this morning. Or thought she'd heard. If anyone could understand what was going on, Corbin could. She cleared her throat.

"Uh, Corbin?" How to explain she'd 'heard' a special message, just for her? The voice had never done such a thing. Any way she tried to word it, she sounded insane.

Without slowing, he slipped his hand into hers. "Hey, I'm so proud of you. I know you wanted to attack those fools, but you let them go."

She sighed. She was glad she'd let them go, too. Mostly.

"Although, I did want to ask…" He fidgeted with her thumb and looked at the ground as if seeking some sort of sign.

She stared down too but saw only brown pine needles amid clumps of springy green moss. She gulped and wondered if Corbin had somehow guessed she was off-kilter. Maybe she looked as crazy as she felt. She'd hoped to be the one to break it to him.

He continued, "I doubt Jasper was telling the whole truth about the Dragon, but this enemy must be deadly dangerous if we need a special sword to beat him. But… Have you considered that you might not be the one who should fight him?"

A hitch broke her smooth stride. "Why wouldn't I be?"

She didn't mention that her heart leapt at the idea of a battle. Corbin didn't need to hear that part. Wouldn't want to hear it.

"Just listen." He faced her finally, and they stopped. Corbin took her other hand as well. "I understand why you have to go on the journey, why we all do. The voice guides you, not us. And you're amazing with a blade, but lots of other people can use a sword. No one else can do what you do now. You have a sacred obligation as the voice of this messenger to keep yourself safe—"

"Stop it. Just stop it." She pulled her hands free to poke him in the chest with a finger. "Sure, this voice talks through me, but I'm not just a puppet. I'm not giving up my whole life."

"No one's asking you to. We all know you don't want to lead Aluvia." His words held no judgment—just a simple statement of a fact she'd made perfectly clear.

"I don't, but I'm not giving up the last four years of

hard work because of some man with a dragon obsession. He could set us right back at the beginning, drain our world dry of magic, destroy everything. No doubt that's why the voice spoke. If stopping him means I need to lead with a sword, so be it. None of us—no one else we trust—can fight like I can."

They lapsed into silence, the awkwardness so painful she was ready to blurt out anything just to slip back into their comfortable place of boy-and-girl-in-love.

"I'm—sorry," she said, not exactly sure what she was sorry for. It sure wasn't for being a strong fighter. Maybe for not being enough of a peacekeeper? For not trusting him to take care of himself in a fight? Maybe she was just sorry she snapped at him.

"No. I'm sorry," he said. "You're right. Of course you're right. You're the best choice to wield the sword." His voice was neutral, but he didn't smile, she noted.

Corbin began walking again, tugging on her hand to pull her along. "What did you want to tell me?"

She hesitated, then fell into step again. She was suddenly not so sure what he'd think of those whispered words. *A sword can be a bearer of peace.* He'd fought battles when he'd had to, and she respected him for it. But he always believed there were better options than fighting.

"Oh. Nothing important," she said.

He knew her past, no question, and accepted it. But

what if her future wasn't squeaky clean and lovely? Did he love her? Or did he love an idea of her?

She didn't want to know. Not now. Life was hard enough without losing the best thing that had ever happened to her.

CHAPTER FOUR

Tall grasses obscured the path to Tuathail. Without Flight business trafficking between the port and Sierra's home, the wilderness had begun to reclaim it. It seemed fitting. Graceful ivy now covered the walls of their crumbling cottage, and Sierra's fairies lived in the trees while dipping in and out of the house as they wished.

Corbin and Nell passed the empty pen on the corner of Sierra's property where Sam, the unicorn, once stayed. He lived free in the forest now but still came around to visit. Queenie's wee little fairies often played in his mane and rode along his back, but today the yard was quiet.

Corbin and Nell greeted Sierra at the door with a quick hug and headed to the table to talk. Phoebe, Sierra's little sister, sat knitting by the empty hearth.

Her simple sleeveless dress showed off the tattoos that swirled down her arms, a reminder of how deeply magic had touched her. Around her neck hung a gleaming mer-pearl, the one she'd used two months ago to warn the merfolk of danger. Though it no longer held power, the elders had given it to her in a golden setting to honor her sacrifice.

After Nell and Corbin explained the events of the morning, Sierra jumped up. "A fiery sword? By all the stars, are you joking?"

"Wish I were," Nell muttered.

Corbin seemed to have shaken off the awkward conversation in the forest. He smiled in his excitement over the magic, even with a sword involved. Nell's heart squeezed tight.

Sierra scowled. "This fairy keeper doesn't know any stories about a flaming sword."

Phoebe said, "It sounded to me like the voice was talking to Corbin, not you. Sorry." She blew her sister a kiss.

Nell snickered.

Sierra rolled her eyes and asked him, "And do you know anything about it?"

Corbin shrugged. "It's a legend. A sword forged by a secretive group that used some kind of powerful magic. That's all I've ever heard, though I do know a bit about the Ice-Locked Lands. The mountains there are always covered with ice and snow, and some are so high they actually disappear into the clouds. Explorers have written about it, but no one's ever reached the highest point of the mountains. And I have no idea what the Tree of Life is."

While Sierra paced, Nell waited silently. She had nothing to offer in the realm of scholarly magical history.

"Does that mean the sword isn't meant for a typical battle? But for some kind of magical one?" Sierra wondered.

"I'm just the messenger. I don't know what it means, either." Nell wished an interpretation came along with the voice. Being little more than a mouthpiece was beyond frustrating.

"Well, at least we know where to go, and what to get," Sierra said. "We might not understand what speaks through Nell, but we know it's always on our side. It sounds like we need to head to the Ice-Locked Lands right away."

Corbin nodded. "Is Micah back yet? It would be helpful if he came with us. He knows a great deal of the history humans lost over the years."

"He's replenishing his magic in the mountains but will be back tonight. I'm sure he'll come." Micah and Sierra hand-fasted two years ago, and they hoped to marry next spring. He returned to his home at least once every moon cycle in his natural shape of a faun to channel magic into himself, just as Phoebe's partner,

Tristan, had to return to the sea in his merfolk form regularly as well.

"I figured you'd all want to go," Nell said. "But I'm just going to say this: Not all of you have to come. The voice may well guide me to this sword, but it's going to be hard and I don't want anyone getting hurt because of some message I was given."

"Stop it," said Corbin. "I keep telling you but you don't seem to hear me: you're not in this alone."

Maybe not, but it felt like it sometimes. No one else had strange voices whispering in their minds or taking over their tongues. "All I'm saying is feel free to stay home this time. I think we all know I'm the best one to wield that sword against our enemy. But you all have lives, and you should get to live them."

Corbin snapped, "You're my life."

All conversation ground to a halt. Nell blinked, opened her mouth, and shut it again. She and Corbin avoided saying such things. Times were just too uncertain to commit to a life together.

Besides, Nell had always secretly thought if she didn't tie herself fully to him, maybe it would hurt less if she lost him one day. Right now, though, denying the depth of her feelings seemed foolish, especially since the thought of a life with Corbin made her knees weak and her pulse jittery.

"I just want everyone to be safe. That's the most important thing." Her voice was squeaky. She hated that.

"We'll keep each other safe," Corbin replied. A copper glow flushed his cheeks, and he wasn't meeting her eyes. Definitely a bit embarrassed by his admission, but adorably so.

Relief warred with worry. His company would be welcome on this long, unknown path. But what if he got hurt? The risks of a harsh journey and dangerous enemy were serious. And she wasn't sure Corbin could stand to watch her fight, which she intended to do. With pleasure. But she knew there was no way to keep him from her side.

She huffed and looked at Sierra, who against all odds had become her closest friend. "Our journey to the fairies was easy compared to the land we're going to."

"We'll deal with it." Sierra crossed her arms in front of her chest.

Yeah, she was going to stick like a burr, that girl. Which meant Micah, too.

Nell blew out a breath. "And it's a lot farther, too."

Phoebe jumped to her feet. "Tristan and Mina can get us there even faster by sea."

Nell would never scoff at the sweet girl but couldn't stop one eyebrow from lifting. "But wouldn't we have to climb up on the ice, soaking wet, ready to catch winter sickness in freezing weather?"

"We can figure it out," Phoebe said. "A boat would cost too much and take too long. The merfolks' magic has grown a lot since you've last been with them. Tristan's on his way here, and we can ask him."

Tristan entered the cabin, tying his dark-green hair back as he walked. "We can ask Tristan what? Sounds like I'm interrupting something important."

He greeted Phoebe with a quick kiss on the cheek. She beamed, but her expression turned serious as she filled him in. He nodded thoughtfully.

"Yes, I believe our magic could mitigate the cold, at least before we fully leave the water. I'll need to converse with Mina. She's learned more about some parts of our magic than anyone. She likes to experiment," he added with a grin.

Phoebe turned to face her sister and Nell. "So, Tristan and I will be going with you."

When Sierra opened her mouth as if to argue, Phoebe scowled at her. The sisters exchanged a long look until Sierra sighed and muttered, "Fine. That's a... fine idea."

Despite her worry, Nell had to smother a grin. Phoebe had definitely grown up. Self-confidence looked good on her.

Nell tapped her foot as she thought out loud. "Okay. What about your magic, though, Tristan? Can you be that far away from your home?"

"The Southern Sea has magic in it as well. I'll be fine so long as we're not trapped on land longer than a month."

"If it takes longer than a month, we'll all be dead anyway," Nell said. "You know where to take us, then?"

"We don't usually swim near the Southern Sea because the ice can be dangerous. But yes, I can take us there. Half a day, three-quarters at most."

Nell's jaw dropped. "Half a day? To cover the entire Southern Sea?"

He laughed. "Merfolk are fast, and I'm one of the fastest, with Mina and a few others."

"Well, that's one good thing. I guess we'll just have to take our chances when we get to the other side of the ocean."

She took a deep breath. Sierra was tough, and Phoebe had proven she was too. Corbin did have tremendous knowledge to offer, not to mention the value of Tristan's and Micah's magic. All of them had carried a lot of responsibility since the fairies returned, and done it well.

"Fine," she said. "I'll get our supplies today; we'll set off tomorrow. It's going to be a fast-paced journey, so be prepared. I want to be back before this Dragon starts any attacks."

"Gotcha, boss." Sierra saluted.

Nell smirked, but then she added in her most serious tone, "One last thing. I'm taking lead on this trip. This one's mine, through and through. Everyone needs to be okay with that."

Phoebe and Tristan nodded immediately. Sierra

sighed and stuck her tongue out. "I'm sure Micah will agree. At least I can keep an eye on my little sister this way."

Phoebe wrinkled her nose back.

Nell wanted to smile at the sisters' antics but couldn't. Corbin had yet to speak.

He wanted her protected and safe, but she didn't have it in her to stand off to the side and wring her hands at a problem. And to be fair, he'd never asked her to do so. He encouraged her to lead as the prophetess—he just wanted her to be safer than a warrior's life permitted. But she couldn't offer him a single statement of comfort. Her words were trapped in her throat.

He met her eyes with a seriousness he rarely showed. For Nell, that moment stretched on and on, like watching a sword twist and fall from her hand, knowing she'd never catch it in time. Her heart fell as fast as her hope.

Then he nodded. "We all agree."

A breath shuddered out. "Then it's a plan."

Her hand had found its way to her sword hilt, gripping it for comfort. She slid it back. Hopefully no one had noticed. Especially him.

"Your life's never boring, Nell." Phoebe said.

Actually, it had been a bit boring. No battles, no challenge. And now that the decision was done, her spirit was rearing to charge like a unicorn racing across the desert. But she didn't say how much she was looking forward to the change. She wasn't sure what they'd think.

"No one here likes boredom anyway," Nell replied instead. "Let's do this. We've got a madman to stop."

The friends agreed to meet at Sierra's again in the morning.

Nell and Corbin set off back toward Covenstead. Nell would collect her coins there and go buy cold weather supplies at Port Ostara while Corbin packed medical supplies and food. He had some books written by explorers he planned on reading tonight. She had no doubt: He had books on everything.

Silence filled the air except for the swish of the grasses along their legs and the crunch of pine needles under their feet. As they neared their little healer's village, Corbin dipped down and picked a steel thistle flower, known for its toughness. It could grow anywhere.

He handed it to her and broke the heavy silence between them as they continued to walk. "You know, I think you misunderstood me earlier about the sword. You'd make a glorious general for any army. You're like this flower: beautiful and strong. A survivor. But I do think you're unique in what you can offer in other ways, because of the voice. I know you're tired of being in the public eye so much, and yet here you're ready to sign up for what could be a long war."

She didn't know what to say, so she said nothing and spun the flower stem in her hands, noting the way the pale gray lines shot through the crimson petals. She lifted it to her nose—rich and sweet—and then tucked it into her braid.

He continued, staring at the ground passing under their feet. "And if I'm honest"—he gulped, and the rest of his words came out fast—"I'm a little jealous all this magic keeps happening to everyone else."

She stopped short and grabbed his elbow. "What? But you were a fairy keeper before any of the rest of us were ever touched by magic."

"I know, but... I've studied magic and magical creatures my whole life, you know? And I'm thankful for Grace, so thankful. But the two people closest to me have more magic than I do, and neither of you wanted it. Sierra has her special fairy keeper mark and extra closeness with Queenie. You have the voice and your prophecies. And it's not just you two. Tristan and Micah are literally magical. Even Phoebe held the power of the entire ocean in her hands. What can I offer that one of you can't? I don't want to ever lag behind or slow you down. I'm not proud to feel this way, but I do." He hung his head.

She faced him fully and tipped his chin to make him

look at her. "Listen up. You're the one who keeps us going. You are hope and light and all the good things Aluvia has to offer. You have more knowledge than the rest of us put together. You have a huge value to us—and to me."

That was as close as she would get to saying she loved him. Too painful to be so close but so far from the commitment she both longed and feared to give.

Flushed a bit, Corbin shoved his hands in his pocket, fidgeting from foot to foot. "I'm glad you think so, but I'm also a coward. I don't want you on the frontline in a war, not a war so big the voice is involved. I'm afraid for you, no matter how good you are, for what risks you'll take. You sometimes seem to think you have to do it all, that you're alone in this battle. And you're not. I don't want to lose you."

He looked up and met her eyes. His sincerity ripped right through her defenses.

A flush burned up Nell's neck to match his, the prickly sensation unmistakable. "I don't want to lose you, either," she replied in a gruff voice. "But I know we'll both do what we have to do. I won't take stupid chances, though. You can count on it."

Half of his answering smile seemed propped up by pure determination. "I will."

"Good. We understand what's at stake, maybe more than anyone else. For me, that means defending our people in all ways, with or without a sword. For the sake of Aluvia." She raised her hand, palm facing forward, and held it toward him in the traditional motion of sealing a deal.

He sighed but didn't move. Her hand seemed to stay poised for an eternity, waiting for his acceptance, his agreement and acknowledgement that she had to protect others from the threat of the Dragon if she could.

Fear gripped her, fear that her refusal to lay down her sword had sliced too deeply between them after all. But then, slowly, he reached out and pressed his hand against hers, palm to palm.

"Aluvia comes first," he said.

While their hands were still joined, the voice whispered, *He believes Aluvia is first in his heart, but it is not. Not yet. But one day he could place Aluvia first and be transformed.*

The voice felt smooth in her mind, so natural she didn't stumble or feel shocked. It felt more like a part of her, woven together, knitted as one thing. The realization sent chills down her back. She wanted to separate from the voice, not grow closer. But she directed her thoughts away from that creepy idea, focusing on the words themselves.

Something else besides Aluvia came first for Corbin? His fairy? Or Nell herself? She didn't dare believe such a prideful notion, though it soothed something in her to think so. She stared at him as they continued along the pine-strewn path. She'd never forgotten that he and his queen had stopped the local fairy swarms that killed her father. Corbin had brought safety to her young life once again. And she'd cared for him ever since, secretly at first, and now openly.

"What?" he asked. His brow wrinkled.

"Nothing. I'm just thankful for you."

She'd tell him about the voice in her mind later. After his vulnerable confession, a revelation about more magic in her life would be a slap in the face. She'd tell him before they left, though. She'd tell everyone. They all needed to know the voice was doing something new. She didn't know what it meant, but she knew it changed things.

CHAPTER FIVE

A journey took careful planning, especially one that could turn into a battle. Nell packed her merfolk-made backpack with a bedroll and first-aid kit, including a flint stone and a small tinder box. She stared at the wooden matches and hoped the merfolk truly knew how to make bags waterproof, or this would be one short trip.

She added a few shirts and pants, a cloak, and would bring all her weaponry, of course—her arrows (only the best, too, fletched with griffin feathers), longsword, dagger. She wore them all the time. She packed an extra bowstring in the oiled cloth that would also serve to polish the dagger and sword. A sharpening stone and a length of rope went into the pack's side pocket, cinched closed for safekeeping. And she still had all the winter supplies to buy.

Her heart lifted as she worked, and she froze at the realization she was preparing for a possible war—happily. Discomfort squeezed her belly.

She thought she'd accepted her calling as the peaceful holder of the voice, and here she was, as eager for violence as ever. She shook her head. No. It wasn't what she felt that mattered; it was what she did. On impulse, she pressed the flower Corbin had given her between the folds of a plain piece of parchment and tucked it in the corner of her bag, a small smile on her face.

After a late lunch, she set off toward Port Ostara for supplies—and information. She'd stop by the local crew's distillery on her way. Two birds, one stone.

Slanted roofs of ancient shacks lined up along the wharf. Since the loss of the Flight trade four years ago, the crew's top alchemist, Carrick, had moved the distillery closer to the big port town where the poison business was brisker.

Smoke was already funneling out of the chimney, smelling of sulfur and burned sugar. The front door was locked, but she simply pulled out her lock pick. A few jiggles and a hard kick and, boom, door open.

"Hey there, Carrick."

"Nell! What are you doing here?" The man had his sleeves rolled up and eyes squinted against the fumes of the distillery.

Nell leaned over and sniffed the vials lined up next

to the door. Acrid, with a hint of ginger. "So, Blind Man's Poison today? A special order for anyone I know?"

She smiled sweetly but pulled her dagger from its sheath.

Carrick threw his hands up. "Look, you know the deal. I don't ask questions. I just make what they need."

"And do they need some kind of magic potion that tames wild dragons?" She stepped to the cowering little man. "Tell me, Carrick, did you create a secret potion for the Dragon-man?"

"No, I swear. He's done that all on his own. I think it uses nectar but something else, too. I can smell it. Maybe dragon's blood, since he can ride them now."

Her head swam. "So, it's true? He really can fly a dragon?"

"Aye, I've seen him riding one. High in the sky." Sweat dripped down Carrick's cheek.

Her heart hammered in her chest. She'd honestly thought Jasper had lied. Carrick, though, she believed. This was worse than she expected. "Is there a way to stop him?"

"I don't know. I've never seen anything like him."

"But you're the master alchemist now!"

"I'm a beginner compared to the Dragon."

"Have you met this Dragon then, personally?"

He paled. "No. And I don't want to."

"But you've declared your servitude to him?" She raised an eyebrow.

"Didn't have much choice. Jasper signed us all up, so to speak. The men over in Port Iona and us, we're one big crew now, all serving the Dragon."

"And you're okay with that?"

"Well, you don't see me dead, do ya?"

Well, he was a little gray, Nell noted, but from fear. The whites of his eyes showed, and his hands shook. She considered the times he'd snuck her healing potions after her training sessions with Jack. With pursed lips, she took a big step back to let the poor man breathe a bit.

"I need more information about him, Carrick. What's his weakness? Everyone has one."

"I don't know, I swear! I just know he demanded our loyalty in payment for our lives."

"You can do better than that."

"Uh, he says he's gonna force the magical creatures to serve humans again. And he never takes off his mask. That's all I've got on him!" Carrick's face crumpled.

Then a familiar feeling stole over her. The voice poured from her, with just the one terrified man to witness it.

"You must look more closely to see behind the mask. Potions won't save the dragons or defeat the one who covets their power, but the fiery sword can."

Her voice echoed through the chamber. Carrick cried out and dropped to his knees.

Nell was struck by a feeling of other-worldly anger. The power behind the voice was growing impatient. She'd heard the voice's words as clear as a bell, not muffled at all. She wondered why.

In her mind, she received an unexpected answer. *There's more magic available to us now...The earth has spoken, and the sea has finally risen to power... Now we are but missing one more... And you can be freed.*

"What do you mean?" she asked the voice. Her heart sped. Freedom? From her role as mouthpiece? Or from the coming tyranny of this Dragon?

"I don't mean anything!" Carrick shouted from his position on the floor.

The only true defense against this enemy will bring your freedom as well as the health of your people and the rest of Aluvia. If you so choose.

What's our defense? And what freedom? Nell thought fiercely back, no longer caring how stupid she felt. *How do I know I can trust you?*

Don't you know us by now, Nell? The voice was warm, laughing. Maternal.

She did. She didn't know what exactly it was, but the voice was on the side of good.

We have waited many years for the strength to reach the one we sensed, one who could carry on as we once did, before so much was lost. You, Nell.

The voice was suddenly far more willing to explain.

It's time for a change, it said.

Carrick staggered to his feet and brought Nell back to the present moment.

"You tell Jasper to stay away from here," she said. "Him and the Dragon, too, or I'll make life a nightmare for all of you, you hear me?"

She stormed out of the stinking distillery toward Port Ostara. So, the sword was supposedly buried in the Ice-Locked Lands, which meant it was in the very same area where the Dragon lived. A man who rode a dragon. Even if he wasn't there right now, what kind of followers did he have living down there? Was that where he tamed his dragons? Going to grab the sword suddenly looked a lot harder. She kicked a stick in her path.

Well, if you had a snake in the house, you didn't stand back and throw rocks at it. You cut off its head. She'd get the sword and hunt the Dragon down, even if he rode a dozen dragons.

But she'd better be prepared. If she wasn't, she wouldn't need a dragon to kill her. The unforgiving land of ice and snow would do that all on its own.

Nell's list of necessary winter weather supplies wasn't long, but fur boots and heavy coats weren't in high demand along the coast. If anyone had them, it'd be Alastair the tanner. His shop sat on the opposite side of town, downwind to keep the fumes away from the port. She'd brought all her money, which wasn't much. No one paid in coppers for prophetic warnings.

She gave a whisper of thanks at the open sign on the door. The strong smell of tanning leather floated out from the shop. When she entered, a bell chimed. Saddles, reins, belts, and bags of all kinds hung from wooden pegs on one wall. Awls and knives were strewn behind the counter within reach. If she'd had a mind to, she'd have a lot of weapons at her fingertips.

"Who goes there?" an older man said, limping into the front room.

Nell laid her coin purse on the table. "Hello, Alastair. I need some of your fine products."

They settled down to business. She had at least enough coin for white fur cloaks and boots for everyone. And the furred boots with special fish-scaled soles might look strange but would grip the snow better while keeping their feet protected.

"Going somewhere cold, then?" Alastair asked as he wrapped her purchases.

"Looks like."

He frowned but said, "Just as well for you. Trouble's coming 'round these parts."

"Oh?" She narrowed her eyes at him.

"There's talk these days about a new man; local crew's serving him now. Sounds bad."

She lowered her voice. "I've heard of him myself. He's moving fast, too, seems like."

Alastair slapped his hand on the counter. "We're no saps ready to show our bellies to a bigger dog. If this Dragon wants us, he'll have to take us over our dead bodies."

She smiled fiercely. "I have no doubts about Port Ostara's loyalty. Thank you."

He flushed. Rubbing a finger under one ear, he added, "And uh, if you're going to be in snow, you might want some of these."

He held up a strange-looking scrap of white gauze, with ties on each side. "It protects the eyes. The sun off the snow will blind you just like white sands in the desert. I'll make a good deal for you."

Alastair looked so sincere she even listened when he recommended light-framed tents for them, ones with removable, bendable willow branches to hold its shape that would pack tight and light. And when he suggested the special water flasks the mountaineers strapped inside their coats to keep their water from freezing solid, she figured she'd better buy some of those, too. By the time she left, her coin purse was empty and her hands were full of packages.

The hike back from the port was long with the new

supplies weighing her down. Halfway back, she stilled, brow furrowed. The woods had gone silent.

She dropped her packages and grabbed her sword. Sweat prickled along her skin and she crouched into a ready position, all senses on alert. The unnatural quiet screamed louder than any sound could.

A man stepped from the trees onto the path.

He was tall, taller even than Corbin, with muscular arms bared by a leather vest. An elaborate dragon mask carved of painted wood covered his features from his forehead to just above his jaw line.

Her breath snagged, but she gripped her sword tighter. The Dragon. It had to be.

He wore two longswords crisscrossed on his back and walked like he knew how to use them. A dagger hung from a scabbard at his waist. With his height, strength, and reach, he would be tough to beat even if they were equal in weaponry. Which they weren't.

A jagged red scar trailed past the edge of the mask, along his right jaw line and down his neck. Dark hair with one thick streak of white lay across broad shoulders. His age was impossible to determine, but an aura of power surrounded him.

"Stay back," Nell warned.

He sauntered toward her. "Nellwyn Brennan. I see you are preparing for a journey. Perhaps to the Ice-Locked Lands, hmm?"

Shock stunned her for a moment. "How do you know me?"

"Who in Aluvia doesn't know you? And you didn't answer my question." His voice was deep, amplified by the mask covering his face, distorting it.

"I don't need to answer your question. Why don't you just go back to the frozen land you came from?" She couldn't tell if he was smiling under that mask, but he rocked back on his heels, looking unconcerned in his pose.

He shook his head. "There's no going back now, even if I wanted to. I'm taking over Aluvia, with all magical creatures placed under human rule. My rule."

He drew one sword from his back and swung it in an arc. The sun glinted on the sword as it fell. A black substance glistened on its tip. Poison?

"I don't think so." She stepped back.

"I'm not asking you to think. You're the girl who united the ports and villages. You have the people's hearts. I just want you to hand them to me." He pointed his sword at her.

"Is that a threat?"

"A request—for now. But if you cause me trouble, I'll kill you."

She laughed. "You can try."

He swung at her then, an overhead strike that blurred with speed.

She blocked his sword with her own. The tremor

from the clash ran up her arms. She licked her lips and shifted her feet, readying to take the punishing blows she knew he would deal. If that was poison on his weapon, all it would take is one nick and she could be incapacitated. Or dead.

Nell warned him, "It's not just me who's brought change to Aluvia, you know. All the keepers have taken the message to heart. They'll stand against you."

"They can't fight like you."

Well, he had that part right. She lunged with a hard stab. Her move should have taken him by surprise—she was fast—but he knocked her sword aside easily.

"You'll have to do better than that. No one is my equal with a blade. Not even you."

She smirked. "Why not just take me now? If you can."

He attacked, but she spun out of range and jabbed at him. He took a step closer and forced her sword to one side.

His breath wasn't even strident under the mask. "None can match my strength, but you could be my equal in power. I don't wish to kill more than I must. If you were on my side, the people would follow me without violence, without resistance. Wouldn't that be better?"

"I'll never help you destroy our world." She struck at him again.

Their feet scuffled back and forth along the path. Steel chimed over and over. Nell kept a close eye on the glistening tip of his blade. Dust rose and coated their boots, dried her throat. If she found an opening, she could end his assault on the ports before it started. The voice couldn't have foreseen the Dragon showing up like this. Killing a man went against every promise she'd made to herself in her new life, but in this case, she was willing to make an exception.

He stabbed. She parried.

She slashed. He blocked.

He was good, she gave him that. Really good.

Above the clanging of the swords, he said, "We would stop the destruction of the mountains by those monstrous dragons. Not like mine, tamed and fireless. All magical creatures will serve me and my people soon enough. We'll take back nectar from the fairies. The ocean will be ours to fish and travel, not blocked by that ludicrous treaty with the merfolk. Of course, I have my own transportation."

He stepped back and gave a sharp whistle. With a shriek, the wind picked up.

A creaking sound came overhead, like a thousand sails opening at once on a speeding ship. A gust of icy wind made Nell shudder, and there in the middle of the dirt path from Port Ostara to Covenstead, a dragon landed, shaking the ground with its weight.

Standing as tall as the tree line, the beast filled her vision. An ice-blue dragon with white eyes. It lifted its head and screeched. Frosty mist blasted from its nostrils, sending the temperature plummeting. Its cry rode down Nell's spine like the sound of metal on metal.

She struggled to take in enough air. She'd never even heard of a dragon like this. She'd seen dragons before—red, fire-breathing dragons. They had been magnificent and terrifyingly deadly.

But this? This was so much worse. Dread seemed to flow from the very skin of the animal itself. Up close, the dragon radiated a hatred she hadn't sensed from a magical creature since their world began to heal.

The beast shrieked and sent a blast of icy breath onto the tree beside it. Not just frosty mist this time—ice coated the branches, thick and hard, white vapor swirling up around the trunk. The dragon blew again, eyes glowing white until the tree suddenly fell with a deafening crack, split right down the middle, frozen brittle and shattered.

Her sword hilt loosened in her hand. Every joint in her body went weak before training swept in and had her gripping her sword in a defensive position. Not that it would do much good now. This dragon could kill her in a heartbeat, a frozen corpse left here on the dirt road.

Frost crackled the grass at the beast's feet, and the man stood there, unafraid. This, then, was the man who Jasper deemed worth his loyalty. Not just a warrior, but something more.

The man calling himself the Dragon interrupted her spinning thoughts. "It's already too late to stop me, so don't waste your energy on that foolish journey. The next time we meet, you'll have to choose: me or death. Consider your options carefully, Nellwyn."

He lifted his empty hand. The dragon lowered its mighty head, and the man gripped its neck frill, swinging up just behind it. When the beast stood tall, he climbed down its neck using the ridges as steps to land in a leather seat on the dragon's back.

He rode a dragon.

"I'll have taken Port Iona before the full moon rises tomorrow, as I should have long ago. And I won't stop there. Know this well: I'm coming for all of Aluvia!" His last words rose to a shout.

He lifted his sword in the air, and the beast rose onto its back legs with a mighty roar. The sound thundered through her bones. Its wings moved, and the air around her smelled of snow and jasmine and musk. Dragons had a scent—she hadn't known. The last time she'd met one, all she smelled was the burning of the forest. She'd never been this close to one since then.

She wished it had stayed that way.

The dragon and its rider rose through the sky above her, flattening bushes and cracking tree limbs. A flurry of wind beat upon her, a blast of freezing air that stole her remaining breath. And then he was gone, along with the white-eyed dragon, flying fast … heading toward Covenstead.

Her sisters.

Her mother.

Corbin.

She snatched up the supplies and ran.

This man knew who she was. He could easily know where she lived, who she loved. As she raced home, the ghost of her eight-year-old self ran alongside her, reliving her darkest memories.

The moment of disbelief when her mother had told them about their father's death. The crying of the babies all night long, their mother unable to offer comfort.

Death had come without warning to Nell's home that day. It could have come and gone again today already.

It was late afternoon when Nell finally reached the healing cabins. Her lungs burned from running with the extra weight of their supplies. The little village was quiet. Maybe the Dragon hadn't come here after all. But when she entered the clearing by her house, she staggered.

Her home.

The thatched roof had collapsed, coated with a thick layer of ice. The door, split down the middle, lay warped on the frozen grass. *No.*

Tears burned the backs of her eyes, but she had no time for them. "Ma! Girls!"

She raced to the front edge of the crumbled home and yanked away one stone after another.

"Nell! Wait!"

It was Corbin's voice. She didn't look away from her task. "Help me!"

"They're okay. Do you hear? They're okay!"

His words finally sank in. She turned slowly, blood on her knuckles. "They are?"

"Grace saw the dragon coming and warned them in time. They're with my parents now and will stay there. They'll be safe that way."

"Thank you. Thank you." She wrapped her arms around him.

"I'm so sorry about your home. We'll rebuild it."

Corbin held her close.

"He… he threatened me, told me to join him or else." Her voice shook but grew firmer. Louder. Her family was fine, just as Corbin had said, but only because they got lucky.

"I can't believe the dragon breathed ice," Corbin said, both awed and disturbed. "In all the books and scrolls I've ever read, dragons only breathe fire."

Nell couldn't care less about the mystery of the man's blue dragon. What mattered was he'd come after her family. Grace had saved them, but the Dragon had made his point. He'd pay for it.

The sooner she got the sword of Aluvia, the better.

"I want to leave now," Nell seethed. "We can march straight through."

"A good night's sleep will help you more than anything. The others won't be ready tonight and he's gone now. The news will hold until tomorrow."

"Fine, but we've got to warn Port Iona before we head to the Ice-Locked Lands. You know that, right?"

"I wouldn't have it otherwise. We'll do it first thing in the morning." He stroked her hair.

Against her will, her thoughts returned to the giant dragon. Its white eyes. Its freezing breath. She imagined it destroying Corbin's home the next time. Or Sierra's. Or entire villages. Death would be swift. Countless innocents would die.

"What if I can't stop him?" The words were pulled

from her in a harsh whisper. She leaned her head against his shoulder.

"You will."

"How do you know?" She tilted her head up to meet his gaze.

"Because I know you." He smiled at her.

His faith in her was a magic all its own.

Nell awoke to the dim glow of early dawn, rested and ready. She'd slept in her healing hut after salvaging what she could from her home, thankful her packed bag was fine. She put on her summer travel clothes, keeping the new winter gear packed away until needed. Her sword and bow came next. With a dagger strapped to her thigh and a quiver alongside the waterproof backpack, her weapons were all within reach.

As a final step, she tucked her small back-up knife inside her boot. Given Jasper's attitude, perhaps not everyone in town would be receptive to the warning they came to give. She wouldn't invite violence, would even seek to avoid it, but she wouldn't allow anyone in her circle to be harmed.

Thanks to the voice, they knew where to go and what to get in order to win. And she would fight with a sword of legend. With a slow smile of anticipation even in the face of overwhelming, dangerous odds, she stepped out and closed the door behind her.

Four years ago, Nell had walked to Sierra's holding a sword in preparation for a dangerous journey. This time, Nell held Corbin's hand. His wonderful scent made her smile, the honey and cinnamon fragrance of his fairies mixed with soap and spicy herbs. His hand in hers lifted her spirits further.

Corbin wasn't a morning person, but that was fine. They both relaxed into the sounds of the forest: the shy wood thrush whistling a welcome to the morning, the crickets chanting their last songs before retiring for the day. His fairy queen skimmed along the tops of the trees with her wee ones. The beauty of the forest built a happy cocoon around them, making yesterday seem like a strange dream.

When they approached the cottage, though, the small bubble of peace popped. Her grip tightened on Corbin's hand.

"Everything's going to be fine," he assured her.

"I know," Nell said. She wished she believed it as much as he did.

Believe it said the voice inside. This time, the voice wasn't a whisper. It sounded like someone had spoken into her ear. Goose bumps raced along her arms.

She'd had a voice living inside her for years, and now it was powerful enough to speak in her mind. Maybe strong enough to take her over completely? She had no idea what this change could mean on top of everything else, but first things had to come first.

Sierra led them to the kitchen, where Tristan and Phoebe already waited at the table, packs at their feet. Micah was there, too, ready to journey in his human form. A nip of cold hung in the late summer air.

"Corbin and I have some news. Bad news." Nell explained her confrontation with the Dragon, including the attack on her family. The recounting fueled her rage further.

"He has to be using magic on his dragon. Dragons would never serve any human willingly, but this one came to his whistle, like a dog. Furious, but obedient."

Micah's eyes widened with horror. "Dragons are fierce, proud creatures. They will sometimes respond to our singing, but they only consider other creatures of the sky as equals."

"Creatures of the sky?" Nell stared at him, baffled.

"Flying creatures, you see," Micah explained. "There used to be quite a few. Firebirds. Windsteeds. Griffins. Snow sprites. Dragons live within caves and forests, which is why fauns can sometimes influence them, but they still consider the sky their home."

"Oh." Nell hoped this Dragon couldn't control all those things too.

"I've never heard of snow sprites!" Corbin leaned forward in his chair.

"They are ancient beings—small, mischievous elementals made of the air itself that live among the snowy lands. It's said they could travel anywhere the wind could go. But dragons are far more powerful."

"And dragons wouldn't voluntarily serve a human the way fairies work with us?" Sierra paced around the small kitchen.

Micah frowned. "No. Dragons are less tame than even the wildest griffins, dangerous but not evil. Though perhaps they have too much magic to keep contained safely now."

Sierra sat down at the table with a thud. "I thought magic was good. We didn't have enough—how can too much magic be bad?"

"Imagine, if you will, a world with a long drought," Micah said. "Then the rains come pouring down. The dry ground cannot absorb the sudden rain well. Some places flood, yet others receive little relief as the water runs off the too-hard surface.

"I think in many ways, Aluvia has been like this. The merfolk have finally received the sea's magic, as the fairies have their own, but the dragons seem to have both too much magic and yet not enough. I don't fully understand, but it might be why they are setting too many fires."

"But this man's dragon didn't breathe fire," Nell said.

"I saw his dragon up close, and believe me, frost is just as deadly. Jasper says they'll all be riding them, an army of them."

Micah's expression darkened. "If what you say is true, their very souls are enslaved. No wonder his dragon serves him. Taking a dragon's fire is stealing the source of their power, their essence, if you will. It's the worst kind of theft."

A heavy silence filled the room before Sierra stated, "Then this fight isn't against the dragons at all. It's against the man who forced them do his bidding. I, of all people, know how terrible it is to enslave a magical being."

Queenie flew over and caressed Sierra's cheeks, bringing a small smile to her keeper's face.

Nell stood and pulled on her backpack. "We've all made mistakes. Aluvia knows I've made my share. But we've fixed what we could and moved on. This Dragon's made his own mistake, and we're going to fix it for him. We'll warn Port Iona he's coming, free his dragon from his power, and then we'll to stop him. Permanently. Let's go."

When they arrived at the cove, Tristan already waited in human form. His bird tattoos were striking against his usual pallor. Even in these dire circumstances, Phoebe's face glowed with happiness when she ran to him.

Corbin reached over and took Nell's hand.

After Phoebe shared the grim news, Tristan tensed as if ready to dive in the ocean immediately. "I'll ask Mina to warn the elders after we reach Port Iona. I promise you, the merfolk will do what we can to help fight this so-called Dragon."

"Thank you," Nell said. "I know your people prefer to avoid conflict when they can."

Tristan lifted his chin. "We will not go quietly into servitude ever again."

As he spoke, his hands glowed. His magic was powerful now, thanks to Phoebe's sacrifice.

Magic. So much magic.

Nell realized that in all the hubbub of the Dragon, she'd yet to tell the others about her own magic changing, possibly growing. As much as she hated to discuss it, she had to.

"Um, well." She cleared her throat. "Before we start this journey, I have something strange to tell. Stranger, I guess. I'm, well, I'm hearing voices. Actually, just one voice. Which is more than enough."

"Come again?" Sierra blinked.

"Inside my mind," Nell pressed on doggedly though the tips of her ears burned. "A few times now, I've heard someone—or something—whisper something to me, but it wasn't any of you, and it sure as fire wasn't me. And it's gotten louder."

Corbin said nothing, but his dark eyes shone with hurt. Nell looked away.

"What did the voice say?" Micah asked in his calm way. Of course he wouldn't find it strange or frightening. He had deer legs at least once a month.

"It's said a few things, little bits at a time. That it was time for a change and that a sword can be a bearer of peace. And it… told me to believe things would be okay." Her gaze went to Corbin, who still stood unmoving, lips tight.

"Do you think it's the same prophetic voice we hear?" Phoebe wondered.

Nell shrugged. "If it is, it's trying something new. But it did say there was more magic now, so maybe that's why it's changing."

"How long has this been going on?" Corbin asked, his voice strangely controlled.

"Not long," she assured him. "I didn't want to say anything because–"

"Because poor Corbin doesn't have as much magic as you, and now you have even more?"

She refused to flinch at his acidic tone. "There's nothing poor about you."

Grace flitted about like a crazed butterfly and finally pressed herself against Corbin's neck. He gave a deep sigh and shook his head. "I'm glad you told us now, at least. Better late than never. But there shouldn't be any secrets among us. Not even ones that might hurt."

Guilt stung. She should tell him what the voice said, about him, though it seemed impossible that Aluvia wasn't really first in his heart.

The voice spoke quickly inside Nell's mind: *The truth in his heart is one he must learn for himself. Give him time. His heart will bring healing when he learns to fully trust.*

Nell bit down on her lip so hard it came close to bleeding. These new words would soothe him, she knew. But the voice said not to tell him, so she'd wait. And have a secret she didn't want.

"I'll tell you what I hear as soon as I can." That was truth, as far as it went. Not even Corbin could argue with it.

Her friends all stared at her like they'd never seen her before.

"Okay, we're done with that. Can we get going now?" Nell snapped.

"Everybody ready, then?" Tristan asked smoothly.

Even with all her preparations, Nell wasn't sure she felt ready. "Let's go."

ell gripped her bag tighter. Going under water had sounded reasonable until she stood along the shore, staring at the glittering surface.

The others trooped into the sea, sloshing water further up their legs with each step. Corbin had already been under the sea with the merfolk several times, much to his delight. Nell was the only one who had never traveled under the waves with them, despite being a strong swimmer. It always seemed too much like drowning for her taste.

Mina, Tristan's sister, waved above the gentle swells. Then she flipped down, her bronze tail slapping against the surface. Young Liam swam up to help transport Micah and Sierra. Though still just a seawee, a child among the merfolk without tattoos yet, he was nearly as fast as Tristan.

The three merfolk's eyes were black as night from their magic, ready to keep the humans alive underwater. Nell trusted Tristan and the others because Phoebe did. She was fine after days in the ocean.

Still, Nell's hands felt clammy. Her lips curled at the sight of the green water, full of slimy algae and slippery fish, but she forced herself into the water. The fairies spiraled up and away from the ocean's surface. If only she could join them, just fly into the sky and disappear into the clouds.

Doubt is natural. It takes courage to act despite fear, the voice spoke up with warmth.

Nell thought back, *I'm not afraid.*

Laughter like bubbles of water danced through her mind. *So you say.*

The voice was getting awfully talkative.

Nell gritted her teeth and dove.

Mina grabbed her hand, and a shock raced up Nell's arm, unexpected and strong. It stole her breath, exploded inside her. Blue and red sparks danced in the water around them. She fought to race to the surface, but Mina wouldn't let go.

"Relax, I'm allowing you to survive." Mina frowned. "Your own magic must be fierce. It's heightening mine, like two instruments complementing each other in a tune. Apologies, friend, but all should be well now. I've adjusted mine."

The swelling of power inside settled to a low hum.

Nell tried to stop struggling, and the sensation of pressure against her lungs eased. *Calm down,* she told herself. But no one else had ever described pain from the merfolk's magic.

The magic of the sea has recognized you as belonging to another power. We're with you, she heard in her mind, satiny smooth.

Belonging? She didn't like the sound of that. And who was this *we?*

Her friends were waiting for her but had missed the strange shock Nell experienced. There wasn't time to explain, and it didn't matter anyway. The voice had already told them everything they needed to know.

"Let's get to Port Iona." She marveled at the clarity of her voice under the water.

The merfolk's powerful tails sent them zooming. The fairy queens and their wee ones followed above the surface.

The sandy bottom sped past at a dizzying rate. Nell closed her eyes. With the merfolk's smooth speed, she almost felt like she was flying.

The trip was over before she knew it. What would have taken two days on land was a straight shot through the ocean, completed in just an hour. The tunnel Tristan had once used to sneak Sierra and Micah onto Port Iona had collapsed in the giant quake. Today, their group stepped out of the ocean just outside the city gates, which stood wide open.

As everyone did their best to dry off, Nell steeled herself. For the last four years, she'd been received in Port Iona with cheers, tears, kisses to her hands. Too many times to count.

The first time they'd returned to the port after Bentwood's defeat, rubble still filled the streets. Nell had climbed the raised platform of the central square, just as on the day they'd rescued Phoebe. Children's grubby faces peered up between terrified adults, and her heart swelled for them. She let go of her tight control and stepped aside for the voice.

"You've done well, our people!" the voice had said through her, rich and warm. *"But you must never forget what has happened here. Strong foundations can be rebuilt, but your ways must remain changed if Aluvia is to be saved!"*

Each time Nell and her friends journeyed back to Port Iona—or anywhere—the crowds came and called her name. No matter if Nell had come to research ancient magic or to warn of a new danger, she'd stand before the people and let that other presence bubble up until all she knew was the voice.

She wasn't looking forward to another performance today. With the voice so newly strengthened, what if it tried to take over more than just her throat?

Nell hitched up her pack and tossed her wet braid behind her. Here came the prophetess, she guessed. But when she reached the cobbled streets, long repaired since the last quake, she stopped, cocked her head, and lifted one hand to her friends.

"Take a look around," she said.

"What are we looking for?" Phoebe asked, eyes dark. Port Iona still gave her shivers, Nell knew, but the brave-hearted girl had come a long way since she'd been kept prisoner on this peninsula. Thank the stars for Tristan and Mina, who'd helped Phoebe heal, as did the magic of the ocean itself.

Corbin whispered, "Where is everyone?"

Nell narrowed her eyes. "Exactly."

At this time of day, the fish mongers should be tossing their silvery prizes into baskets. The metal smith should have his forge heated, smelling of melted copper and money. Girls should be giggling over hair ribbons at the morning market.

Instead, only a handful of people skulked among the shops like thieves. A few men drank ale with low whispers. Not one person turned to greet them. No shouting crowd gathered to call her name.

Nell felt invisible. What should have brought relief sent a chill through her instead, warning of a dangerous change. Too sudden a change.

Jasper's words came back to her. *They won't see you as a savior forever.*

Which was fine. Better than fine. She wasn't their savior; they were their own saviors. But if this Dragon had brainwashed them already, maybe the people would forget just how bad things had been before the voice intervened.

Their group paced down the street, the sound of their boots loud in the silence.

"This is creepy," Sierra muttered, holding hands with Micah.

Nell wished she could disagree.

A few people met Nell's eyes, opened their mouths as if to offer a greeting, but then fell silent. Their gazes darted around, like people afraid of being watched. Even worse, some stared and then turned to whisper to a neighbor, like snakes rustling through the grass.

In the city square, none awaited them to hear their message, but they gave it anyway.

"People of Port Iona, a new enemy is nearly among us!" Nell called. "He plans to take your city soon. You must protect your home. The voice has given a new message! Come hear and heed it!"

None came. The voice didn't make an appearance either, as if it knew there was no one to hear.

"Something's really wrong." Corbin murmured in Nell's ear.

"Agreed."

She lifted her hand and waved her friends over. "Everyone split up in pairs and dig to see what you can learn about whatever's going on. We don't have much time."

"Shouldn't we each go in different ways then? We'd cover the port a lot faster," Sierra suggested.

Nell shook her head. "I have a bad feeling. I want everyone to have backup and be ready to retreat into the ocean if need be."

They parted without another word, each pair taking a different direction.

Nell and Corbin went first to the sweets shop that often gave free candy for her sisters.

"Hi, Jeannine," she said, not even bothering to pretend cheerfulness. "I hear a man named the Dragon has been 'round these parts, talking about a take-over. Have you been in danger?"

"We're fine, Nell. Just real busy." Jeannine nodded at Corbin but said nothing else. Her hands shook as they formed balls of chocolate.

Nell stared hard at the woman, who turned red and still did not speak.

As they walked to the tailor, Corbin said, "Maybe let me have a go?"

"You couldn't do any worse than I just did."

He nudged her shoulder. "You say what you're thinking. Everyone loves that about you."

She laughed low. "Not everyone."

"They're the fools, then. But sometimes people prefer a more round-about conversation."

"Okay, you're up, then. I'm out of my league. Sweeten him up for us."

Brett the tailor glanced up when the two approached his counter but then stared at his needle as if he were stitching up a critical wound instead of a torn pair of pants.

"Have you had a good summer, Master Brett?" Corbin asked, his tone light. He leaned on the counter and flashed his happy smile, the one that always got a smile in return.

The tailor looked past Corbin's shoulder and squinted before returning to work. Nell pretended to settle her weapons better on her back and glanced back casually. A man leaned against the rough-hewed wall of the pub across the street, one leg bent so his booted foot tapped against the building.

She faced Brett again, raising her eyebrows. He gave a slight shake of his head, and though his eyes were dark with apology, he said only, "Everything's been fine, thank you kindly."

They received the same reception at the money lenders, the candle shop, and the market. Everything was fine. No one had anything to say.

Life had indeed gone on, but it didn't feel natural. Jasper had to be at the root of it, preparing this city for an easy takeover by scaring the people half to death before they ever saw the first dragon.

Nell's throat burned with unshed tears as they returned to the square. Corbin didn't say anything but kept his arm around her waist, a reminder that at least one person still trusted her.

When they met up with their friends, Micah murmured, "The news I've gained is not pleasant. Discretion would be wise." He pointed to the ancient temple just beyond the square, near the water. They'd explored it several times before, but no one had used the space in years. It sat just far off enough from the square to be left alone.

The temple was exactly like they left it, crumbling along the edges. The hallway ushered them down a narrow corridor with a small room on either side and emptied into a rotunda that opened to the sky through a small circle in the ceiling. The skylight was matched by a similar circle inlaid on the floor. The curved stone walls held rows of carved nooks where scrolls were tucked away.

Everyone had the same story.

"I can't believe it," Nell seethed, hand gripping the hilt of her dagger. "Are all of them stupid? They can't go back to the way things were. It'll all start over again." She wanted to punch someone.

"If the voice tells them to stay true, I bet they'll snap right out of it," Phoebe said.

Sierra shook her head and met Nell's eyes. Both practical people, they knew the golden era was over. They couldn't preach to a crowd that wasn't there. The real work had begun.

"It's harder for healers and alchemists to make elixirs without nectar," Sierra said. "And people are tired of supporting fairy keepers with food offerings for nothing."

"They've got a safe world! Isn't that enough?" Nell snapped.

"I know it. You know it. But not everyone has magic in their lives like we do."

Corbin nodded. "A clever person could easily fan dissatisfaction and fear into jealousy and hatred. Like the Dragon seems to have done."

Sierra added, "And if dragons—the fire-breathing kind—start burning lands outside the mountains, the people might believe this man could contain their threat. Some are more than willing to hand over their freedom if they think it'll keep them safe."

"Admittedly, this situation doesn't look good," Tristan said, "but you've warned them as best you could. We have to continue to the Ice-Locked Lands and focus on what's within our reach to affect."

Nell swallowed her roiling frustration, knowing it didn't help to get angry with people you couldn't fight. Corbin was always saying how violence wasn't the answer.

Not all anger leads to violence, the voice slid through her mind. *It can instead lead to revolution.* The voice was louder than before. A tremor ran through her. Revolution. She didn't feel like a revolutionary. She felt like someone who'd failed the very ones she was supposed to care for.

Nell looked around the room to settle herself. During the early months of desperately trying to preserve Aluvia's magic, she and her friends had gone through each part of the temple, reading everything. Whoever had built this place knew a good bit about conserving the magic of Aluvia. Unfortunately, much of what Nell and her friends had found only left them confused.

Today, though, she had a strange, new feeling, as if she had been here many times before, years ago. The image in her mind didn't quite match the room in front of her, and she squinted under the open skylight, trying to figure out what seemed different.

Someone bumped her, hard, and she staggered. She dropped to one knee to catch her balance, hands pressed against the cool stone floor.

"I'm sorry! I was staring at the ceiling! My fault," cried Corbin.

"I'm fine. Don't worry," she said. Corbin bumping into something or someone wasn't new. As she pushed herself up, her gaze sharpened. "You guys, look at this stonework. Why is the center circle a darker stone than the rest of the floor?"

Corbin lit the oil lamps along the wall, and Nell examined the floor more closely.

"Maybe they were artistic," Corbin suggested.

That didn't feel right. Nell shook her head. "There aren't any other floor decorations in the whole building. And the sun should have faded it through the skylight, not darkened it."

Corbin knelt and examined the floor. He pulled out his boline knife and picked at a strip of clay-like grout that edged the inner stone circle. The strip came out in one smooth chunk, leaving behind a clean separation. A deep and clear line appeared all around the center circle as he worked.

He broke out in a grin. "Well, look at that. We found something!"

Nell said, "It's probably just a trap door to the wine cellar, down in the damp."

A heavy pressure grew in her, though. Like an itch she couldn't scratch. There was something important about the circle, but she couldn't explain why she felt so sure. This unexplained knowing bothered her. It smacked too much of magic.

"There might be a way in to whatever that holds, but the Dragon won't put off his attack while we excavate here. We've got to go." She forced the logical words out, but her voice lacked the strength it usually held.

"Magic is rising around us right now," Micah said. "Can't you feel it? With all respect, we must find out why." He placed his ear against the wall and tapped it, eyes closing in concentration.

Nell's mouth went dry. More magic? She already had plenty, thanks.

Corbin winked at her, easing some of the tightness in her chest.

"Are you using magic to search?" Phoebe asked Micah.

He laughed, his dark brown eyes sparkling as he paused. "No, I suspect a trap door in a building so old will be mechanical. I'm no builder, but I've worked with the mountaineers who use many contraptions to move giant fallen trees from the forest path."

"We can all help then." Phoebe stepped forward to examine the wall, too.

Tristan fell in beside her, their heads bent close. They prodded each crevice near them, their unique tattoos on display as their bare arms moved quickly along the wall. Tristan's flying birds and Phoebe's merfolk tattoos were so different yet perfectly matched.

Nell gave in with a huff. The trip wouldn't continue until this mystery was explained, not now. Everyone was too excited.

She scanned the room, noting the carvings and the spaces while keeping her gaze soft and open, willing the knowledge to come to her in the way it sometimes did when she was tracking, be it pheasant or wild boar. It was a level of observation she was rarely conscious of, but she knew to trust it. Maybe this rising magic would help speed the process if she let it.

One of the carved cubby holes in the round room seemed to be slightly uneven from the others. Shaped… wrong. Different.

An urge to reach inside it teased her fingers. Her body surged with energy as if it might walk over there of its own volition. Without thinking, she tensed her muscles. She'd accepted the voice of prophecy using her as a mouthpiece, but she wasn't keen on it using her body like a puppet, too.

It wouldn't hurt to look, though. Then they could get a move on.

As soon as she made up her mind, the itchy feeling dissipated and her body relaxed.

She walked over and reached up to the cubby hole. It was too high to see inside. What if a snake was in there? But she hadn't come this far to quit now. She shoved her hand inside, fingers questing, and brushed a lump with smooth edges. She pressed on it and hoped she wasn't making a horrible mistake.

CHAPTER EIGHT

A loud creaking filled the chamber. Nell stumbled back with a jerk, and Corbin steadied her with a firm hand. The others gasped at the unexpected noise.

The circle in the middle of the room dropped down, scraping stone, revealing a short tunnel with a ladder. A whoosh of air flew through the rotunda, bringing with it scents of melted wax, cinnamon, and paper.

"What do you think?" Sierra whispered.

The tingling along Nell's spine grew. "I think we have to see what's down there."

Phoebe groaned. "It's in the dark. In a basement."

"Just wait for us here, Phoebes," Sierra said, but Phoebe pressed her lips together and peered down into the darkness.

The new space became pitch black within a few feet,

so Nell lifted an oil lamp from the wall. When she returned to the opening, her nose twitched, but there was no smell of mold. Odd, so close to the sea, but the tiny chamber must have been tightly sealed.

Or magically sealed?

She shivered again.

A deep part of her, perhaps part of her woven with the voice, insisted that they explore. Demanded it. The others waited, as if everyone knew this space was meant for Nell.

She peered into the opening. "It looks like some kind of library. I'm going down. Corbin, can you give me a hand?"

He reached to her without hesitation and took her lamp.

If only everyone was as trustworthy as Corbin. She lowered herself into the hole. Then, taking back the light, she inched down the ladder. The climb down was easy—the room was situated exactly under the one above. A curving table lined the entire circular wall of the room. Books stood in tall stacks and papers were spread about, as if waiting for someone to return.

Memories not her own flashed along Nell's mind, of this exact building with the door to the secret room wide open. Instead of the room being dark and empty, it bustled with life. Women in deep red robes came and went, consulting scrolls and books. The mood was intense but peaceful. Filled with purpose. Sacred. She lost her breath at the images, so real she almost expected to see a red-robed woman smiling next to her.

The memories felt eerie, like waking up from a dream and being uncertain if you were still dreaming or awake. Yet part of her unfurled toward the idea with longing. The sense of belonging, of purpose. Being not a mouthpiece, not a chess piece, but a chess master.

Corbin's voice broke into her flood of memories that could *not* be memories. At least not hers. She'd never been here before.

While she stared at the images seen only in her mind, the others had joined her in the small space, even Phoebe. Corbin carried his own oil lamp. The two lights wavered in the darkness, mingling and casting long shadows along the curved walls.

"Nell, look at this," Corbin's voice stayed low but vibrated with urgency.

On the wall above the table, his fingers hovered over a carving of a longsword over a giant tree, with wavy lines coming out from the blade.

Corbin whispered, "It's the sword of Aluvia—it has to be. The tree, the sword, the flames. The people who were here must have known about it. Maybe they wrote about it!"

Nell blinked, and the room swam.

Another memory that couldn't be hers flooded her mind, starkly vivid: a silver sword with flame billowing from the blade. Superimposed on it came an image of a tree, impossibly tall with deep green leaves. A woman with a red cloak held the sword aloft in both hands, fire crackling wildly around them both. Nell *felt* power humming down the blade into the hilt. Her clenched palms stung.

In response, her throat tightened, and words poured out for all in the room to hear. *"The fiery sword can rekindle that which has been extinguished. It can bring victory, but the cost will be high. Choose wisely."*

Nell gasped and came to full awareness with a jolt. For the space of a heartbeat, it was almost as if she had been two people. Or many people. Not pushed aside. More like… a joining.

Shock stole any words she might have produced.

She'd never held that sword, but her memory produced the perfect image of it, far beyond what her imagination could make up. Deep-gold handle. Bright silver blade. And orange-red fire flickering all around it. As if she had lived that experience.

"But how do we find it, exactly?" Corbin asked. "Does the voice know?"

The voice seemed done for the day, but Nell couldn't gather wits enough to tell him.

Sierra grabbed a thick volume that lay off to the side of the stacks on the table. She ran her fingers along the book. "No dust."

The leather cover creaked as she opened to the first page. Her jaw dropped, and she looked up with a gasp.

"This is from over five hundred years ago. When Port Iona was established."

Phoebe looked over Sierra's shoulder. "Does it tell this building's purpose?"

Sierra shrugged and handed the book to Corbin. "This is your expertise."

He sat on the floor with the wide book spread across his lap. An artist's illustration covered the two pages in rich color, the paint pristine. "Look at these people. They must've been the ones who stayed here. See how they're all lined up in front of this building?"

Nell glanced at the painting, and her gut trembled. Women in red cloaks. Like the ones she had pictured. Goose bumps marched up and down her arms.

She was losing her mind.

"Let's just find what we can about the sword and get going. Fast," she urged.

Magic was always suspect in Nell's book, though if it improved a weapon, she could accept it. But having some other presence inside her, talking to her, making her see things? That wasn't the kind of magic Nell was excited to experience.

The others pulled down books, flipped through pages. Nell stared at the carving on the wall. The sword looked plain and simple… except for that bit about the fire. She snorted and joined in the search.

Much of the information they found was practical: making this potion or that, properties of certain herbs, lists of magical creatures. Corbin noted that blue dragons were never mentioned.

Some of the information seemed like rules guiding the group of women, who remained separate from everyone else, going about their job without others much noticing. No interference, no distraction. Nothing to sully the purity of their purpose, whatever it was.

A lonely life, thought Nell.

Finally, after an hour or two—hard to tell inside the tomb-like building—Phoebe crowed with excitement.

"I think I found something!" she called. "This sounds like there was a special sword forged by the women who lived here. It had some kind of magical fire, and after the death of their last high leader, the remaining women felt the flames were too dangerous, so they hid the sword away, buried it at the highest point of the Ice-Locked Lands."

For once, the weapon in a story didn't capture Nell's attention. She was stuck on the red-robed women. "If they focused on magic instead of combat, what were they doing with a sword, much less a flaming one? And if they were real, why haven't we grown up with stories of them?"

And yet if they weren't real, why did she have memories of them in her head? Not a question she was willing to ask out loud. Not yet. It made her sound crazy even to herself.

Corbin answered, his eyes fixed on the illustration.

"Maybe there's more to our history than we have even guessed, history we've lost. But whatever they were, none of them are here now. It might be that none of us can safely use that sword, not even you, Nell."

Nell examined the book's careful illustration. The blade was narrow, almost delicate, but she bet it would all but sing in the hands of its owner. Her heart panged at the thought of it held by another.

"A sword like that would turn any fight into a glorious battle." The words dropped from her lips without intention.

Corbin bit his lip. "That's what I'm afraid of."

His words were like a kick to the gut, but before she could react, the voice spoke to her.

My sword will bring healing as well as justice. The voice slid through Nell's mind slower this time and brought a peaceful balm to her heart. She could almost feel a hand brushing down her hair, cradling her cheeks as a mother would. The whisper didn't seem strange at all, or frighten her now. It soothed her.

As if in a dream, she lifted the book up and flipped through it. The final back pages had a map drawn by hand and a short bit of writing scribbled in a cramped style. Nell hadn't known she was looking for it, but once she saw the hand-drawn map, her heart thudded with recognition. She simply knew the red-robed women had written this.

Sierra and Corbin were debating the nature of the

magical flames, but Nell interrupted. "Corbin, what language is this? And isn't this the Ice-Locked Lands?"

The argument cut off and everyone crowded around the open book to stare at the map.

Corbin studied the short phrase. "It seems to be in some sort of code or ancient language, maybe. I bet I could figure it out if I needed to. But, yes, the map shows the whole continent down there, with a lot more detail than the maps I've seen."

"Like landmarks and where to go!" Phoebe piped up. "Those red areas might be unsafe for walking, see how there's a dotted path to follow around them, and look—that's a little tree drawn at the top of that mountain. That must be where the sword is! The Tree of Life!"

Nell had no way to explain her certainty that the women in red had left this book as a guide.

Yes... the whisper curled through her.

"How high is that mountain, though? And can we even get up to the highest peak if no explorer ever has, even with a map?" Sierra said doubtfully.

Sweat prickled Nell's brow. It was use this map or risk wandering around in a frozen land without a clue. Those who never took chances never took the victory, either. Time to move forward.

With the decision made, her nerves settled despite herself, like fluttering wings going still. "The voice will guide us and help me with the sword. It's never let us down yet. If I can trust its magic, you can, too."

She lifted her palm to Corbin and waited, hand extended, facing him. The others fell silent and looked quizzically at them. Corbin's eyes closed, and when he opened them, they were filled with resignation. He reached his hand to hers and pressed, palm to palm.

He was no fool, this boy she loved, and he knew the stakes were higher than just one girl.

Corbin wove his fingers through hers before he spoke. "I'll believe in the voice within you. But more than that, I'll believe in you."

"We all do," Micah said.

Tristan and Phoebe nodded solemnly.

Sierra said, "Until the end. We all stand together."

Love tightened Nell's throat. They were so loyal, so full of goodness and light. It made her fiercely glad that, in the end, the one holding the sword was the one most likely to die, magic or not. She'd rather it be her than any of them.

Sierra cleared her throat. "Okay then. Nell, do you feel anything else left for us here?"

Nell searched inside. The itchiness was gone now. *Well?* she asked the voice though it felt awkward, as if she were expecting her mirror to talk. Nothing replied, but she felt a sense of closure and chose to trust it. "I think it's time to head south."

They opted to take the one book with them,

protected by another waterproof bag. The sentences scrawled on the last page were clearly added on later. Corbin wanted to try translating it, in case the message involved the sword or its magic.

Nell would be glad to get out of the building. The feelings it evoked were too strange, too powerful. She couldn't think about what those not-her-memories could mean. She'd think about them later. Talk about the images with her friends later. Just not now.

When they made their way to the square, the sun was much lower in the sky. Nell was prepared to head straight to the Ice-Locked Lands despite her empty stomach, but a crowd was gathering.

Finally. The citizens of Port Iona had come.

But this time, they were not happy.

A haunting silence rode the summer breeze, like the storm about to break. The faces along the street were drawn and angry.

"I don't think they're here to say thanks. Let's send the fairies to wait by the sea," Nell whispered. "No sense in anyone getting killed if Queenie loses her temper when you do, Sierra."

Sierra snickered, but the fairies left in a swirl toward the sea. A flash of white shimmered near the water's edge, far into the distance. Nell squinted but couldn't tell what it was.

No matter. Time to take the initiative.

"People of Port Iona! You are in grave danger! A man comes to siege your city; you must prepare to defend yourselves! The voice says we can stop him, but we must travel far to reach an extraordinary weapon first."

A door swung open across the street.

"You!" the butcher's wife hollered. "You've brought a curse with all these messages of saving the fairies!"

"Our message was what saved you in the first place," Nell replied, voice cool.

The woman's face contorted with rage. "That man, the Dragon. He told us he'd return on the full moon. That's tonight! His bloody dragons will kill us all when the sun goes down."

"Not if we make him king!" someone in the crowd said.

The butcher in his leather apron came alongside the angry woman. "I have no wish to serve another like Bentwood. What can you do to keep us safe? Some far-away weapon won't help us now."

The woman muttered, "Nothing. She can do nothing."

Another man yelled at the butcher from the window. "Shut your wife up! She'll bring suffering down on all of us! The crew told us not talk to them!"

"When it's your wife up all night weeping, let's see how you feel," the butcher snapped.

"None of us want to die, you old fool. But talking to fairy fanatics is the fastest way to bring death now! A fairy sting won't stop them dragons."

Nell glanced back at the man yelling from the window, and something along the horizon caught her eye. Another flash of white, just visible between the buildings, like a curl of hazy fog. What was going on?

All the eyes in the street bore down on her. She felt their weight but had nothing else to offer them. Then Corbin clasped her shoulder, giving her a hard squeeze. He believed in her.

She touched his hand in silent thanks, gathered her wits, and tried again. "I've met this Dragon myself. He made a lot of threats and promises he can't keep. And he's wrong. We must honor the magic in our lands. Stealing from our magical brethren isn't an option anymore."

Anger was beginning to heat the forge in her belly. The familiar feeling gave her power to stand tall.

A bearded man she didn't recognize shouted, "We're better than any fairy fanatic or fish-lover. If we ruled over them all, life would be better. The Dragon's got that part right."

He came closer. He had the look of a crew member, with heavy scarring on his hands and arms. The growing crowd tightened, muttering among themselves.

Two more men stepped out of the pub, hands on their swords.

"And who is this Dragon? Do you even know?" Nell asked.

The bearded man sneered. "What do you care? You've not been here in four or five months, Nell. The Dragon's been talking to folks around here about lots of things. He makes sense. We've made our choice."

"Sounds to me like this Dragon's just preying on your fears," Sierra snapped. "Is that who you want to serve? The people of Aluvia have no kings."

"He says he can bring us untold riches. He'll keep us safe from the dragons."

Corbin spoke up. "And is life so bad now? Have you actually been threatened by any dragons, other than his?"

Nell scanned the area. More people had arrived, filling the only road out of the port.

The butcher said, "Life's been better. Cost of everything's gone way up since the merfolk started charging for things that used to be free, and our healers say a little nectar in their potions could help cure plenty of illnesses faster."

Nell tried once more. "If we lose magic again, life will be far worse than now. Have you forgotten the earthquakes?"

The bearded man replied, "If we lose our homes, it'll

be worse sooner rather than later. Better to move with the tide and take our chances."

The crowd whispered among themselves. The crew members had definitely been preparing the way for their new master.

Nell looked over at the horizon again, and this time, a shape had taken form. Dots in the distance grew larger, the same deep blue as the sea, but high in the sky. They were large, with wings.

Corbin followed her gaze, along with Sierra. They both stiffened.

"Is that—?" Sierra began.

"Dragons." Corbin bit out the word.

Nell's mind finally made sense of the shapes, and she stifled a gasp. The wide bodies were clear now, along with the pointed wings and long tails. Three dragons. Though they looked small from this distance, she knew each would be as big as a cottage.

She narrowed her eyes at the dark speck on the back of the biggest. A man riding it, the Dragon himself, no doubt.

Everyone needed to run. Nell opened her mouth to shout, but she couldn't move. The voice rose up through her without warning.

The prophetic voice spoke, loudly, urgently to the crowd, *"It's not too late! Reject the enemy and stay faithful to what you know is true! If you return to your old ways, all of*

Aluvia will suffer. My children, my people, do not forget who you are!"

"Who we are?" the butcher yelled. "We're dead. Unless your magic can save us from those beasts right now!"

The voice relinquished its control of her body. Nell gasped and stood stunned, unable to move. *Help us defeat the Dragon!* Nell cried to the voice. *Prove yourself!*

You *must show them the way. You can do it.* The voice came quickly.

I don't know how! Nell yelled back in her mind, prickles of sweat beading her brow.

The butcher shook his head, eyes narrowing. "The Dragon was right. You're a fraud. He may be a hard master, but least he'll give us back our dignity. Any leader's better than you."

Nell dragged in a breath and threw back her shoulders. "No. I'll protect you from him and his dragons. We must continue to preserve the world's magic. The voice has said so."

The dragons were closer now, in a triangle formation. White mist blew from their noses like fog, the source of white flashes she'd seen. The man on the back of the lead dragon wore solid black. She waited for the voice to speak, to inspire, to give hope. But there was silence.

So she made a promise, just from her. "I might not be able to defeat him today, not with those dragons, but I'll find a way. I'll help you take back your city even if he claims it."

"Big words for a little girl." Jasper stepped out of the crowd.

Nell reached for her dagger. "Following me, now, Jasper?" Her lip curled in a snarl of loathing.

He laughed, but it held no humor. "What, no fairies to protect you, little fanatics?" Jasper sneered at Sierra and Corbin. "That's okay. If Nell gives herself up, the rest of you can go. He doesn't care about you, not even you keepers. He's beyond you now."

Sierra stepped closer. "Nell's not going anywhere."

"Oh, so you'll let all these nice people die, then? If Nell doesn't submit, the Dragon won't show them mercy." He waved his hand back toward the inner city streets.

Sierra and Corbin exchanged horrified glances.

"You're lying," Nell said.

"Was I lying about the dragons flying toward us right this minute? I told you I'm in tight with him. I know his plans, see, and they don't end with this one puny port. Why would I lie?"

Nell said, "You lie because that's what liars do."

The butcher scowled, holding his weeping wife. "I think that 'voice' of yours is the liar. You've done nothing for us but tell us what to do, how to live."

During this exchange, an even larger crowd had gathered in the street, spilling into the square. People cried out at the sight of the approaching dragons, bracing against their door frames. Their eyes turned calculating as they stared at her, then back at the approaching threat. Nell took in their expressions, and her lips pressed into a hard line.

Jasper turned to the crowd. "Let's hand over Nell to the Dragon and live! Take back our lands from the wretched magical creatures pushing us from the sea and mountains! She's already proven she's worthless when it really matters! Who will save you? Not Nell! The Dragon! *The Dragon!*"

CHAPTER NINE

The faces in the square warmed with hope. Nell could tell they'd hand her over in a heartbeat, but she had no intention of giving herself up without a fight. "You know that going back to the old ways would destroy our world. Giving me up to him won't prevent that."

"The only ones benefiting these days are you and your fanatic friends," Jasper said. "The people here are finally seeing through you, Nell. I told you they wouldn't love you forever."

She cursed under her breath. He was right. There was no easy way out of this now. Retreat would be the smart thing to do, but not enough people would be able to escape even if she convinced them to abandon the port. The best she could do was try to spare most of them.

Nell whispered to her friends, "You all run. Regroup and come back to fight with the sword once you find it."

Before any of them could react, she spun to face Jasper. "I'll duel your Dragon. If I win, he leaves the ports alone. If he wins, you'll get your king. How's that for a deal?"

Corbin didn't bother to muffle his curse behind her. She'd rarely heard him use such language. "What do you think you're—?"

Jasper leapt on the square's watering well and pitched his voice to carry down the street. "What say you, my people? Shall we let her fight the Dragon? Are you ready to see what a real leader looks like, a king who will keep you safe from the abominations in our world?"

For a second, silence filled the square. The last chance of resistance hung like a trembling leaf clinging to its branch. Then the crowd yelled, "Let 'em fight!" Throngs of bloodthirsty people pushed into the square. The trembling leaf broke from its branch and was lost, floating away on the wind of fear and rage.

Her dagger was in her hand, but she couldn't use it, not against the very people she'd worked so hard to save all these years. Wild rage and desperation coated the faces in the crowd like soot over a beautiful painting. These were people ruled by fear, a mob.

Her friends gathered behind her, and she yelled at

them over her shoulder, "Get back. Go to the sea; call the other merfolk. I'll come for you after I fight him."

A sacrifice from you now will not save them. You first need the sword to defeat his wrath.

She startled at the voice in her mind, which had a new sharp tone. It sounded... worried? Upset? With her, maybe.

I can't give up now, she told the voice. *I'm sorry. But these people need to see me fight for them. And if I win, he won't use his dragons to destroy the port. I can do this.*

Sadness dripped from the voice's words like rain. *You will do what you must. But pride has no place in a war for survival.*

"We won't leave you," Corbin said, stepping up beside her.

"We're all in this together," Sierra added.

Micah, Tristan, and Phoebe lined up next to her like a wall, but these people would tear them down in a heartbeat. They would be safer with her plan. The Dragon wanted her.

He could have her—if he could take her in an honest fight. She knew what she was up against now. And she excelled at her craft.

The approaching lead dragon bellowed, and people cowered and shrieked. Its growl was so deep it crawled up Nell's spine like rumbling thunder.

One, two, three dragons swooped over the skies, spiraling in to hover above the center square, close enough for Nell to smell snow, jasmine, and musk heavy on the wind, and see the white where black should be in their eyes. The sun glared bright as she looked for the enemy himself. A dark silhouette of a large man and wings stretched across the sky.

One of the beasts blew a white breath at an abandoned shop along the edge of the square. Frosty ice crackled the thatch rooftop, collapsing it just like her home. If that breath hit the crowd today—she shivered. Three dragons were more than enough to destroy a port.

People were screaming, ducking, shoving. Taking advantage of the distraction, Nell tossed her traveling pack to Corbin, along with her quiver and bow. He clutched them, eyes stunned.

"Go!" she shouted again.

But the crowd already gathered in front of them, blocking off the escape route through town. She turned in time to see Sierra push Phoebe and Tristan toward the temple just beyond the square. They shook their heads, but Sierra pointed fiercely, and they ran around the far corner of the temple that led to the docks and the sea. Sierra, the stubborn girl, raced back to Nell.

The dragons circled above the city, their huge wings casting sweeping shadows over the square. The jostling crowd shoved Nell back and forth among the fleeing citizens.

One dragon dropped suddenly and landed on the far

side of the square, blocking off the main street out of the city. The second hovered near the docks, blocking the water.

The last of the creatures to land was the largest. Ridges ran down the long neck to where the man sat atop its back, the man who had come to conquer. The large blue dragon, just as astounding as the first time she saw it, landed on the tiled roof of the port's school house, one front claw grabbing the spire. The beast mantled its wings so widely they touched the buildings on either side. Its claws sank into the angled roof, cracks spreading from each foot like spider webs. A thatched roof would have never born the weight. The dragon defiantly threw back its head and shrieked.

The sound blew through Nell, and she wanted to clap her hands on her ears. She stiffened her back instead.

High above them, the man raised a sword and shouted a long battle cry through his mask. It was time to do what she'd agreed to. She swallowed hard.

"Cease your running!" The Dragon's voice boomed across the square, loud and deep. "Stand and proclaim your servitude, and live. Defy me and die!"

People pushed to escape. Some were trampled in the stampede. The man raised his other arm, and in response, the dragon by the dock swept upward, faster than should be possible for a beast of that size. People turned to stare, mouths agape, as if watching a horrible accident, unable to turn away.

The riderless dragon spun in the air, tightened its wings along its sides, and plummeted toward the ground until its wings opened with a giant crack, sending the dragon swooping low across the crowd. People dropped to their knees and covered their heads, as if that would help at all against such a beast.

As it reached the edge of the square, the dragon rose over the port's city hall and blew a mighty breath. Cold rushed through the air but concentrated along the snowy mist that hit the building with a shriek. The solid stones cracked and split, coated with ice.

Blustery winds like a winter squall buffeted the crowd as the dragon hovered above them. With a hair-raising screech, it blew another flurry of ice and mist at the building, collapsing the stone roof with a thunderous slam. The beast landed in front of it, huffing.

Silence fell across the square at the sudden destruction of one of their oldest and finest buildings made of the hardiest stone.

The man—the Dragon—spoke into the shocked stillness. "You knew dragons could kill, and now you see how quickly. But I have no wish to destroy you. Serve me, and I will make humans strong again, masters of the magical world!"

The crowd roared. Nell cried out in denial but couldn't even hear it over the noise.

He stood in his stirrups, raising both arms left bare by his leather chest plate. "What will it be Port Iona? Are you for me or against me?"

Port Iona's people, some with joy and some with fear, shouted back, "For you!"

The man climbed down the dragon's back and long curving tail to the ground. Then the creature climbed higher along the bell tower, leaving deep divots in the orange-tiled roof. After speaking with Jasper, the Dragon strolled to the middle of the square to where Nell waited. The crowds opened for him and closed right behind like water filling in the wake of a boat.

Her palms didn't sweat, but prickles ran along her scalp.

"I hear we are to have a duel, Nellwyn. Didn't you learn your lesson the last time?"

"A duel of honor requires using only your own strength, your own weapons. Dragons don't count. I'm not sure I can trust you for that."

He laughed. "I won't need my dragons to defeat you."

Anger burned a flush along her cheeks. Nell pulled her longsword and strode away from Corbin and her friends to meet the Dragon in the center of the square.

Her friends shouted at her to stop, but she didn't. Couldn't. For once in her life, her cool head in battle failed her. He'd come after her family, threatened everything she loved. The need to defeat him beckoned too powerfully to resist.

She stood alone in a wide circle in the center of the square. The crowd pressed away from her even as people crammed into open windows to watch. Silence was heavy.

With the people contained and quieted, the two dragons without saddles lifted as a unit and circled around the city. Each time they soared directly overhead, the people hunkered low. The sun still burned in the summer sky, spreading light like icing along the rooftops.

The ringing of a sword pulled from a sheath snapped Nell to attention and called to the deepest part of her, the tough young girl who fought her way to a top position in a dangerous crew for the sake of her family.

The people of Port Iona had betrayed her—her and their own world, but there was no time for tears. She braced herself for the first strike.

The Dragon moved fast. The blows came one after another, quicker than he'd fought before. She had just enough time to realize he must have been toying with her, and that she was in deep, deep trouble. Then her focus tunneled until she only knew movement and response.

She ducked a fast strike, heard the whistle as it cut through the air. Lunging, she thrust her own blade, but he knocked it aside and slammed his heavy fist on her shoulder. She staggered but threw off his following sword strike and jabbed one of her own.

"You can do better than this, can't you?" He sidestepped past her.

Rolling her sore shoulder, Nell ignored the taunt and circled him, crouching slightly on the balls of her feet. He pressed his attack, and she blocked one hit after another with the flat of her blade, her fingers tingling from the force of his attacks. Her eyes narrowed. Taking advantage of a small opening, she slipped her sword past his guard and sliced a thin red line across his shoulder. Before she could feel any sense of triumph, he picked up the tempo without missing a beat, pushing her backward step by step with a series of rattling strikes.

She glanced around to quickly check her location. Her lips tightened. The ancient temple was visible behind her —she'd been pushed to the edge of the square. With a shout, she threw herself at him and delivered a dozen fast blows. Her foot snagged on an uneven cobblestone, breaking the rhythm of her swings, and his sword jabbed at her ribs. She missed her parry but pivoted away fast enough so he only sliced her leather vest, not her skin. Too close, though.

Nell's breath burned in her lungs, and her hands were nearly numb. She danced back, light on her feet, to take a moment to breathe, but he followed her, sweeping his sword in a whirling arc. Her blade blocked his with a clash and trembled, close to breaking. She deflected the strike downward, the sound of sliding metal screeching. This fight needed to end fast. She licked her lips and considered her limited options.

Then the Dragon pulled the second sword from the sheath on his back with his free hand. The entire edge of the blade shone with the same dark liquid she'd seen on his blade the first time they fought. The sticky-looking glaze was the wrong color for Flight but could be any number of other options, none good.

"Impressive, Nellwyn. But you've never been as skilled with two weapons as with one."

She reeled at the implications of his statement. He knew her. Knew her personally?

He spun the swords so they whirled in circles, becoming one continual slicing blade. She pulled her dagger from her sheath, struggling to keep up. She cursed the decision to not bring her second sword, but he was right. She'd always favored fighting with a single sword over two.

Clang, clang, clang.

His swords kept knocking her blades away. She was going to lose. Again.

The knowledge shook her.

"Why not just submit now? Is being dead really better than ruling at my side?" the Dragon said, his voice gruff with anger.

"You have a funny way of trying to recruit people.

Destroying my home. Trying to kill me. And if you use up Aluvia's magic, you'll kill us all," she shouted.

Their swords met overhead, and she pushed back as hard as she could. They held there, two warriors locked in combat.

The glint of his eyes shone through the mask, so close to her face. He whispered to her, "I saw your family flee your home before I had my dragon strike. I didn't kill them. No, I want to save us all, with your help. Don't you see? Any war brings causalities, but the world isn't balanced—we all suffer without the magic we're due."

She couldn't process what he was saying, not now. He lunged at her. She blocked, but he struck again.

"You've taught people we're servants of magical creatures," he said. "That we owe them protection. It's so, so wrong. Come with me now, and we can lead this world. Dragons, fauns, fairies, merfolk, and more—they'll all respect and serve humans as they should. Together, we'd be welcomed as rulers, and lives would be saved."

She shoved hard, and her dagger slipped.

He spun. With a quick twist of his wrist at the last second, he sent her dagger flying. It fell to the ground with a clatter. She'd only seen one person do that maneuver.

Her eyes snapped up to the man, searching his

mostly-hidden face, his body, for clues. It couldn't be. Could it?

Her distraction cost her.

He reversed his grip, and the pommel of his second sword came up hard under her chin. She tasted blood and saw stars, slamming onto her back. Her breath left in a whoosh, leaving her stunned. Her hand barely held onto her sword, but he walked over and stepped on the blade.

"Come on, Nellwyn. Weren't you going to save these poor people with the strength of your sword arm?"

Faces swam in front of her eyes. The crowd had gone quiet. She'd expected jeers, but she only heard the rustling sound of dragon wings in the sky. She turned her head and caught Corbin's horrified expression, Micah holding him back. Sierra stood nearby, shocked.

Blood dripped from Nell's mouth. She wiped her face with one sleeve and growled. But she couldn't force herself to sit up. Her head was ringing.

The Dragon's masked face loomed over her, growing nearer until it filled her vision. His strip of white hair fell past his mask, and his eyes glowed with a sinister light.

"Kill me now, then," Nell said, and she spat blood to the ground. Hopefully Corbin and her friends had the good sense to run. Someone had to find that sword.

He laughed, a low, cruel sound. "Killing you would be like melting down a perfectly balanced sword because your enemy once held it. You and I, Nellwyn, we're meant to fly. The sky has no limit for us. Don't you feel it?"

"The name's Nell, and what I feel is you're crazy." She gritted out the words through the fiery ache along her jawbone.

His next words came so softly she barely heard them. "I've been watching you a long time. I knew you'd be powerful, though not even I guessed how closely our paths would dovetail. We're the same, you and I."

He knelt and lifted her to a sitting position. The world spun until colors resolved again into shapes. He was so close she could pick out the intricate carving along his mask, the careful dye work.

"We aren't the same at all." Nell shook off his touch and swallowed more blood, salty and metallic. She tried to stand, but her body refused. At least her voice wasn't shaking. "Why don't you show me who you are, if you want me to join you."

"Don't you know me yet, girl?"

She'd been disarmed like that before, by her weapons trainer, Shane McConnel. *But Shane died,* she thought groggily. Murdered by Jack and Bentwood. And Shane wouldn't have white hair. Or magic.

Especially not evil magic. He'd never be like this man.

The unknown man leaned even closer, the scent of leather mixed with something both sweet and sour rolling off him. "No matter. The point is I know you're a worthy warrior to join me, with or without the sword you seek."

"You already know where the sword is?"

"It doesn't matter. You'll never find it in time."

He turned and faced the crowd, sword extended high. He raised his voice so loud it echoed in the square. "The creatures in the frozen continent listen to my commands, as all magical creatures should. Without someone leading them, they're no better than wild monsters."

He gestured at his scarred neck. The scar's center was white and jagged, but skin puckered around the long red seam of it. Pity pushed at her fear. She recognized the sheer amount of pain represented by a scar like that.

Struggling to her knees, Nell left her sword behind. His strength was incredible. She was lucky he hadn't broken her jaw.

She was going to die right here.

No. The word was clear in her mind. It wasn't the prophetic voice speaking in her mind, though. It was just herself, Nell, refusing to die.

A tiny knife could still pierce a heart. She only needed the strength of her right arm for this maneuver.

Nell slid her hand smoothly to her boot and palmed the tiny knife she kept hidden there. Ignoring the pain, she stood and shifted her weight to the balls of her feet, waiting for an opening.

He turned back to her and she glared, raising her chin high.

"That's my girl," he said, and she snarled.

She was nobody's girl.

Then the familiar tightening of her throat cut into her concentration.

Not now! Not now! she screamed to the voice.

Usually, being taken over by the voice felt like being pushed underwater, but not this time. Her vision didn't waver at all. A strange taste touched her tongue, like heartbreak in winter.

The crowd froze. Even the Dragon paused, eyes widening behind the mask.

"People of Aluvia, remember this moment. Salvation can be regained, but suffering will now be had in equal measure first. The sword must open the sky with fire to defeat the icy death of the enemy." The words rang clear but held worlds of sorrow that broke Nell's heart.

"What power! I must have it," he murmured, staring at her eyes, which she knew must be pitch black. The voice's power slid from her awareness and left her fully herself, fully angry. Grief always made her mad.

She couldn't let him win. Wouldn't.

Nell steadied the thin, hand-sized knife. He might kill her, but she'd take him down with her.

She flung herself at him, two steps, three, a blur of motion.

Her arm felt unsteady, but she stabbed him as hard as she could. The knife slide into his chest, too high for the heart, and she cursed at herself for missing her target.

She shoved hard anyway, hoping to hit an artery. Blood poured down his chest, covering her palm. The people shrieked, stumbled backward.

"Nell!" she heard Corbin cry. But he was too far away, trapped in the crowd.

The Dragon sucked in his breath but smiled. Her stomach twisted.

He chuckled, staring down at her from his full height, not even hunched over from pain, blood dripping down his body. "A warrior queen, that's what you are."

She stared at his blood coating her hand. She may have missed his heart, but she'd struck a solid blow. Perhaps he had some sort of magical strength, the way fairies were tougher than their size suggested. As if she needed the scales tipped any further against her.

Dragon bellows filled her ears, drowning out the crowd. Their roars shook the ground. He wouldn't hold those beasts back once she went down.

A dragon landed in the courtyard with a rippling thud that sent people screaming into the safety of the buildings. His dragon, the biggest of the blues, coiled up like a spring to fit in the remaining courtyard behind his master. The man didn't flinch.

He grabbed her wrist and sliced a thin line along her palm with the black edge of his sword. Blood dripped down her fingers, and roaring filled her ears, followed by pain like she'd never known.

Liquid fire ran up her arm. Nell screamed and fell back to the ground. The black stuff on his blade had to be poison. Was she dying? She almost wished she was. This made Jack's beatings feel like a loving caress. She struggled to catch her breath. Loose rocks in the courtyard dug into her back.

The Dragon leaned over her, his mad, wild eyes showing through the mask. "We are alike, touched by magic. You don't really want the power, I know. I'll take the burden from you." He stood and held his hands over her as a cold traveler might warm their hands against a fire. His eyelids drifted half-shut, his fingers questing in the air until he clenched his hands into fists above her prone body.

Pain ripped through her again, a sword edge slicing at her very essence.

The voice inside Nell shrieked, a chorus of voices breaking at once. *He's taking your magic, taking our strength! Don't let us go, Nell. Fight his power!*

Nell gasped, clutching at her chest, back arching as he raised his hands higher. It felt like her limbs were being torn from her body. Her sight warped as she stared at the blue sky above, trying to breathe. Corbin and Sierra's voices, shouting threats and curses, drew nearer, but not close enough. Nell's awareness of them slid away.

Something was unspooling inside her, the glowing magic that had dwelled within since the fairies infused her with it. The magic that somehow sustained the prophetic voice.

Wind spun up around them, blowing hard. Fire and ice coursed through her veins, smashing into each other, warring for control. Her hands clenched. The battle inside her was the hoof beats of a thousand horses thundering through her, the rushing of a million wings sending her high into the sky, surrounded by air, by mist, by light, by pure energy.

Hot, cold, hot, cold… Her lips chattered, and she burned as if with fever.

He leaned down and said, "My elixir traps your power while allowing mine to absorb it. It's my best creation, a powerful potion like no other. It's easier on you if you give in to it."

She gasped, struggling to contain the surging power

rocketing through her. "You can't take this magic. It's not for you."

"We'll see," he murmured, flexing his hands over her like a puppet master pulling on invisible strings.

She screamed again. When the sharpest pain eased, she panted and turned her gaze to the blue dragon behind them, who seemed, perhaps, solemn? Sad?

The man followed her wide-eyed gaze and glanced past his shoulder. "He remembers how it feels, I imagine, to have his magic taken. His fire burns inside me now, just like with all my dragons. They do what I ask and give me power. So much power."

He flexed his hands, tightening into fists again. She lost all breath from the pain.

Knives were stabbing her heart, she was sure. The voice inside her wailed.

We can't stop him, it cried. *He's placed us in a web, a trap...*The voice grew fainter. *He's locking us away from you, Nell... separating you from your magic...*

The world continued to shudder and buck as Nell fought the theft, the loss of the voice. She shivered as cold ripped through her again.

Let us help... the voice urged. *His power is like yours, but wrong, too cold to be safe...We can hide in your heart and protect you there, keep your magic from him until you can reach the Tree and be healed.*

"Give it time, Nellwyn," he said.

Nell fought to listen to both voices.

"You might be able to keep me out for now, but not for long. My elixir will strip you bare soon enough, and you'll come to me."

"Stop it! Leave me be!" she screamed, focusing on all the magic she'd ever touched.

The dragon behind the man threw up its head and wings as if it had been stung. It lurched back, away from her, out of her darkening vision. She heard a dragon roar, a flurry of feet, a clatter.

"Look at her eyes! They've gone black," she heard someone say. Sierra?

Then someone was dragging her, her back scraping hard against the stone ground, but she couldn't stop to see or think. She could only feel, and she wished she couldn't. This was far worse than the fairy swarm.

Quick, Nell! We are almost too weak to help. Open your heart to us.

"What do you mean?" Nell cried aloud. Her will to fight was fading. She was plummeting into unconsciousness. This time, she might not wake up.

You didn't want this, it's true, but if you don't fully accept us into your heart, you'll die. Our legacy will die, too, along with Aluvia's magic. Our world will sink into an ice age it might never recover from. We need you, Nell. The fairies chose you; we chose you.

Why? she wanted to cry. This hurt too much. Wind whipped through her along with the Dragon's evil magic, freezing her, killing her. She was powerless to stop it.

Because you're a fighter, a warrior.

Who are you? Nell had to know.

There's no time. His magic is twisted and will corrupt anything it touches. He won't be able to steal your magic—yet—but he could turn it to darkness—turn you to darkness. We'll protect you as best we can. Let us into your whole heart, Nell. Now!

Fine, she said. She couldn't even remember why she had once resisted the voice at all. Nothing mattered now. *Take whatever you need. I give you my life. I accept you fully and forever.*

And warmth filled her like a tide, gentle but strong. It slowed her descent into darkness, lifted her until she was drifting among clouds on a summer day full of light. The warmth soothed the freezing places, even healed her jaw, her knees, and her back. But his poison was still there, one icy knot beneath her heart not even the voice could undo. It burned in its coldness.

It's the best we can do. The source of his magic is the most mercurial of all magics, easily corrupted, and the first lost to our world long, long ago. Be warned—you don't have much time to find healing. We can't fight off his poison forever. Find the Tree at the summit of the icy lands. Follow the map. You'll have to be strong, our child. But you are. You can survive this.

The voice was fading now. A mere whisper, growing

softer and softer still, as if locking itself behind a closed door. The door was almost shut. Soon, it would be gone.

Who are you? she asked again while the sky swam around her.

A series of images flooded her mind in response:

Women in red cloaks lifting hands toward a tree that touched the clouds.

A group of women living separate from the world, living in a unified purpose and study.

Each leader among them binding herself to a sword that blazed with orange and red flames, one woman after another through generations.

The sword forever holding some part of the soul of each woman who wielded it.

The fiery sword of Aluvia.

We are the ones who have lived years beyond measure, giving up all to mend and tend Aluvia's magic.

Nell fought to remain conscious. *Why did you give up so much for our world?*

We chose to.

But why?

We are the guardians.

The blackness overtook her.

"Forget this temple. Let's get her in the sea! Now!"

Nell awoke to Corbin's voice. He sounded unlike himself: demanding, angry, insistent.

"She's still unconscious, even after Micah poured magic into her! I don't think even mer-magic could keep her from drowning." That was Sierra. Angry, too. Why?

"The people will break in here any moment. The dragons may be gone for now, but the villagers made their allegiance known."

"I think they regret their choice." Micah's voice came from farther away. "Did you not see the old woman and her husband crying at the end?"

"I couldn't see anything but Nell," Corbin said.

There was such pain in his voice. She sucked in a breath, and the others exclaimed, their presence surrounding her.

"Nell, we really don't want to relive the fairy swarm black-out. We don't have time," Sierra said, strained teasing in her words.

Nell forced her eyes open and focused on Corbin's relieved face. Tear tracks stained his cheeks.

"Hey, I'm okay," she whispered, tracing the paths of his tears with shaking fingers.

"I'm not," he said. "I nearly lost you. Don't ever do that again!"

His voice was rough, and she wanted to close her eyes against his audible pain. He'd shed tears for her.

Nell tried to think past the fog in her mind. "I

remember he was winning. But what happened? Why aren't I dead?"

Micah said, "When you told the Dragon to stop, it seemed his servant dragon felt your command. It fought its master long enough for us to drag you away during the man's struggles to control the beast."

"We used the chaos to hide in the temple." Sierra picked up the story. "Micah tried to counter the poison with magic. It helped but didn't seem to work completely."

Micah shook his head. "It was all I could do."

Those words sounded familiar for some reason.

"And now?"

"Now we have to go," Corbin answered. "It sounded like the dragons flew away. This is our best time to leave, before the villagers or the dragons come back. Phoebe and the merfolk are waiting for us. Can you travel?" He touched her face softly.

Nell took inventory of her body. Her bones ached, but not as bad as she feared. She was breathing, so that was good. But there was something strangely different inside...

The silence in her mind.

And the stinging coldness under her heart.

Memory flooded in of those last minutes with the Dragon. Nell staggered to her feet. The magic she'd grown used to was locked away deep in her heart with the voice. This idea left her hollow, empty, more alone than she'd been in four years.

She refused to even consider the silence within or what it could mean. Instead, she focused on her enemy, always her preference over self-reflection.

"He knew me. He knew my sword style, knew I don't fight with two swords. He used Shane's old trick on me, even."

"Shane McConnel?" Sierra asked. "It can't be him. Jack and Bentwood had him killed, what, five years ago? Right after you came back from studying with him. He was too much of a threat."

"Yeah, I know." She'd been devastated when Jack mentioned it. Shane had expected great things from her. He'd believed in her and treated her with a gruff kindness. Not many in Nell's life then had been kind.

"And he didn't have any magic," Sierra pointed out.

"Neither did I, once," Nell murmured. Lifting her left hand, she examined the red scar along her palm. Micah's magic and the voice's last effort had healed the physical wound, but the small icy space under her heart still burned. Even so, the pain was much reduced.

"Well, whoever the Dragon is, he sure isn't dead." Corbin's eyes were tight.

Not yet, thought Nell, but she was too tired to say the words.

"Not yet," Sierra said.

Nell smiled, until a memory of those glowing eyes

loomed in her mind. She shivered. No doubt one of them would have to die before this battle was over. Whoever he was, he didn't seem like the kind of man who'd accept defeat gracefully.

"What did he do to you when you fell?" Micah's voice was low, and he spoke slowly, as if he was choosing each word very carefully. "The level of suffering you experienced did not come from any edged weapon."

She didn't want to think about what happened at the end of the fight, but she had to. Even without access to the voice, she could imagine what it would say: trust the others with this.

"He—he's done something to me with magic, something that's silenced the voice inside me. I can't hear it anymore; it's locked away." She swallowed hard.

The world went dark for a moment, and she caught herself against the wall. Corbin wrapped his arms around her, but as much as she loved him and was thankful for him, she couldn't relax. She wasn't just a girl with her boy. She was Nell, holder of the voice, the one with the message. The Dragon wanted to silence that message and had done so, at least for now.

"I've never seen you hurting like that, ever. You still look ill, even with Micah's magic helping you," Sierra said, studying Nell's face.

Nell rubbed the spot under her heart, where pain came and went. She thought of the voice's warning: *He may not be able to steal your magic yet, but he can turn it to darkness—turn you to darkness.*

She couldn't bear to tell them that. If Corbin knew her very soul was in danger, he'd never let her do the necessary fighting to save her family, or herself.

And maybe they wouldn't trust her anymore. She could tell from Corbin's downcast gaze that he was already disappointed in her for dueling in the first place. To admit that her own nature led her to this place of vulnerability made her angry—and ashamed. Still, lying didn't sit well. She'd promised them the truth as best she could, so she compromised.

"I think he used a poison that's trying to take all the magic the fairies gave me. If it reaches the voice, it'll take the power forever. The voice said I could be healed at the Tree of Life."

Corbin ran his hands along her forehead, as if checking for temperature.

"Not that kind of sick," she said, gently. "His power is inside me, somehow. With magic. The only way to stop it is to get the sword at the Tree of Life."

Magic. The word lay heavy in the room. For so long, the scarcity of magic was the danger. Now, too much of the wrong kind of magic could kill her and the people she loved most. She could already feel the spot pulling energy from her, even as the voice, she presumed, fought against his contamination.

How will a sword heal me or our world? Nell cried silently.

But there was no reply from the gravelly voice. Just a flutter along her heart. She had long wished for the voice to go away, but what good was a voice of prophecy if it didn't speak when needed?

Nell shook off the pain and pulled on her backpack. She arranged her bow and quiver. Someone had thankfully grabbed her sword and dagger. She strapped those back on like armor against her fears. All she could do now was complete her quest and hope the burning icy place inside would be healed.

"We've got to go. There's a sword to find." Battle didn't seem exciting now, but it did seem necessary. And inevitable.

Micah gave her an understanding smile. "Then it's time to return to the sea."

The sun still had hours yet to set in the long summer day. The four of them slipped past the shadowed front of the temple and around the corner toward the ancient pier.

Micah shaded his eyes with a hand. "I see Tristan and Phoebe in the water with Mina and Liam."

Sierra let out a quiet sigh.

Clatters came from the other side of the square.

Shouting, growing nearer. Nell looked over her shoulder. They still had a bit of time, but not much. People had heard or seen them leave. She guessed they didn't want to lose their bargaining chip.

"Let's go," she whispered.

They raced to the narrow entrance of the dock. Nell let the others run ahead. One splash… two splashes… She faced the pathway, holding the rear, sword drawn. At least the narrow path around the building wouldn't allow more than a couple of people to pass at a time.

Queenie and Grace arrived, darting around in agitation.

"Don't attack!" Sierra called to Queenie, who glowed brighter.

"In the water, in the water—now!" Nell burst out.

Killing off half the frightened townsfolk wouldn't be a way to win back their sympathy, and as much as Nell hated to admit it, the fairies and the rest of Aluvia's magical creatures still needed the people's help.

The largest dragon and its rider soared over the building and above the water, silhouetted against the sun. The flying beast wheeled and headed toward them, ready to charge right at her, a prime target on the docks with nowhere to hide.

"Come on!" Sierra yelled.

Glaring at her enemy, Nell backpedaled down the ramp to the dock, and townspeople surged around the building. The first few fell off the narrow walkway into the surf, pushed by the raving crowd. Their faces were contorted with rage, but Nell knew that deep down, fear was what drove people to act like cornered animals.

Everyone from their group was already in the water except one. Corbin waited for her, hand outstretched.

She took four giant bounding steps down the dock, sheathing her sword as she ran. They clasped hands and jumped into the sea together.

CHAPTER ELEVEN

Under the water's surface, the roar of the crowd cut off as if it had never been. Bubbles obscured her vision and brushed across her skin, the water warm from the summer sun. Then a tailfin flashed, and Mina's concerned face appeared. The mermaid touched Nell, and after an initial shock coursed through her body, lightness filled her.

"You're okay!" Mina said, grabbing Corbin too.

Nell allowed herself a breath, still hesitant, but the water swirled inside her harmlessly even as that same touch of claustrophobia closed in on her.

Gurgles and watery shouts accosted her ears.

A dark shadow fell over them in the shape of a dragon, growing larger by the second. Above them, the surface frothed, and then sheets of frost formed along the white caps, shards of ice falling around them like daggers.

Mina called out, "We must go!"

They darted away, the surface of the ocean glittering with ice behind them. With the merfolk on their side, no one would catch up with them. Thank Aluvia for their magical allies. Now if only they could all be saved from humanity's short-sightedness.

Nell hated how blind the people had become. And she hated she'd lost to the Dragon—again, in front of everyone. Her hands twitched when she recalled how he'd flipped her blade away as easy as shooing a fly. Shane had tried more than once to teach her that move—and how to deflect it—with careful, clear instruction. If she'd learned it, she might have won today.

Who was this Dragon? Maybe he was one of the other young students who'd studied with Shane, someone who must have mastered what she couldn't. Three boys her age had been training with Shane before he died. One of those boys had looked down his too-long nose at the girl who'd come to learn to fight. He'd been tall enough to match up with the body of the Dragon and prideful enough to try to conquer the ports. He'd once suggested Nell would make a better tavern wench, serving warriors instead of trying to be one herself.

Just thinking back to that time sent her stomach

boiling, but her disgust at today's defeat stung far worse. It didn't really matter who the Dragon was—as long as she beat him.

The journey farther south was more somber than Nell's first underwater experience. The water already felt cold, despite the magic protecting them. Maybe the coldness was from her fear.

The Dragon wouldn't likely kill the people of the port—he couldn't grandstand without subjects to rule over—but she couldn't help being afraid for them. Fear was something Nell was beginning to better understand, but she'd rather not. It stole her excitement, robbed her of the certainty that directed her next course of action. She did her best to push the fear away, but it clung to her like a spider's web, invisible but unmistakable.

The sea turned bluer, a clear, vibrant shade. The fairies followed above the water in a dancing string of lights. When the sunlight grew faint above, Nell was grateful for the bright silver light radiating from the merfolk's skin. They sped through the water so quickly that it frothed and churned in their wake.

The merfolk were swimming too hard for any conversation, and the silence allowed Nell to consider the surreal images of the red-cloaked women. She kept coming back to the image of the flaming sword—with pieces of the guardians' souls inside.

How was such a thing possible, and what did it mean for anyone who used it? She didn't know how she'd explain the strange visions to her friends, especially if it made Corbin even more reluctant about Nell using the sword. And she had to use it, she was sure.

That soul bit might be best to tell later. A lot later.

As they traveled farther, the creatures around them changed. Fewer brightly-colored fish, fewer jellies. Instead, giant sea turtles now skimmed along the currents, and playful seals and sea lions darted by. After a while, white chunks dotted the top of the water, jagged puzzle pieces long separated from the whole. Blue daggers of ice pointed downward like skewers, and the merfolk slowed their speed. Their swim became a delicate dance, dodging between icebergs large enough to hold a house atop them.

The murky lower waters hid the deep-sea floor from them now. They might as well have been suspended in midair, but Nell couldn't imagine it feeling the same way. To fly would be the ultimate in freedom. The depths of the ocean felt too much like a watery tomb.

Words wisped up like water vapor, so faint it sounded like an echo from furlongs away, but she recognized it.

The sea's magic is not for you. Something else awaits you, our child.

Relief thundered through Nell, followed closely by shock at her own response. Was she happy the voice could still speak to her, albeit through a tenuous thread? If it could still speak past the walls around her heart, it could still control her life. Yet joy rose spontaneously at the connection with the magic that had long been a thorn in her side.

And when the whispered words sank in, only Mina's tugging hand kept Nell moving through her shock. What awaited her? Was it an ominous warning?

But the message didn't feel that way. It felt like a promise.

A promise of something good from something much bigger than herself, something that understood her true nature and valued it.

And there, amid the chunks of ice, a long-frozen part of Nell began to thaw.

She wasn't alone. Not just because of her friends, but because of what she carried inside. Maybe it was time to embrace that.

Nell looked at the ocean and caught glimpses of the beauty others saw. The ice glittered like diamonds against the merfolk's light. The waving seaweed forests looked like a field of wheat spreading out for miles. The low, sonorous notes of a whale's call echoed majestically.

She met Corbin's gaze. He was awe-struck, as she knew he would be.

Suddenly, Tristan stopped. "Sea snake. A big one. Do we hide or fight?"

"No more hiding, brother," Mina said.

Nell could see it now. A gray snake slithered toward them, undulating through the water like the sidewinders of the desert. The creature was thicker around than a grown man's thigh.

The snake swung its head in their direction, thin flaps around its eyes opening and closing like nostrils. Could it smell her fear? She fumbled for her knife.

"No, this is for me to do," Mina said. Then she lifted one hand toward the snake and shouted, "Go!"

A flash of blue light shot from her palm like a sheet of lightning filling the sky. The light hit the snake, and it reared back, dashing away as quickly as it had come.

Nell's breath snagged in her throat, and she eyed Mina with new respect. The laughing little mermaid had some claws. Impressive. "That's what you can do now?"

"Phoebe showed us the way, but we've honed the tool to a fine point," Mina said, her smile smug.

Nell laughed. "As sharp as my sword!"

Corbin grinned at both of them and squeezed Nell's hand.

"If we mer could learn to fight back and defend ourselves, I know you can find the magic you need to win against this new enemy," Mina said.

"Thank you," Nell said.

They regrouped and kept moving forward,

remaining wary. The sea became a labyrinth. Sometimes the ice only floated on top like a giant barge, but often, inverted pyramids pushed deep underwater, with few openings for passage. The sheet of ice above them thickened into a solid mass.

"We need to stop here and move to the surface," Tristan said. "I dare not risk going further under solid ice floes."

"You've taken us farther than I thought possible," Nell assured him, turning to include Mina and Liam. "We're very thankful."

"Liam and I would go with you, but we have not been gifted with landwalking," Mina said. "Here is where we must say goodbye, after we see you safely onto the ground."

Micah said, "I will go first and set up the tents and begin a fire. I am the most hardened against winter temperatures."

Tristan warned, "You will be in severe danger of freezing until you put on your dry winter clothing. As long as a part of you touches the water, Mina and Liam can channel enough magic into you to remove the worst of the chill. I'll go with you. No one should be out there alone, and I, too, am hardier than humans."

"Thank you. I'll take the help gladly," Micah replied.

Nell had wanted to be the first on the ice, but common sense won out. Micah had much more experience surviving in snowy mountains. He'd shift to his faun form as soon as he left the water, so at least his lower half would have the added protection of his fur. Tristan had no fur, but as a merfolk, he was used to transitioning from cold waters to land and had magic to keep him strong.

Micah scrambled onto of the surface of the Ice-Locked Lands, followed by Tristan. Time seemed frozen down in the dark, icy waters where the rest waited, but after a while, glowing dots of fairy lights danced just above the surface.

"That's our sign," Sierra muttered.

"It'll take just a moment to ease you into the winter weather with our magic," Mina said.

Nell pulled herself from the water along the edge of the ice and onto land. Mina's hand on her ankle felt warm, but the rest of her shivered and ached immediately.

"Hurry!" Micah wrapped her in a towel and lifted her straight off her feet to whisk her into a tent before she caught more than a glimpse of moonlit white all around.

Inside the tent, a little brazier glowed, its red coals already sending out much needed heat. Nell's hair had begun to freeze into solid chunks in the arctic air. Her teeth clacked together so hard she feared they might break. She'd never been so cold in all her life.

Micah briskly rubbed her arms. "The sooner you change into proper, dry gear, the better." He dug in her pack and pulled out the warm winter clothing from the top layer.

"I'll get Corbin out while you change." He laced the tent shut when he left.

She set to work immediately, unpeeling her swim layers, cursing as the cold bit at her wet skin. Her hands shook, but she managed to pull on her winter clothes, complete with jacket, hat, and gloves. Then she huddled next to the brazier, closed her eyes, and hoped to survive. Hunger gripped her belly, but she didn't even have the energy to eat.

The spot under her heart throbbed with a new pain in her exhausted state. Whatever magic Micah had invested in her must be running thin. She rubbed her chest and kept silent. Already the merfolk were pouring out magic like a bleeding wound just to keep all of them from freezing as they left the water. She couldn't take more magic now.

Each member of the group followed the same procedure, one by one, until the whole team was tucked away inside their tents along the edge of the shore. The moon hung high in the sky, marking the late hour. They needed to rest and be ready to go first thing in the morning.

She hoped the ice didn't break off and float away. They should have pitched tents farther away from the shoreline.

Tristan said goodnight to Phoebe and eyed Nell

sharply. "Is the wound from the Dragon flaring? You must tell us, so we can stop its spread until we can reach the Tree."

"I'm fine." She clenched her teeth.

He raised one eyebrow. She couldn't blame him for not believing her—he was right not to—but still, she closed her eyes against his suspicious doubts. Soon, the draft from the open flap and the sound of buttoning fabric told Nell she'd won. She had the voice protecting her heart, after all. She'd manage. The thought of the voice, not completely lost, sent a pulse of warmth through her that chased back the icy pain. She sighed in relief.

The cold dragged her down into a heavy drowsiness, and she fell straight to sleep.

When Nell woke in the morning, the others were still unmoving lumps in their bedrolls. She wiggled her toes, thankful for no signs of frostbite. She'd slept in her winter clothes, from her hood down to her boots. The icy spot in her chest remained, sharp but bearable. After a short struggle with the tent, she stepped out, staggered, and found her footing. Only then did she look up, blinking against the brilliance before her.

Though the sun barely reached above the horizon, the light already glittered on the panorama of white. A long vista of snow and ice spread out from the shoreline like an unfurled carpet. Nearby icebergs in the ocean were tinged with a sapphire blue that matched the sky. In the distance, a rugged mountain range reached so high that clouds obscured the tops. Blue, white, and silver painted the terrain here, laced with hints of deepest black. As alien as it appeared, this land was more beautiful than anything she'd ever seen.

Also more dangerous. Nell's well-trained eyes picked out crevices and holes in the ice, death traps for the unwary. Whole strips of ice near the coastline bobbed in the water.

But the mountains beckoned.

From deep in Nell's heart, a wave of homesickness rushed through her so profound she was humbled. She wasn't the one feeling such longing. The emotion of the voice must be powerful to seep past the web of the Dragon's poisoned magic.

She shook her head. Who were the guardians exactly? Where did they come from?

The voice didn't answer.

Can you hear me? Are you okay? Nell asked, just in case.

Only silence. She guessed it couldn't squeeze another message past the toxin's barrier.

She looked back up into the empty sky and wondered if she'd ever hear from the voice again.

Across the expanse, something moved, far above the

snowy ground. She narrowed her eyes. The shape looked familiar and appeared deep blue. Could that be a dragon? Already looking for them? She stared longer.

Yes, their enemy had indeed sent a dragon after them, one circling the skies in a patrol. His pride would demand some kind of hunt. Queasiness shot through her, and she crouched low, thankful for the white fabric of their tents. From this distance, not even a dragon would see them, but it meant everyone would have to be on guard.

Hating to look away from the threat for even a moment, Nell stuck her head in the boys' tent. "We've got to get moving before we have company! A dragon's on the prowl."

The others staggered out, alarmed, but the dragon had already dropped behind the mountains.

"At least it stayed far away. Maybe it wasn't even actually looking for us," Corbin said.

The others nodded without enthusiasm. Nell didn't express her doubts, not wanting to argue, but everyone packed up fast anyway.

After a cold and unsatisfying meal of hardtack and dried fruit, everyone turned to face Nell. Their scrutiny was obvious in the examining looks they gave her, all but counting her teeth. She rolled her eyes.

Micah said, "I believe Nell needs another healing before we begin. Even with the time pressure we are under."

Tristan nodded and stepped closer. "I'm happy to help."

She shook her head. "You need your magic more. You're both far from your sources of power."

"Perhaps you could compromise?" Corbin asked. He leaned over and whispered in her ear, "Let them help you at least a little. They'll feel good, and it'll tie our team tighter."

She sighed. He knew people better than she ever would. If he said this would help everyone somehow, she'd have to believe him.

"Fine," Nell said, both grateful and irritated. She might not want her friends' magic, but she couldn't deny the Dragon's darkness was already sapping her strength. She couldn't afford pride.

"Only give me a bit though," Nell told them, frowning.

Micah and Tristan smiled in response with exasperating calmness. They laid their hands on her shoulders and closed their eyes.

This time, awake and aware, she felt the tingle of the magic as it entered, searching out something inside her like a magnet seeking iron. The power spiraled around her heart, its warmth soothing the cold ache there. Her breath came longer, easier.

"Thank you. That was generous of you." Her voice was husky, and she cleared her throat.

"Think nothing of it. You would offer yourself for us

the same way," Micah pointed out. At least neither he nor Tristan looked worn by their expenditure of energy. Micah's deep brown skin glowed with health, and the naturally-pale merman moved with ease.

Phoebe, Sierra, and Corbin joined them, so the group of six stood in a circle, together in the wilderness. The wee fairies danced around with Grace and Queenie despite the temperature.

Nell compared the view to the map from the temple's book. "If I'm reading this map right, the highest mountain point is that way."

They all turned to follow the direction she pointed, toward the tallest mountain peaks. Where the dragon had been.

Sierra sighed. "Yeah. Through the plains, through the hills, and then up… and up… and up."

"What's that marking to the left of the mountain? The circle with a dot inside it?" Corbin asked, looking at Nell expectantly.

A pinch of irritation flared in her. What did she know? With no voice guiding her, she lacked the one ability she'd had to lead them safely here. Being wrong could get them all killed, if they didn't starve or freeze first.

She frowned.

It wasn't like her to be so irate toward Corbin for no reason. Or to doubt her own abilities, dragon or no dragon. It had to be the poison already affecting her heart.

Nell smiled at him, a little wanly. She'd have to be on guard against those traitorous thoughts. Because of the Dragon's poison, the enemy wasn't just outside her.

It was inside her, too.

"I don't know what that symbol means on the map," Nell said, "but we know we need to head toward that mountain where the Tree is, away from the coast. We're going that way, keeping an eye out for dragons and anything else he might send our way. This is his territory, and don't forget it." She gestured to the mountains. "Let's get going."

As soon as they set off, the icy wind chilled Nell's hands, her nose. Thank Aluvia it was summertime. She couldn't imagine the depths of cold here in the winter. The sun rose higher, and she blinked against the light reflecting off the snow, eyes watering.

"Ach!" Sierra threw her hands up, trying to block the brightness.

"Right." Nell dug in her bag and handed out the gauze strips that reduced the glare. She hadn't really believed Alastair's tales of how cold, how bright, and how harsh things were here. She'd have to thank him later, if she made it back. *When* she made it back.

With the gauze in place, the world was even more surreal, hazy, white, seemingly endless. The bits of black visible only highlighted the incredible whiteness of their surroundings.

"I'm surprised there's not more snow." Phoebe huffed as she picked her way across the surface.

Their new boots kept them from sliding, but with every step they took, they crunched through the thin, sharp top layer of ice to the powdery snow beneath.

"Don't say that too loud," Tristan joked, nodding toward the clouds near the mountains.

"The air feels pretty dry," Nell said. "I imagine that's why the snow is thin. For now."

The winter probably saw the entire land covered waist-high with snow. She shivered.

Surely this place was as foreign as the deepest ocean depths ever were. Where were the birds? The insects? Here, it seemed nothing grew, nothing lived, though she suspected she just didn't know where to look for life in this strange place. The stark simplicity called to her, reminding her of the clean emptiness she often felt after the voice spoke. The guardians, she reminded herself.

Are you there? she asked. No answer came.

She'd often wished to be totally alone even just once over the last four years, but now loneliness tapped Nell on the shoulder. She ignored its attempted greeting and walked faster instead, the crunching of snow harsh in her ears.

Micah fell into step beside her, his faun legs a stark

deep brown against the white background. He said, "I've been thinking, Nell. Now that I have seen the dragons, it's clear the animals are in servitude, their natural power stolen. But if the sword frees the beasts from this man's command, he would be far less dangerous, no matter how good a swordsman. After your healing, I believe freeing the dragons is our top priority, above even defeating the man."

With the silence broken, everyone moved within speaking distance as they hiked.

Nell sighed. "I like the plan, as far as it goes. The voice said the sword will free the dragons, but it didn't say how exactly to use the sword to heal anything or anyone. We don't even know why those dragons obey him. He says he takes their fire, but how does someone do that? And how do we reverse that with the sword? And if we do, will the dragons just burn everything instead?"

And now it was silent again.

Micah offered, "If nothing else, maybe you can make his beasts uncontrollable again for long enough to fight him with the sword."

"I don't know what I did to that dragon," Nell replied. "If it stayed out of control, I'm not sure our weapons would stop them. Unless they were unicorn-horn-tipped arrows, and maybe not even then."

Corbin frowned but said nothing.

Unicorn-horn arrows were deadly to magical creatures—one had nearly killed Micah and Queenie.

Nell only had one such arrow left. They were quite rare now. With more magic available, unicorns' horns remained gloriously atop their heads all year now, their entire long lives.

But unicorn-horn-tipped arrows could maybe kill a dragon, or even the Dragon himself, despite his strange magic. Her heart squeezed with dark satisfaction of that last thought, but then she frowned. Their new enemy would no doubt enjoy killing. She wouldn't be the same.

Besides, she'd left her last unicorn-arrow back in the house, buried at the bottom of her weapons chest. She should have destroyed it—a weapon specially designed to kill magical creatures served no good purpose—but she couldn't bring herself to waste it. At least she wouldn't have to make that particular moral decision here.

She shook her head. "We'll have to trust the voice's promise and keep moving."

CHAPTER TWELVE

*P*reparing for their second night out in the snow wasn't pleasant, but it was better than the first. Nell suggested they conserve as much of their rations as possible and sent Phoebe and Tristan to search around the camp for any hidden dangers, keeping a wary eye out for another dragon patrol. Nell gritted her teeth against the cold, her nose long gone numb, but set about making camp with careful, calm motions. The burning cold around her heart had returned stronger than before, souring her mood. She struggled to keep her face blank.

But Micah, ever aware, stole over and laid a hand on her. He whispered, and a rush of energy poured inside her, pushing back the darkness and pain. A gasp slipped out of him when he pulled his hand away.

She burst out, "You shouldn't have done that. I wouldn't have let you if you'd asked."

"Which is why I didn't," he said. "And even so, I can't heal you fully."

"I'll be fine." She fought to make the words gentle.

"At least I'm not the only stubborn one around here." Sierra smirked.

"Sometimes, we need our friends to help us, even if we wish it were unnecessary." Micah lifted one eyebrow.

Nell grimaced and avoided his gaze. He was right, but she was supposed to be leading this quest, not dragging behind half-dead.

Corbin sat down beside her. "It takes strength to accept help, Nell."

She balled her fists and then purposefully shook them out, along with the worst of her attitude. Maybe the worst of her weakness wasn't even coming from her. The Dragon would gain victory if she were to collapse here, defenseless.

"Thank you," she told Micah.

Corbin bracketed her in a hug. "Tell us if it gets bad. Okay? We need you to stay strong. They'll share their magic until we get you to the Tree."

Unless the darkness gets too big to stop, she thought. She felt his power even now, working diligently at the shield around her heart. Digging little doubts, insidious irritations. Amplifying her flaws, setting her own traits against her.

Micah and Sierra cleared a space and set up a small fire between the two tents with a bit of the tinder they brought. It was a risk, that beacon in the darkness, but they had to have the heat. Phoebe and Tristan reported nothing of concern around the camp, adding there was brown tundra grass in the distance that might burn well for future fires.

The two funny little tents Alastair had sold Nell worked surprisingly well. Flexible willow tree branches threaded through the slick material that created a cozy dome with space enough to include a tiny brazier. The branches could be removed and coiled up to store in the packs. Three girls in one, three boys in another.

Nell much preferred sleeping in the open. Tents muffled noises and blocked views, allowing enemies too close without warning. But a place like this gave no choice. The temperature dropped lower at night, and she wasn't going to risk anyone's life.

The tired group of friends gathered around the fire, cooking porridge to go with a precious helping of dried pheasant. The sun took its blazing light below the horizon behind them. An eerie blackness remained, with millions of stars scattered across the sky. She was thankful to be clearheaded enough now to appreciate their beauty.

The six friends banked the fire, but the fairies kept a warm glow in each tent, lining the bedrolls. Nell took a final glance at the sky before heading to bed. She sucked in a breath and pointed upward.

"Does anyone else see that?" Between the voice's influence and the Dragon's poison, maybe she was imagining things.

The others looked up and gasped.

She wasn't going crazy, then. At least not right now.

In the sky far above the distant mountain peaks, glowing ribbons of red and silver lights swirled and loomed with questing fingers that tried to reach beyond the tallest mountain but seemed unable to. Roiling flashes of red and silver flickered among them like lightning.

"It's like the sea at high tide, restrained by the breakers," Phoebe whispered.

The light was eerie but beautiful.

"What is it?" Nell whispered, her eyes glued to the slowly undulating colors, twisting as if in an invisible breeze.

"I don't know," Corbin said, his own voice hushed. "I've heard of lights in the night sky far up north, but those were green and blue. Steadier. Not like these. These are something else."

No one had an answer.

They seemed to call to her, those lights, like a beacon drawing her home, but she had no idea why. They didn't fade, just continually swelled, shrank, and swirled. As fascinating as they were, though, she couldn't watch them all night. There were always going to be strange things when magic was involved, she reminded herself. She didn't have to understand it. She just had to do what she'd promised.

The next morning, Nell awoke with a jolt. She lay still, waiting. A shadow swooped against her tent and then quickly disappeared. Darkness flashed over their tent again, as if circling above them. A shadow with wings and a long, pointed tail.

"Sierra!" she whispered. "I think we've got company again. Another dragon."

Sierra rolled out of her bedroll, grabbing her knife. "An attack?"

Nell laid a finger by her mouth, nodding at the still sleeping Phoebe. "Not sure. If it's another dragon watching for us, the white tents will hopefully be camouflaged. But we need to hurry today and get to a less flat area of land. Without the Sword of Aluvia, we're dead if a dragon finds us."

"Agreed."

The dragon had disappeared by the time they peeked carefully through the tent flaps, but the scare pushed the team hard.

As they hiked farther inland toward the hills and cave systems shown on the map, they moved fast enough that no one had breath for conversation. Nell brooded over how the Dragon knew her. It made the back of her neck cold to think of him spying on her, for long enough that he even knew her fighting preferences. But the streak of white hair, the wide build of his shoulders, his obvious magic… none of it was familiar. She gnawed on her worry until she gave it up as an impossible puzzle. Whoever he was, he'd be dead soon enough.

Focusing instead on the practical matters of the landscape, she was glad to see it wasn't as bare as she first thought. Patches of tundra dotted the snow with its spongy brown grass, which would attract animals. Two bird nests nestled in the craggy rocks jutting from the ground like unexpected monuments. She stopped and gathered three oblong eggs to add to their rations.

Beyond the rocks, there were strange shadows in the snow. Tramping over quickly, she stared at tracks in the ground and swore. Each print was big enough that she could have sat in it and had room left over.

"Guys. Are those what I think they are?" she called back to them.

Corbin reached her first. "Those look like dragon tracks. Look at those gigantic claws."

"That's what I thought," she said, casting a glance at the empty sky. The others gathered, dismay written on their faces. "And those brush marks in the snow were probably its wings when it took off. Keep an eye out. There may be more dragons here than we know."

But they had to keep going, dragons or not. The afternoon was quiet, as their breathing grew more labored. By the end of the day, they'd at least reached the sporadic beginnings of the hillside, which offered a bit of shelter, but the mountains were still so far away. Too far.

Before bed, Nell and the others sat around a smoky peat moss fire cut from the tundra. The swirling lights above began their dance again. Despite their beauty, Corbin stared at the strange notations in the back of the book from the ancient temple, frowning, his lips moving occasionally as if thinking to himself.

Nell stared dully at the low fire. They'd marched hard all day, and they had so much farther to go.

Another healing session with Micah and Tristan before dinner had shored up most of the pain around Nell's heart, but their faces were drawn afterward. She wouldn't take their magic again; it was too risky for the faun and merman. They'd better find the Tree soon, or she'd be lost to the Dragon's magic after all.

Creaking groans like a ship on rough seas echoed through the valley, noises Corbin said came from ice floes around the Ice-Locked Lands. Without the distraction of the hike, her mind kept drifting back to her fights with the Dragon. She imagined different moves she could have tried, but the honest truth was she couldn't think of any other way she could have beaten him. Whoever he was, he was just too good. The thought made her grit her teeth.

A long howl echoed through the night, sending goose bumps along Nell's arms.

Everyone lifted their heads and stared at each other.

"Wolves live here?" Sierra asked, pulling out her bow and arrows.

"Snow wolves." Corbin glanced at the darkened hills surrounding them. "There's also ice cougars, basilisks, and other creatures native to this region. Snow giants are really dangerous, if they even exist, but they supposedly prefer the high mountains. And now, of course, we've got dragons, too."

"Nice place." Nell rolled her eyes.

"I think we'll be okay in the tents," Corbin offered.

"I sure hope so. But, if the Dragon's hunting us like I think he is, he'll have more tricks up his sleeve. Wolves could be the least of our worries."

She looked up at the mountains that remained stubbornly far away. The Dragon could have taken all of the ports by now, even while directing one of his dragons to keep watch on them here. The urgency of the quest drove her to stay sharp even as despair at their situation pulled at her, at all of them. Weariness was doing the Dragon's work for him.

Nell watched the dancing ribbons of lights, and let the wonder of their beauty soothe her tired heart. She could breathe deeper, even with the air stinging her lungs.

I'm coming, she told whoever might be listening up there at the mountains, among the lights. *Don't give up on me.*

She wouldn't give up on herself, either.

That night, her sleep was punctuated with the cries of wolves. And in her dreams, she was among them, wild and free, the moon calling long cries from her throat, gilded crimson magic racing beneath her paws along the ice.

In the morning, heavy clouds covered the bright blue sky for the first time, providing relief from the glare. As the friends moved farther inland, hills rolled around all sides of them like scoops of cream. The map indicated a series of caves maybe a day or two ahead.

By lunchtime, a strange haze hovered over the snowy ground in the distance. Half the mountain range was hidden behind a solid wall of white.

"Please tell me that's not a snow storm coming," Nell said, pointing in the direction of the whitened sky to their left.

Corbin squinted into the distance. "I've read they can spring up in minutes here."

Micah frowned. "But there's something else there. The clouds hold some sort of power in it, magic."

"What do you mean?" Sierra asked him, paling.

He narrowed his eyes. "I do not think this is an ordinary storm but is a magical attack."

Nell swore under her breath. "Let's get as far away as we can. Maybe we can reach the caves before the storm hits. Alastair said wind slides right around these tents, but a blizzard isn't the way I want to test his word as a tradesman."

Snow drifts were already forming as they hurried through the hills. At times, they were blocked from the wind's fury, but at others it came from all directions, forcing them to lean forward to keep from being blown over. Fat flakes of snow stuck on their packs, their furry jackets, their eyelashes.

In between gusts of snow, something billowed toward her, pale but translucent. In the darkening light, Nell could swear she saw small, almost invisible creatures riding the wind, swooping and swirling closer. Shriveled, ghostly things with gaunt faces and angry, teeth-filled glares full of hate. She stopped in her tracks.

"Are you seeing what I'm seeing?" Nell called to Micah. "Faces in the wind?"

He narrowed his eyes and lifted one hand. "I do not see faces, only shapes, but I feel the power. Magic has pushed this storm to us, most assuredly. It feels the same as the dark magic the Dragon inflicted upon you, Nell."

Tristan wrapped his arm around Phoebe and called over the howl of the wind, "I see something, too, but it's not clear, like looking in a mirror in a dark room."

"I don't know how you can see anything in this," Corbin said, arm raised to block the wind.

Another blast of freezing wind hit them. Micah staggered. "Whatever it is, I can feel it radiating hateful power."

Two more swirls of white spun around her. A face brushed by: sunken cheeks, eyes completely milky white, no hair, but a mouth full of teeth.

She bit down on her tongue to keep from screaming. The taste of blood was salty and metallic.

"Micah's right. Something dangerous is here," she warned.

Corbin replied. "So, where can we go?"

They were all looking to her. Frustration spun up faster than the winds. Those ghostly creatures could attack at any moment. She had no idea what damage they could cause. Even if they could only force a blizzard, being buried in freezing temperatures was deadly enough. Nell squinted against the increasing whiteness. To their left, a small overhang between two rocky hills looked big enough to help shelter them.

"This way!" she called and took off running. In her rush, she slid on a patch of ice and fell. Pain jolted through her bones.

Corbin exclaimed and tried to help her up, but she shook off his arms. "I'm fine."

She might not be in top shape after her pathetic defeat, but by all the stars she could still get off the ground on her own. He looked at her with wounded puppy dog eyes, but she ignored him, brushing her coat off with jerking sweeps of her hands.

Turning away from him, Nell pointed ahead to the overhang, where the snow hadn't piled up as much. "We'll set up there. Hopefully the storm won't last long!"

Just as they reached the spot, the haunting faces in the wind blew by her again and sent her heart racing. No one else said a word about seeing anything strange, though, so she simply reached for the bags. She willed herself not to look for the horrifying creatures but to focus only on the task.

The others worked with her, and they got the tents up with amazing speed. Corbin tied a rope between the two, saying, "If it gets bad enough, you can follow the rope to us. Whatever you're seeing in the wind doesn't seem to be hurting us directly, but this storm could get even worse."

Nell couldn't imagine it getting any worse but felt better nonetheless to have a physical tie to the other half of their group. The wind outside the tent howled louder than a dragon, and the material of the walls rippled and jerked. But none of the frightening white ghost creatures appeared in their tents. Nell gave a tentative breath of relief. Snow, they could deal with.

The flurries hissed against the tent.

Sierra said, "What did you see out there, exactly?"

Nell described the faces, the fury in the eyes. "I wish I knew why you couldn't see them, too."

"I guess I should be glad I got left out of that."

"Weird creatures or not, that's a lot of snow out there." Phoebe shivered.

"Definitely."

Nell's whole body and face ached from the arctic air. Her hips and knees felt bruised from her fall. Her insides still felt coiled up from those howling ghostly faces that others had not seen.

She thought back to Corbin's expression when she'd refused his help after she fell, the way he'd bit his lip and turned away. Nell ground her teeth. She appreciated his concern, but she didn't need help for a simple hike.

She'd be glad for some magical assistance, though. Ironic, since she was once so afraid of magic that she'd had to steel herself to walk through Corbin's fairy field. She'd come a long way since then, but it didn't matter. She had to muddle through this mess on her own, facing the Dragon's magic without the guide she'd come to trust. She shivered, and the coals of resentment smoldered inside her.

CHAPTER THIRTEEN

The winds of the snow storm picked up, screaming with a frightening intensity. The edges of the tent ruffled, flapped, and danced. How much more could it take? They couldn't survive without shelter.

"Get ready to run to the boys' tent!" Nell called. Hopefully the other tent would still be there. They pulled on their packs and crouched at the door of the tent.

Another gust hit. Fabric ripped, and the top of their tent pulled away and soared off like a child's kite. Nell looked up into a spinning tunnel of white, and blinding snow filled the tent.

"Quick!" She reached past the ragged remains of the tent until she slapped up against the rope. Steadying herself, she yelled, "Put your hand on my shoulder!"

Sierra called back, "Phoebe's with me. Let's move!"

Nell pushed her way into the blizzard. White filled her vision in every direction, but at least there were no faces, no teeth, no glaring dead-looking eyes. Only the rope in her hands. It took just four or five steps, but her coat was caked before she managed to scrape on the outside of the boys' tent. "Let us in!"

Winds howled in her ear and lying down began to seem like a reasonable idea. The snow would be soft, at least.

Then hands pulled her inside, with Sierra and Phoebe falling in behind.

Fairy lights made her blink. Queenie, Grace, and all the wee ones lined the fabric, lending their brightness and strength. Though she would have preferred more space, there wasn't any. Nell sat pressed next to Corbin. Everyone huddled around the meager heat of the brazier and whispered about the strange creatures in the storm, the risks of the blizzard, their strategy should the last tent fail. The winds continued to blow.

"We might as well eat," Nell said, hunching against the cold. The needs of the body didn't stop because of threats outside of it. Everyone ate crackers made of sunflower seeds and a bit of dried fish. When no more creepy beings appeared and the tent walls held up, her shoulders began to drop.

Such haggard ghostly creatures surely were impossible. Not even Micah had seen the gaunt cheeks, the filmy white eyes. Maybe the extreme cold had made her hallucinate. The Dragon clearly sent that storm at them—Micah sensed the deliberate power, too, after all—but those creatures riding the wind must have been her imagination. That was it.

Despite the storm, the heat in their tent rose, and her eyelids grew heavy. The time spent in stillness made her earlier irritation seem out of hand as well. Corbin would help anyone up out of the snow, she knew. He wasn't suggesting she was weak. He knew better than that. So did she. She allowed herself to lean against him, and he wrapped one arm around her shoulders.

She rubbed her forehead. Perhaps the Dragon's poison had progressed further than she knew. She took a deep breath, swearing to be more kind and patient with everyone, no matter what those dark impulses muttered.

When the sounds outside finally faded, Nell said, "Let's find out what we're up against."

It took two tries for them to unlace the tent flaps, but finally the group ventured outside. Snow covered everything at least two feet thick. The ruined girls' tent was full of snow, the top hole not even visible.

Nell cleared her throat. "Well, on the positive side, he's given up on attacking us for now, I guess. Sky's even clearing."

"That's a lot of snow, though," Sierra said. "Guess we'll be sleeping six to this tent somehow?"

"We can figure out something. Sleeping like sardines will help keep us warm, at least." Corbin wiped snow off the top of the surviving tent.

"I guess we were pretty lucky." Phoebe eyed the huge mounds of snow drifts all around.

Corbin nodded. "Just one tent down—we got off easy. The layer of snow probably helped keep us warmer, actually. Some animals burrow under the snow to survive the deep winters here."

His voice had taken on its lecturing tone. Nell listened respectfully, even fondly. She never thought she'd be thankful for a snow storm, magically induced or not, but it had given her the time she needed to regain self-control.

She forced a grin at him, lifting one eyebrow. "So you're saying if I need to hunt, I may have to crawl under the snow?"

He blinked twice before he answered. "I, uh, imagine there's something to find above the snow, if you're lucky. Maybe I can hunt with you tonight? With those storm creatures you saw, we should probably stick in pairs, at least."

"That'd be nice," she said.

He ducked his head before glancing up with a pleased smile.

She was glad she'd spoken her thought aloud. It really would be nice. Besides, two hunters were better than one, practically speaking. Their foraging had been limited to a few bird eggs and some very bitter tundra weeds. A savory hot meal would push some of the cold out of her bones.

After packing up quickly—saving the remains of the tent material, just in case—the friends pushed through thigh-high snow drifts until Nell's leg muscles burned. Corbin marched alongside Nell. He didn't offer his arm, his help, or his sympathy. It was nice. Eventually, the drifts thinned out, and Nell gave a sigh of relief under her breath.

"Found anything new in that book of yours?" she asked Corbin. He'd been so quiet.

"The words added in the back are important, I know it, but I can't quite figure out the language yet. It's like it's in a code. I'm almost sure one of the words means 'tree.' Maybe."

"If anyone can figure it out, you can."

He offered her a bright smile, and his response warmed her.

When Nell finally called it a day, the sun sat on the horizon with thick packs of clouds scurrying past, but the heavy clouds of the storm had not returned. "We didn't get as far as I'd have liked, but we need time to hunt, no matter what dangerous creatures are out there. If another storm comes—natural or otherwise—fresh food will carry us through better than our packed stuff."

"Good luck." Sierra scanned the steep hills beyond their camp. "Looks empty."

Corbin nodded. "I imagine the dragons have scared off or eaten all the larger herd animals, but I'm sure a few rodents and birds are still around, hidden."

Sierra wrinkled her nose at the mention of rodents, but Nell had eaten worse.

"Come on then, Corbin." Nell pulled her bow out. "Let's see what we can find."

The air had a heavy stillness after the wild snowfall. The light was luminous even in dusk, reflecting off the curve of the sky and the white of the snow in an endless loop.

Nell checked for animal prints but found nothing. "We'll have to go farther from camp."

"That's fine with me. I've got your back."

She hoped so.

They searched until darkness fell. Nell shook her head. "Looks like another meal of cold porridge, unless you can talk Sierra into being less stingy with the dried meat. Sorry."

"Hey, you can't make game appear. Even hunters as good as you have limits."

She grinned. It seemed like forever since they'd spent time alone, especially without an immediate crisis brewing. She reached for his hand, weaving her fingers through his. Moments like these mattered, even on dangerous journeys. Maybe especially on those.

Her hands were calloused where his were smooth, but they fit together perfectly. He tightened his grip.

As they picked their way back across the ice, Corbin asked, "Do you know if there's anything we should grab for potions or poultices while we're here? When we get back, you could mix up some really unique medicines."

Nell pressed her lips together. The ground passed under her feet, right foot, left foot, one after another.

He cleared his throat. "I mean, when we get back—and we will—you'll pick up training with my mother again… won't you?"

Words, words, words—so hard to handle, unexpectedly pointed and sharp sometimes, and other times so unclear and fuzzy. But she couldn't fight the Dragon, the land, and her own heart. Not all at once.

She stopped and faced Corbin, reaching to take his other hand. They stood linked. "I love your mother and appreciate all she's given me. But I think we both know if we survive this, everything could be very different."

He looked a little too carefully at the sky. "You may not have time to study for a while, I know. The people will need you now more than ever after the Dragon's lies."

"You mean they'll need the voice more than ever. But unless we find this Tree of Life, they won't hear it again. I might not be special for much longer," she reminded him, pointing toward her heart. It was the most she would reveal of her struggle.

She continued, "I'll either walk out of here with a

magical sword, or, if the Dragon has his way, I won't walk out at all."

"He wants you to join him, not die." Corbin jutted out his jaw, finally meeting her gaze.

"If I don't join him, he's not going to let me go peacefully. And honestly, let's say we win, the Dragon's gone. Even if that happens, I'm not sure I'm meant to be a healer, Corbin. When I think about the sword of Aluvia, I feel—"

"I don't think now is the best time to decide your future, do you? We should talk about this later." His words were sharp. He dropped her hands, took a step back.

Nell's stomach clenched.

"I'm not sure my future's even my decision to make anymore," she muttered and pushed past him.

At camp, she sat silently by the fire, aching with cold. She glared at the scrubby bushes burning fitfully.

The others exchanged meaningful looks but said nothing, asked nothing. Corbin sat across from her, gazing at her with those big brown eyes, begging for her to choose a quiet life as a healer. To never risk her life as a warrior.

So she was good with a sword. What of it? She'd worked hard to become so. He should trust her to take care of herself. She shook her head and forced herself to watch the fire instead of Corbin's pained expression.

He just didn't understand. Nell loved that he was

soft-hearted, she did, but she couldn't help being more like a hawk than a dove. The voice hadn't condemned her for being a warrior. It seemed, in fact, to have encouraged her.

At least one person—or thing—seemed to understand her around here.

Everyone got ready for bed in awkward silence. Six in a tent meant for three required everyone to lie on their side. At least it was warmer, but anytime someone moved, Nell startled awake. After everyone else had gone to sleep, she found herself stepping back outside the cramped tent, too restless to lie still.

Without the campfire, the darkness had a rich depth like velvet. The cold stung her face, but her eyes couldn't stay away from the undulating ribbons in the sky. The lights felt so… restrained. Held back from the fullness they could be.

Nell saluted the roiling lights with a sardonic smile. "I know how you feel."

She breathed deeply, white fog puffing from her mouth before blowing away in the wind. It was too cold for this sort of rumination. She shook her head at her foolishness, pulling her gaze from the sky. But as she turned, she glimpsed a flash of red and orange from the corner of her eye. Not the silvery red of above—this looked like a spurt of fire. Fire, in a land of ice.

CHAPTER FOURTEEN

Heart racing, Nell spun toward the flash but nothing was there, just a silent night with starlight glittering against the snow like diamonds. Her breath hitched, and she rechecked her surroundings. Nothing. She was sure she'd seen a glimpse of fire.

Maybe exhaustion and the cold were playing tricks on her eyes. With one last suspicious look around, she crawled back into the tent, burrowing deep into her sleeping bag without taking off a single layer of clothing.

In the morning, her vision of fire seemed to be impossible. Nell felt it definitely must have been a hallucination, maybe from exhaustion. Maybe it was even caused by the Dragon's toxic poison, who knew? Better not to mention it, especially on top of being the only one who had seen faces in the howling wind.

They'd reached a flat area that spread between the rocky hills, giving level footing for the first time in days. Moving faster lifted everyone's spirits.

Phoebe and Tristan paced across the slick ice in front of Nell. A few pieces of their long hair escaped from each of their hoods and entangled in the wind, red and green together. She found it sweet, not that she'd ever admit such a mushy feeling.

Up ahead, a creature suddenly dropped below the cloud line. It remained far enough away to blur details, but the vivid blue coloring was clear enough.

"Dragon!" Phoebe choked on the word.

"Quick. Move back into the hills, and we'll search for the caves." Nell pitched her voice low, but the command carried clearly over the ice.

Following her lead, everyone turned and scurried toward the bigger, jagged hills. If the dragon saw them, they wouldn't need to worry about making good time to the mountains anymore.

Nell glanced over her shoulder. "It's coming closer. Move it!" It would freeze them solid. Kill them in a single breath.

They ran faster, skidding and sliding. Nell reached the edge of the hills first but waited for her friends. She'd never leave them out there like ripe berries for the picking. They shouldn't have exposed themselves on an open plain, no matter how much time it saved them. Sierra and Micah pounded up beside her, followed by

Corbin. Only Tristan and Phoebe were left exposed on the flat open ground, arms pumping as they raced for cover.

The dragon landed hard on the opposite end of the oblong plain and lifted its head with a screech. Plumes of white mist shot high in the air.

A loud crack resounded through the frigid air, and Nell's heart skipped a beat.

"Come on!" she screamed.

"It's too heavy for the ice!" Corbin gasped.

Cracks broke away from the dragon's feet, spreading like spider webbing. Popping sounds echoed through the hills and breaks jagged their way closer and closer across the ice. The dragon stomped one foot and bugled. The land under the beast suddenly split open with a roar, water spewing upward as the chunk of ice sank. With a shriek of rage, the dragon floundered in the icy hole before launching itself back into the sky, water dripping from its tail and belly.

"Run! Get off—it's a lake! The surface ice is breaking from the dragon's weight!" Nell yelled.

Another loud *crack* resounded through the air, and Phoebe fell through the ice. She was there one second, gone the next. She didn't even have time to scream.

"Phoebe!" Sierra shouted, voice echoing off the surrounding hills.

Tristan skidded to a halt and jumped feet-first into

the hole after Phoebe. The water swallowed him up without a ripple.

Nell cursed and her gaze flashed to the dragon, flying away now, snapping its tail and shaking out its feet. The cold had been too much for an *ice dragon*.

"We've got to find the caves and set up a fire for her. That thing could come back or bring more. Grab the warmest thing you can find!" Nell threw her pack to Corbin.

He took off into the rough hillside, with Micah joining him.

Sierra ran the opposite way, toward the hole in the ice. Before she got three steps in, Nell tackled her.

"No, you'll die under there! Tristan's got magic."

"Let me go!" Sierra bucked and struggled to escape.

"Promise me"—Nell ground her teeth hard—"you won't dive under the ice. He can't save you both, and she'll need you. We'll get her inside a cave, get her warm."

Blue light flared under the ice.

Sierra stilled. "I promise."

When Nell moved, Sierra scrambled to the edge of the hole and knelt with wide, bleak eyes.

Corbin appeared at her side, pressed a fur cloak into Nell's hands. "We found a place. It's not far. And… Phoebe?"

"Not yet." Nell let out a breath.

"Micah's starting the fire." Corbin laid his hand on Sierra's shoulder.

More blue light blazed beneath the ice, rays spearing up through the hole before fading.

Sierra gave a strangled sob.

Then Tristan's green hair floated up, followed by the vivid red of Phoebe's. Her hair filled the hole like blood pouring from a wound. Tristan pushed her out of the icy water, her eyes closed, lips blue.

"Quick!" Nell bellowed.

Sierra, weeping openly, bundled Phoebe in the cloak, crying, "Thank you! Thank you!"

Corbin helped Tristan out the hole, and Nell wrapped him up. Then they all followed Corbin to a shallow cave, snugged between two rocks, nearly impossible to see.

Nell gave thanks, too. At least the dragon wouldn't find them here, should it return. Hopefully it wouldn't, not after its own obviously unpleasant encounter with the lake.

Inside, Micah had a small fire going near the edge of the opening. The smoke hovered at the top of the cave like haze, but the smoky warmth was the best thing Nell had ever felt.

Sierra laid Phoebe by the fire. The sunlight dropped off fast inside, cloaking them in dimness even with the light of the low flames.

"Thank Aluvia for the waterproofed pack!" Tristan tossed Nell a dry set of clothes.

Sierra and Nell got Phoebe changed, and everyone huddled in the cave until her breathing grew steady and her skin flushed with warmth.

"She'll be okay. They both will," Corbin said, eyeing Phoebe and Tristan.

Tristan had changed into a new set of clothing as well. Their wet clothes would have to be left behind if they didn't dry out in time. The near disaster would cost them an entire afternoon, but at least Phoebe was alive.

"We might as well camp here tonight," Nell said.

"You think the dragon's still out there?" Corbin asked.

Nell shrugged. "Either way, Phoebe needs to rest. We all could, really."

"You don't have to convince me." Sierra ran her hand down Phoebe's hair.

"I'll take first watch," Corbin said.

"Mind if I join you?" Nell asked. "Two are better than one if we can arrange it."

"Always glad to have you with me," he said. Warmth unrelated to the fire spread through her.

After dinner, Phoebe stirred a little more and insisted she was fine, as did Tristan, who said, "I could draw enough strength from the water to fight off the worst of the cold for both of us."

Nell didn't really believe their assurances, but she

understood saying one thing when you felt another. She rubbed at her chest and turned away.

They skated in and out of the rocky hills during the next day, staying in another cave that night instead of their cramped tent. Phoebe and Tristan kept up without complaint, as did everyone else. Though the tinder they'd brought with them was nearly gone, Corbin found scrubby bushes buried under the snow along many of the caves, and the dead branches burned well.

But even with the added warmth, the space beneath Nell's heart seemed colder, especially when anger flared. The worsening of her attitude had to be from the poison, but she waved Micah and Tristan away when they offered magic.

Mountains now ranged almost all the way around like two hands cupping a delicate ice sculpture. Behind them lay the ocean, somewhere too far to reach now.

Before they'd traveled more than a half a day on their sixth day, another blizzard blew up, drenched with hateful magic that seemed to feed on their fears. It kept them trapped in a cave all afternoon and night. Thanks to the shelter, the friends remained warm, but hunting had been impossible. Their stomachs growled all day.

By the next morning, Nell decided enough was enough. They'd been here a full week already. Maybe if she went hunting on her own, she'd find success. She'd wake the others with a delicious surprise.

The morning sun had not yet topped the mountains, but a faint rosy glow spread along the whiteness. She followed a narrow gorge between the hills, and a frozen stream glittered like pink diamonds. It was beautiful. A place worth fighting for.

The spot under her heart pulsed sharply, breaking her stride. A memory flashed: She saw herself falling again in battle with the Dragon, her weapon knocked from her hand.

No. Shaking her head hard, she crouched to study clumps of lichen on the rocks poking up from the snow. Something had nibbled on the bits of green, leaving bite marks so tiny, few would have noticed.

It took only a quarter-hour more until she found a little tunnel in the snow, paw prints around it. Excellent. She laid out a piece of dried fruit near the hole and drew her bow. It wasn't as sporting as she'd like, but sometimes a girl had to do what a girl had to do. The little animal never even heard the thud of her arrow and hopefully never felt a thing beyond a second of shock. She'd never want to cause undue pain to an innocent creature.

The Dragon, though, was a different matter. He wasn't helpless or innocent. Some pain might do him good. Her lips twisted.

She picked up her prize and whacked it against a

nearby rock for good measure. Some kind of rodent with thick white fur, tiny ears, and a scrawny tail. She sliced along the rodent's thick skin—far tougher than it looked—and wondered how it would feel to cut the Dragon as he had cut her. The red scar line along her palm still showed. The voice's desperate healing attempt hadn't been enough, clearly, nor had the magic of her friends.

She jerked her knife harder, and blood pooled on the snow, deep red, shockingly vivid in the bright sunlight. She cut out the creature's heart, and if she imagined her enemy as she did so, well, he had pushed her too far. Attacking her home, trying to steal her magic. She buried the skin and other inedible bits of the creature and arrived back at camp with the freshly cleaned animal in tow, pleased with the offering she could make to the morning's meal.

As soon as she reached the cave entrance, Corbin rushed up to her. "Where have you been? I've been worried sick!"

"What does it look like I was doing?" Nell held out the rodent.

"You shouldn't go off on your own like that! Not here. Think about avalanches, blizzards, treacherous ice—not to mention our enemy waiting to attack."

Nell opened her mouth to argue, but he didn't give her a chance to speak.

"I barely slept before we left because I was reading

everything I could that would help us. You don't know how bad it is here, Nell. We have to stick together."

She jerked up her chin. "I can take care of myself."

Corbin touched her arm, pulled her to face him. "I just don't want to lose you."

She wanted to hit him and hug him at the same time.

He lifted his hand, palm out, and waited.

With a deep breath, she met his gaze and pressed her palm to his without a word. She let the warmth from his hand soak into her skin and tried to imagine the heat finding its way into her heart. Corbin would help shield her if she let him.

"I know," she finally said, voice breathier than it should be. "I won't forget. I promise."

She promised herself the same thing.

CHAPTER FIFTEEN

$\mathcal{A}$ loud pop from the low flames broke the silent tension, and Corbin turned to build up the fire. "You caught breakfast. I'll cook it." He took the skinned creature from her without flinching. He'd really toughened up a lot in the last years, her soft-hearted fairy keeper.

He set to work, melting snow in the little pot, helpful as always. She really should learn from his humble and forgiving nature. He only wanted her to be safe.

Sure. Safe and wrapped in a blanket for safe-keeping. She couldn't stop the thought. Maybe he just needed a reminder of how well she could take care of herself. Hadn't she proved that already? She'd almost died twice, after all, but lived despite the odds.

The first time had been when Jack tested her for the rank of enforcer. She always thought she'd die by a blade, but that time, Jack's bare hands had almost been enough. He'd left her bruised and battered, yet she'd passed his miserable test and won the position she'd needed.

The second time Nell had nearly died, of course, had been when she was attacked by a swarm of fairy queens. Sometimes when she lay awake at night, she wondered why she'd lived when her own father had died from a swarm like so many others. During those moments alone in the darkness, guilt could sting as harsh as the fairy stings themselves. But she couldn't regret her life.

After they packed up and began the day's hike, Nell walked ahead of everyone, alone. Her muscles burned with the pace she set. It felt good to push herself. Sure, a warrior faced some danger, but what was life without a bit of flavor? Risk was like the hot sauce at the Salty Dog Tavern: Corbin could only stand a drop of it, but she poured it over her whole plate. No one else understood.

She hunched against the icy wind, consoling herself with plans of how she'd get rid of the Dragon in the end. Should she stab him? Drown him? Poison him with his own toxin? There were so many options.

Occasionally, more flashes of fire danced in the sky along the edge of her vision. Great. She'd glance up only to see nothing. But she could have sworn that, for one split second, the shape of something familiar was outlined against the piercing blue sky, with wings gracefully flowing over its head, aflame with orange and red and gold flickers. She tore off the gauze protecting her eyes, blinked hard, and shook her head. Hallucinations on top of seeing flashes and bizarre horrifying faces.

You got that? she snapped at the silent voice inside. *You've finally driven me mad.*

The lack of response was more depressing than expected. She missed the steady calmness of the voice, as well as its support and guidance, though it galled her to admit it. If the voice was gone forever, she wouldn't know quite what to do with herself. But as the silence inside continued, she feared she'd have to figure that out.

All morning and into the afternoon, she stayed a few footlengths apart from everyone, glowering at the ground. She chose to squint rather than put back on her gauzy eye covering, preferring clear, crisp vision to reducing glare. The others followed her lead. Eventually, Corbin fell into step beside her. He reached for her hand, and she let him take it, the connection easing a tightness in her belly she hadn't realized was there.

"Nell, are you going tell me what's upsetting you—beyond the obvious?" His voice was barely audible over the crunching of the snow.

"As if the obvious wasn't enough?"

He smiled, but the corners of his mouth didn't lift far. "I'm sorry if I upset you."

"This morning or when you refused to even discuss that I might not end up as a healer?" Nell said.

He winced. "Both. I'm sorry if I've made you feel like I don't trust you."

Her heart felt like it was hovering in mid-flight, about to soar… or crash.

Corbin squeezed her hand. "You're a smart, strong person—you know I believe that. Of course you can take care of yourself, but I worry for you anyway. I've made you mad plenty of times in the past, but you've never gotten this upset. Is there something else going on?"

Only that she hadn't heard from the voice in so long she feared the Dragon's poison was winning. And even if they won this fight, Nell didn't think she'd be able to live like Corbin wanted her to and still be happy.

"I—I…" The words hung on her tongue, but a quick glance at his gentle expression had her swallowing them. "I miss warm weather. Our mountains back home aren't nearly this bad."

That was the truth, if not all of it. And it wouldn't hurt either of them.

She wasn't going to bring up the flashes of fire she saw in the sky, either. She was tired of being the strange one, and if it was indeed more magic Corbin was missing out on, mentioning it would only ruin the tentative stitching up of their torn trust in each other.

"Me, too. Right about now, the meadowlarks would be calling with the sunrise, and we'd be in short sleeves." He sighed.

"And then later, we could sit by the beach and watch the sun set over the waves."

"That'd be nice." He bumped her shoulder with his. "I *am* sorry, you know. I don't want to fight."

"I'm sorry, too," she whispered.

Words sprang unbidden, as if jostled loose from his touch. "What if I can't find this sword? If I can't defeat him? Or if any of you die because you came with me? It'll all be my fault."

"Hey, now! That's not true! No one blames you for our choices."

"Choices made because of me."

"Because you were choosing the right thing, and I wanted to support you. We all do."

"It didn't feel like much of a choice." She couldn't believe she'd been secretly excited to battle again, even against a foe like the Dragon. So stupid of her. This trip wasn't a sword duel. It was a grueling, exhausting marathon to prevent a war.

Corbin looked at her steadily, calmly. He'd always anchored her, the one who first saw beneath the surface to the real her.

He said, "You know the reasons why you chose to come here, to seek the sword and fight. You know them better than I do. Why don't you tell me?"

She kicked at a rock. "Save the world, save our magic, blah blah blah."

He laughed. "That's the Nell I know and love."

She unbent enough to smirk, but then her smile faded. "My family needs me still, Corbin. And if something were to happen to me, if this poison does something to me—"

She cut herself off. That was a distraction Corbin couldn't afford.

"We're going to stop that from happening." He sounded serene, so sure of himself.

Anger sparked, fast and sharp. She snapped before she could stop herself. "What makes you so sure?"

"Because I know you," he said simply, taking the heat from her sudden fury. He took her other hand. "I know us."

They walked in silence after that, but it was an easy one, not the dreaded thick silence that had been spooling into an inky pit between them. Everything else in her life might be going up in flames, but at least Corbin still knew and loved her even at her worst. She'd nearly forgotten that, but it was as clear now as the mountains before her. And she loved him, even when he was being ridiculously idealistic. Maybe they balanced each other out, if she could figure out a way to serve both her mission and her heart.

By the time the sun was setting, everyone walked closely together, eyes trained on the ground for any weaknesses. Another fall at this stage would be more dangerous, with energy and resources already low. Far fewer words were spoken. Even the little fairies had stopped their frolicking and flew straight as arrows alongside them.

Urgency nipped at Nell's heels. *Faster. Faster. Faster.* A full week had gone by already. Two blizzards full of malice and an attempted dragon attack—who knew what their enemy would send next? Every day, he grew stronger and more entrenched in his power.

Nell ignored the sting beneath her heart.

A long howl echoed through the dusky air. Everyone halted.

A second howl poured through the rocky hillside, followed by another wolf picking up the call from the other side of the valley.

Nell kept her voice low and calm. "They're close."

She scanned the area. So little to see in the purple-shaded dusk, at first. But then she noticed a jagged opening alongside one of the cliff-like chunks of ice to their left. Beyond the small cave, black hills dotted the ice, like lava cooled and frozen.

The howl filled the air, and this time was answered by a chorus. Nell and the others circled up, back to back.

"Do you see anything?" Tristan whispered.

"Not yet," Corbin said.

"How many can we expect?" Nell asked, gaze roaming the land.

"They hunt in packs of up to a dozen," Corbin replied.

"And just think how hungry they must be. We're starving, and we've only been here a week," Phoebe said.

"These could be sent from the Dragon, too. Like the storms—and the dragons." Nell pulled out her bow and drew an arrow.

The first wolf to slip forward was almost invisible: White fur from nose to tail, but the eyes were black as coal. The animal stared at them from the opening in the ice which had to lead to a cave.

Icy cold ran up and down Nell's back. The wolf's eyes looked angry, like the eyes of the face in the wind. This beast wanted to kill her, too. "Sierra, do you have Queenie nearby? It's an attack."

"No, don't use the fairies!" Corbin grabbed her arm. "Look, it's a mother wolf. You can see she's been nursing pups. We can scare her away; her pups will die if we kill her."

Was he kidding? Let her friends be attacked? She growled.

The wolf growled in response, and its fur bristled.

Sierra said, "I don't know, Nell. Queenie's not sensing—"

"I know what I know," Nell interrupted. "That man wants us dead, and Aluvia under his foot, or have you forgotten? If I have to take down some of his creatures to defeat him, so be it." She took aim.

"Stop!" Corbin pleaded.

He was going to get them all killed. Her vision tinged red with fury.

Then singing filled the air with poignant, heart-rending notes. Her anger floated away on the music. She'd forgotten about Micah's skill. Using his magic, he sang a song of peace that held power beyond its beauty. His song had been lovely the first time she'd heard it, but now her heart fluttered at the haunting melody, as if something inside was trying to take flight.

Like dust motes in the breeze, Micah's song drifted through the air as a glowing series of lights, bright gold with hints of green like moss in springtime.

Nell's eyes widened. No one else was watching the colors. Was she the only one who could see the magic carried along by the power of his singing? It was breathtaking.

The magic shimmered, vibrant and full of life. It sank into the wolf, fading under its skin, bringing with it a deep sigh of relaxation from the animal. The bristles of its fur settled, and the wolf sat, tongue lolling like a pet dog.

Throat full, Nell closed her eyes. She'd been wrong. She'd nearly killed an innocent creature.

Even without the use of her sight, the colors still swirled in her mind. Goose bumps tingled along her skin, and her hands loosened on the bow and arrow.

The pain that never left her faded to a distant noise. Even her guilt slipped away in the beauty of the song.

Micah stopped singing, and the golden notes softly faded into the fast-darkening sky.

Two white pups trotted out of the cave and pressed up against the bigger wolf. The mother yipped at the babies and then padded away into the cave, the pups trailing behind.

The danger was over, but Micah's power still filled the clearing.

Tied into the rush of magic around her, Nell saw flames along the edge of her vision, clearer this time. She spun toward the flash in the sky.

A glorious mare—rippling white body and mane, clear muscles flexing as she pawed the sky. Wings twice the length of her body extending from her back, with licks of gold, orange, and red flames lighting along the length of them. She was magnificent.

If she were real. Because the next instant, she was gone.

The dark-blue sky was stunning—but empty.

"Did the rest of you see that?" Nell asked, her voice cracking. Sierra had once seen strange things during their first journey together. That had been her fairy queen calling her, though, and Nell had no such creatures to care for.

Corbin said, "Let's move on before we talk. Other

wolves may decide to attack if we stay. They may be natural, but they're still predators."

Micah nodded. "We must camp away from here, and quickly. My calming influence will be short-lived."

The sun had dipped below the horizon, and the temperature was dropping.

The group of friends backed away from the cave, picking through the craggy land. Nell followed, swept along by their urgency, shock still reverberating.

She had seen magic. Magic must be growing in her, even with the voice silenced.

ell kept the words bottled inside until the tent was up—no cave tonight—and the fire going. Then she grabbed the conversation by the reins. A girl had to take her medicine when it was time, no matter how bitter. "First of all, Corbin was right about the wolf. She wasn't sent from the Dragon, or Micah's magic wouldn't have calmed her. I'm—sorry. For refusing to listen. A good leader always listens to her team, and I didn't."

Corbin nodded. "We understand. You're on edge."

True. No one else bore the responsibility she did, did they? It was all well and good to be kind and generous when it wouldn't cost anyone's life. But she had to hold the line.

"And no harm was done," Phoebe pointed out.

That's right. No one and nothing was actually hurt.

Sometimes toughness was necessary. Nell still believed that was true, but she could admit—at least to herself—that being too quick to use her weapon was something to watch out for. She'd try harder to listen to Corbin next time. Irritation flared at the thought. Being wrong galled, even with the grace the others offered so easily.

"There's something else, something really important," she pressed forward. "Did anyone else see something while Micah was singing? I think… I saw… his magic."

Sierra said, "Really? That's new, isn't it?"

"You could say that."

"Hmm. Well, I didn't see anything," Sierra said. "I don't see magic most of the time. I have to focus on Queenie and our bond to see it. It takes work."

"I saw it," Tristan said.

Nell sighed with relief. "Was it golden?"

Tristan nodded. "I assumed it was Micah's magic. Ours is always blue."

"Why couldn't I see it before?" she asked, licking lips dry from shock.

Micah pursed his lips as he thought. "I suspect the magic Tristan and I have shared with you has sensitized you. Add in the voice's own magic and the Dragon's, whatever his power springs from, and it is actually unsurprising you would be able to see some form of magic."

"There's more," Nell said, stealing herself for the hurt Corbin might feel. "Didn't someone say something about a"—she coughed into her hand, feeling ridiculous—"flying magical creature much like a horse?"

Corbin nodded, a new chill in his eyes that had nothing to do with the weather.

Feeling humbled, she took a deep breath and tentatively wrapped both hands around his. "Could you tell me about it? It's relevant; trust me."

His eyes thawed a bit. "Windsteeds are in the old stories, creatures made from the wind itself, temperamental and wilder than any unbroken stallion. They can wink out of existence and reappear in another place far away, instant travel through the air. But the stories of them faded many years ago, far longer than those of dragons and even Baleros among the merfolk."

"The fauns have passed down stories of them throughout their history, along with many other magical creatures," Micah offered.

"And did these windsteeds have wings of fire, by chance?" Nell asked.

Corbin stared at her, eyes huge. "You've seen one? Tonight?"

Nell shrugged, trying to downplay the intensity of the moment. "I've seen *something* a few times. This was different than those faces in the blizzard. Like a mirage of fire playing at the edge of my vision. When I looked straight at it, it disappeared. But I caught it clearly once during Micah's magic. And I realized maybe it wasn't just a hallucination. Maybe it was real."

"What did you see, exactly?" Corbin enunciated each word a little too clearly for Nell's comfort.

"Well, about what you described, honestly. A great white steed, high in the sky. Strong, confident—you could tell. Its wings were huge and flamed brighter than a midwinter bonfire."

"You saw a windsteed," Corbin confirmed, with an unusually flat tone for such an occasion. Being left out of the magic again had to sting. "There's nothing else like it."

"This would be good news indeed!" Micah said. "Windsteeds could carry us to the mountain immediately. They could be the answer to our time and distance dilemma!"

"Have you ever actually seen one?" Nell asked the faun.

He shook his head. "No one I know ever has. They are legend only. But we who were also thought to be legend know well that many things exist that would shock humans."

"I'll keep looking, then," Nell said. "Though I wish Aluvia would stop all the surprises."

Corbin leaned closer. In the cold air, heat emanated from his body like rays from the sun. He said, "Speaking of surprises, do you have anything else to tell us?"

She sighed. It was time to tell them about the visions

of the red-robed women. Past time. It was the only way to repair any breaks she might have caused by keeping silent.

"Remember how I told you all the voice was talking to me? Sort of privately?"

"Yes?" Corbin's gaze narrowed.

"It also sort of, well, showed me things. Visions. Things from the past, I think. I didn't say anything because I didn't want to sound like a lunatic."

"Look at the company you keep. None of us can throw stones," Sierra said, putting her hand on Corbin's tight shoulders, as if giving a silent warning. Then she waved to her fairy, Micah's faun legs, Tristan and Phoebe's tattoos, Corbin's keeper mark.

"I know, but these visions seemed a bit much for even me to believe."

"What is it you couldn't tell even me?" Corbin asked slowly.

"When we were in the old temple at Port Iona, I had a vision of red-cloaked women studying in the secret room. Before you found the picture of them." The words came out in a rush. Tingling in her chest spread to her neck. Her cheeks burned even in the freezing air.

"What were they studying? Did you see?" Micah asked, the only one not glaring.

Corbin was more than glaring. His eyes were dark with hurt. Betrayal. She should have told him sooner;

she really should have. By trying to spare his feelings, she'd made things worse.

"I don't know. But I knew it felt familiar. I think it's tied to the voice. It's like she… it's… they've"—she decided to use the singular pronoun since it usually sounded like one person when it spoke—"she had woken up more fully, and I was getting some of her memories."

"What, like a haunting?" Corbin asked.

"No. More like sharing my mind with her. It's always been like that, but it had grown stronger, just as the magic in the world has. Until the Dragon's magic silenced her, like I said." Nell met his eyes. "I saw them wielding the sword, and she said they were the guardians. Guardians of Aluvia's magic."

She couldn't quite bring herself to mention anything about the souls in the sword.

"Then it's good these guardians are on our side, isn't it?" Corbin let out a deep breath.

True. But what if saving the world required a sacrifice? What if *that* was what the voice was preparing her for? The guardians weren't alive and weren't quite dead. Whatever they were, Nell didn't want to be like that.

The lights boiled above them again, as they had each night, like a bubbling soup pot about to spill over. Nell wished she knew if that would be good or bad.

The next day passed without major problems, if one discounted the constant freezing wind and two distant dragon sightings. The Dragon assuredly hadn't given up, though. Not a man like that. Maybe he was too busy conquering the ports back home, laughing at how their group was walking through never-ending snow. Nell glowered at the thought.

They were barely into the second week of this journey, and already it seemed endless. The tallest mountains were still too far away. Food was stretched thin, even supplemented with hunting and gathering. She woke daily with her heart on fire, smothering her cries so as not to wake her friends. Her gaze roamed constantly, watching for dragons, wolves, ice patches or any other dangers.

They stopped to debate which way to take toward the highest peak. The map showed two possibilities—one took them by the unknown circle on the map; the other avoided it. Corbin wanted to scope out what that symbol represented, but Sierra felt it best to avoid any possible risks. Despite the urgency thrumming in Nell, tiredness weighted her down like piles of rocks in her boots. Her friend's drawn faces suggested they felt the same.

Corbin held the book now even as they walked, leaving him no free hands to hold hers. He muttered to himself as he walked rather than engaging in conversation with anyone else. She told herself it didn't matter.

Rocky boulders littered the steep land rising and falling as their group inched higher into the mountains. Dark clouds gathered in the sky. *Please don't let it storm again*, thought Nell. She kept plodding forward, leaning into the increasing wind, eyes on the ground, and as she marched, her thoughts turned into a downward spiral.

Why couldn't everyone move faster? Did they *want* her and everyone else to die? *Of course not*, she reminded herself quickly, but there was a new edge of despair to her monologue, built of doubts placed there by the Dragon's poison, she supposed. *He* was toxic, not just his magic. He deserved to die a hundred painful deaths.

Somewhere behind the thick clouds, the sun sank along with her mood, but she wasn't ready to stop moving yet. If she stopped moving, she might cry at the impossibility of it all, and this was no time for tears. Tears solved nothing.

When another dark shadow crossed the ground at her feet, she scowled. More clouds, darker this time. Great. Another blizzard, even. But something in the line of the shadow did not suggest a cloud. She stopped, startled, and glanced up at the exact moment a white-feathered griffin burst through the low clouds, claws extended, shrieking and heading right at Nell.

"Watch out!" Phoebe shouted.

Everyone darted behind the giant stones jutting up around them. Crouching, Nell fumbled for her bow, keeping her eyes on the giant beast. With hindquarters of a lion and the body and head of an eagle, griffins were beautiful, powerful, and rare. They were also not native to the frozen lands.

Nell stepped out from behind the rock. Her bow was in her hand, her arrow nocked.

"Get down!" Corbin cried from his hiding spot. "Griffins are too powerful to die without a perfect heart shot."

Eyes as white as its feathers glared down at her, and Nell gasped. Something about the raptor reminded her of the faces in the wind, white and dead-eyed.

"I think it's one of his," she shouted.

"No, it's like the wolf—just leave it alone!" he urged.

"But griffins don't live down here in the cold!" Still, she hesitated. He'd been right before.

She knew something of griffins, one of the few creatures she'd paid attention to when Corbin lectured. They were considered noble creatures. She had griffin-feather arrows that had cost her a pretty penny, but none flew straighter or faster.

She touched the dark-brown fletching of her arrow and looked again at the mantling griffin above. No, the white eyes and feathers of this one weren't right. Weren't natural. If their enemy could drain dragons, he could do the same to griffins. They were magical beasts, too.

The raptor gave a hoarse battle cry and dove, right at Nell.

She held the string lightly, waiting for the giant bird to come in close enough for a hit. Three… two…

Corbin pushed her out of the way, landing on her with an *oomph,* fairies squealing in distress. The griffin soared high, back into the clouds.

"Corbin!"

She pushed her beloved off, ready to punch him in the face. Like old times.

The others peered from behind rocks. No doubt the beast would be back. Soon.

"What. Were. You. Thinking?" Nell squeezed her hand into a fist. The scar along her palm stung. The bitter cold spot in her flared and she shivered, fighting down the urge to scream.

"Don't try to kill it, Nell! It's not the only way—it's not. It's not like you to shoot an animal like this without thinking twice; it's something the crews would do. We aren't like that. Micah can calm it like he did the wolf, right?"

Micah shook his head. "It's under some other magic's power, Corbin. I can see it— something like a tie to it, the same one as in the storm. Besides, the griffin would not listen to a faun. Just as mature dragons do not listen to us, griffins are just as proud."

Sierra said, "This time, Nell's right. I'm sorry, Corbin."

High in the sky, the griffin dipped back below the clouds to the left. It shrieked in defiance, then tilted dangerously on its wing and plummeted back toward Nell.

"Don't do it! If you miss the heart, it'll kill you," Corbin said.

Nell took a deep breath, and raised her bow but couldn't stop the question: What if Corbin was right this time, too? If she had killed that mother wolf, it would've been a win on the Dragon's part, to make her more like him, too quick to kill.

"Please," Corbin said into her ear from behind. "Trust me."

The temptation to lower the bow tugged on her. She couldn't decide. Couldn't put down the bow, couldn't release the arrow. For the first time in her life, Nell was in a battle and didn't know what to do next.

The giant bird dropped like a rock out of the sky, and there was no more time. It collided with her, its feet balled up like fists, and everything went black.

CHAPTER SEVENTEEN

She awoke curled up in a tiny space. The smell of honey mixed with the putrid scent of rotting flash made her gag. She sat up, hands over her mouth and nose, and blinked hard.

Bars surrounded her. She was in a cage, inside of a large stone room with other cages holding different animals. Noxious fumes filled the space, and white mist floated along the low ceiling. The room reminded her vividly of Flight distilleries. A smaller stand near the door held vials and bowls already full of fluid, some of them smoking. And a man stood with his back to her at a table, a dragon mask sitting beside his project.

The Dragon.

The griffin must have carried her to him, in a lair somewhere in the mountains.

Corbin had been wrong this time. So, so wrong. But instead of fury or self-righteous indignation, all Nell felt was heartbreak. What had happened to her friends? To Corbin?

The Dragon stood with his back to her, clearly unconcerned with her as a threat. The tinkling of a spoon against glass resulting in a new whiff of mist rising from the table. She didn't watch the mist, though: she watched the man, noting his broad shoulders, the thick arms, remembering his ferocious strikes. Who was this man who'd defeated her repeatedly? She was his captive now.

Flashes of the beating she'd taken sent a thrill of terror rocketing through her. The icy place in her chest spasmed, and she hid a gasp, clenching her fist on the scar he'd given her. She didn't want to draw his notice, not yet. She still wore her winter gear, as if she'd been dumped unceremoniously in the cage. Silently peeling off her gloves and tucking them away, she wiped sweat from her forehead and focused on memorizing her surroundings.

The cages in the room were coated in glowing, viscous nectar. She knew the liquid on sight, could smell its sweetness. Nectar, altered in some horrible way the way Flight used to be. He'd gotten fairy nectar somewhere.

Rage filled her. Like her, the magical creatures were

trapped not just by bars, but by the Dragon's twisted magic.

Nell couldn't tell how many different kinds of creatures filled the cages of brass and silver, but a quick survey told her they were all flying magical creatures. The white feathered birds were firebirds deprived of their fire and their red plumage. A huge cage near the back held what seemed to be a sleeping griffin, perhaps the very one that had attacked her. She hoped the giant raptor was only sleeping, not dead. Even though she'd been right about it being sent to attack them, she was glad now that she hadn't killed it. It was a victim, too. She and Corbin had both been right.

The cage closest to her held something Nell had never seen, though. The creature was barely visible at all, merely a sheer outline of white with the rest of it lightly shimmering and transparent like the ghosts of old wives' tales. Its barely visible skin seemed smooth and sleek, and its rounded head had tiny pointed ears and a short cute nose.

A snow sprite, she thought, recalling Micah's description of them. His measured and academic explanation seemed a century ago. Snow sprites hadn't been seen in generations—and the Dragon had trapped not just one, but *many,* she realized with growing horror.

There were at least two dozen of them in the cages farthest from the door. They jostled and squealed at each other, but the sounds reminded her of upset children, not dangerous creatures. Snow sprites were supposed to be pranksters, but this creature in the cage near the Dragon wasn't laughing. It was huddled in the center, carefully not touching the bars, whimpering in fear.

What was the Dragon doing?

She could only watch, powerless, as he turned to the cage, reached through the faintly glowing bars, and poured a black sticky potion over the quivering sprite, a liquid as black as the one that had poisoned Nell. Immediately, the sprite's body smoked, and the poor creature screamed. The smell of blood and dragons flooded the room, followed by the ripe stink of rotting flesh.

The snow sprite bent in on itself, slumping, its shoulder blades growing sharper. Its face thinned, and fangs grew from its mouth. Its ice-blue eyes emptied to white, and a red mist tinged with silver flowed from its shriveled skin, floating over to the Dragon like a cloud. The red mist slowly faded into him like blood soaked up by a cloth. Taking a deep breath, he glowed with a smoldering red light right before the magic disappeared.

Nell choked back a cry of disgust and horror. The faces in the storm—this was what they had been. She might not know much about magic, but she knew enough to understand he had just changed the innocent nature of the poor sprite to darkness, just as he turned the dragons, and tried to turn her. Not only could the creatures attack with the weather, they could appear anywhere the wind could go, spy on anyone. An army of those combined with his army of dragons would be unstoppable.

How could one sword do anything against this?

The smell grew worse, and the change was complete, leaving a ravaged-looking creature where the adorable snow sprite had been. It was definitely the things she'd seen during the storm. Nell gagged, burrowing her face into her sleeve. She couldn't help it.

The Dragon spoke without turning around. "Well, it looks like it's time to introduce myself officially, Nellwyn, since you haven't been able to guess who I am."

He turned, face exposed to her for the first time. The man's dark eyes shone with black magic, and a white scar outlined in angry red ran along one cheek, under one eye, down to the jaw, and part-way down his neck. She gasped, but not from the scarred face and neck. She did know him. He'd trained her.

Shane McConnel, the sword master from Port Iona. The man she'd respected so much. The one who supposedly died shortly after she left his training five years ago.

"Ah, so you do remember me," he said. "I'm flattered."

He'd been impossible to forget: a prodigy with amazing skills, the kind of sword master she'd only hoped to be. When Jack told her they killed Shane, she'd secretly grieved the loss of a fine swordsman, a good man, despite his work with the crew. She'd been in the crew then, too, after all.

Confusion beat against her mind.

"But what happened to you? You barely finished my training before you took off to the south on some assignment, and then Jack told me he killed you. Is he the one who—" she gestured along her cheek and jaw.

"As if that cowardly assassin could ever lay a knife on me." Shane glared, but then his expression cleared and that was somehow even worse. "No, he didn't give me this scar. My dragon did, with a bite that nearly ended me."

"But if the dragon tried to kill you—"

"Tried and failed, though he succeeded at making me what I am now. After that, magic grew in me, calling me further south, to here, just as my magic will draw you ever stronger to me as time goes on, like a compass needle pulling you true north. It knows its master. Other traces of magic may be on you, puny magic of the earth and sea, but they can't stop mine. It's almost completed its work in you, Nellywn. Tell me, what do you think of my realized dream?" He gestured at the creatures in the room.

"I'd call this more of a nightmare." Nell reached automatically for her sword and stilled when her hand brushed her hilt. He hadn't disarmed her? How arrogant was he? And where had he taken her? Where was the *here* he had found?

Shane gave a low laugh and unlocked the door to her cage. "You think you can defeat me, knowing who I am? Here, in my stronghold? Come on out. We both know the only smart move now is to join me."

The Shane she had known would never have acted like this, but Bentwood and Jasper would have. She knew just how to handle men whose egos outweighed their wisdom. She dropped her arms and hung her head. "You're right. I couldn't beat you years ago."

She stepped out of her jail cell. He waited, watching, and she didn't reach for her sword, not yet. Instead, she spoke softly. "Knowing who you are changes everything. Let's talk about what you really want from me, Shane."

He closed the space between them and reached out suddenly, holding a thin knife. "Stop pretending to be meek; I'm not a fool like your old bosses. If I have to force you to cooperate, so be it."

She grabbed for her sword, and even managed to pull it from her sheath, but he knocked her hand aside.

With one quick motion, Shane grabbed her free hand and sliced along her left palm along the scar. She screamed, pain racing up her arm, worse than the first cut in Port Iona. She heard the sharp clatter of a weapon hitting the floor. Her sword.

Black ooze dripped from her hand. It had burned

before. Now her arm felt full of boiling oil. Her heart lurched, pulsing against a tightening net of rage and evil.

"My friends will stop you even if I die here," she gasped, putting all her strength toward not falling on the floor. Not in front of him.

"I know who came with you on this pathetic journey, and I'm not worried. My snow sprites have been reporting to me for some time now." He smiled over at the horrifying creature with a look suggesting affection.

Nell gagged.

He snapped his gaze back to her. "But perhaps Corbin Lannon in particular needs a lesson on how to treat his soon-to-be-king and savior. I'll slice him the same way I've done you."

"This isn't about him. Or you. It's about what's right." Breathe. Breathe. She had to get out of here. She started inching toward the open doorway. Her sword could stay.

"Ah. A righteous warrior. Tell me, Nellwyn, is it right that humans perish at the whims of dragons? Is it right the fairy keepers withhold their fairies' nectar? I can use their nectar to create a shield for humans to protect them from many magical beasts. My elixir even gives me the power to take their magic. Can you imagine how much better off we'd be if humans regained their rightful place as rulers of our world?"

Anger broke, mixing with the painful pulsing of her heart. "You've warped the sprites' magic into something unnatural, just like you've become twisted with evil. You'll destroy Aluvia with this madness!"

He lifted a finger to hush her and sauntered to the table. Reaching one hand out, he tapped the mask hard once. The thud echoed in the room. The griffin stirred in its sleep.

Licking her lips, Nell mentally counted the number of steps it would take to get out and slam the door on him. Five.

"Be careful, my little queen. The changed sprites and their storms are nothing compared to what else I've conquered. This whole building was built by people who hoarded Aluvia's magic, but now I am the one who lives here. They exist no longer, and I am the one who will deliver the future to Aluvia's people."

Not hoarded; conserved. And we are with you still… The voice was almost impossible to hear, but Nell recognized it with a thrill.

"You've already shown us your dragons," she snapped, drawing courage from the smuggled message of the guardians.

This was an ancient temple held by the women in the red cloaks. Perhaps the place on the map had been intended as a sanctuary, maybe. But it didn't matter now. Now it was a prison.

Five easy steps. If only she wasn't so winded. So hurt. The ground beckoned. Her blood burned.

"And all but one of them have been molded to my

hands through my own special elixir. All but the first. He and I have a special relationship, you might say." He gestured to the scar visible along his neck.

"We can stop your dragons with the sword of Aluvia. We will." They had to.

"Does the lie comfort you? My three dragons took a city in hours. We've taken two more ports since then. Now imagine scores of dragons. Port Ostara is next on my list to conquer."

She could visualize it too clearly. Her breath left in a rush.

"You can't win," Shane said softly, weapon no longer in hand. He didn't need one. The truth had sliced Nell open to the bone.

Those dragons would sweep over Aluvia. The twisted snow sprites would terrorize people. If the ports didn't crown him willingly as their king, he'd just take their cities by force, as he took Port Iona hardly breaking a sweat. Port Ostara would fall next. The smaller fishing villages wouldn't stand a chance.

He nodded. "Yes, you see now. I always could defeat you because I can read your face. I know you. Your Corbin will never embrace the warrior you truly are. He'll always hold you back. But I formed you into the swordswoman you are, and, like a sword, I can re-forge you, replace your magic with a new, stronger power. Just like these dragons, I can make you more powerful than you've ever been."

He held out his gloved hand. She could remember him as he'd been, a worthy teacher, even a respected friend.

For a single moment, her mind produced a new image, one in which she was powerful, respected, loved. No one asked her to lead. Shane led the war, but she could fight the battles.

Grim satisfaction sprang up at the mental picture. No one judged her for being strong. No one worried for her. Shane celebrated her skills without care for her gender. She could do what she enjoyed without thinking about leadership and dependents. Master as many weapons as she chose. No more people needing her. No more people hanging on her skirts. No more… family.

She gasped and stumbled backward, shaking her head. Her sisters. Her mother. Corbin's parents. They couldn't hide from the Dragon forever. This man would kill or enslave them all simply because they stood in his greedy way. The warped rush of pleasure shriveled from her horror.

He said, "I'll only kill if I have to. It's about the mission, Nellwyn. You understand that."

The truth of his words landed on her like a hundred-pound weight. She did understand. She'd often felt the end justified the means and had been proud of her ruthlessness. They were more alike than she wished. Looking at Shane now, she felt a wave of fear.

She had to find that sword or she was going to die or

fall victim to Shane's power, like that poor sprite just did. Everyone she loved would face the same horrific fate.

She couldn't allow herself to end up serving a madman, her own heart corrupted beyond recognition. Only three footsteps would carry her to the doorway now. But her feet wouldn't move.

"I'll beat you," Nell forced out through lips numb with fear—or perhaps with the new influx of poison.

"I doubt it. I was your superior years ago and still am, but the people will follow me without bloodshed if you're at my side. Why allow a war when you know my kingship is inevitable? Isn't it better to spare their lives?"

She couldn't breathe. He finally made one argument hard to battle. They were all going to die anyway. What if she spared some lives?

But were lives worth saving if spent suffering under a tyrant? She thought back to the years she spent serving Jack, unable to do what was right without jeopardizing her family. She couldn't go back to that life again.

She shook her head. "You have no idea what you're asking."

Shane's gaze sharpened. "Well, now. I'll give you one last chance to make the smart choice. I'll keep you here until you do and my creatures will be happy to drink the life from your companions if they step too close to what's mine. Down here, in my lands, my servants are more powerful than you know."

He reached toward her and grabbed her wrist. Pain like lightning shook her.

A bolt of pure terror shattered the heavy weight that had held her feet immobile while he boasted. Through blurred vision, she grabbed one of the smoking bowls of liquid from the nearby stand and flung it at Shane. Liquid spattered his face, ran down his chest. He yelled and covered his eyes with his arms. Hissing filled the room as the unknown liquid hit the floor. It smelled like burned roses.

Taking her chance, she shoved him hard and ran out of the room, yanking the door shut behind her. A harsh gust of wind flew through the hall, nearly knocking her over.

A shrill shriek came from the long corridor on the left. She turned the opposite way and ran on trembling legs. The hallway seemed to stretch forever, never ending. Maybe he'd bewitched the building to keep her trapped. Another scream came from behind, closer. Something inhuman, coming after her. A dragon wouldn't fit in here, but the sound was huge, filling her ears, pushing fear along with it. She'd never reach the door.

A quick glance behind showed a glimpse of pure white fur, triangular ears with tufts, and wide paws with long claws. Some kind of giant snow cat, it looked like, ready for its next meal.

Shane was going to kill her now anyway, no matter

what lies he spun about using her to sway the people. She thought of Corbin and Sierra, and the others, no doubt frantically looking for her, with no warning about what could come for them from Shane.

In a fury, Nell jumped and grabbed hold of a vent grate in the hall ceiling. With a grunt, she yanked the grate open, swinging from the hinged metal bars. The snow cat snarled and jumped at her legs, but Nell kicked and then swung her legs up into the opening of the icy air shaft and lifted the grate shut behind her. The furious sounds of the snow cat muted immediately, but the cold grew worse.

Her breath was loud in her ears, her eyes nearly useless in the dim light. Her darkest fears swam up, whispering she'd die alone here under the ice. This was too hard. Too much work for no good reason. His poison burned like ice pressed too long to the skin. If she fell now, she could rest.

But Nell stubbornly shook her head.

"I won't leave them alone," she declared. Not her family. Not her friends. Not Corbin.

She tightened her lips and reached to pull herself upward. She braced her legs against each side of the icy air vent. Narrow hand holds had been dug into the ice. Her fingers screamed at her, palm on fire along its cut, but adrenalin spiked like the hit of a strength elixir. Whatever toxin Shane had used must be slow-working, or maybe the guardians were succeeding at holding it back. She could do this.

With each reach of her hands, she thought of being back home. In her mind, she wasn't alone in the dark. She was standing in the fairy field with Corbin. He was smiling at her in that way he had, holding out a steel thistle flower to her. Just the two of them and his fairies, peaceful and happy. The love that rushed through her was more potent than battle rage.

The cold air seared her lungs, but she pulled herself up again and again, arms burning with the effort, until she could see glowing light above. The ice against her palm numbed the worst of the remaining pain, even soothed it. The tunnel turned, angling more sideways. She moved faster, sweat pouring down her face despite the freezing wind blowing down the tunnel.

She finally reached a grate to the outside. Beyond it she could see whiteness, but it wasn't snow. Was that sand? Maybe.

Chest heaving, Nell kicked open the metal grate, pulled herself out of the vent, and hastily looked around, fearing a flight of dragons descending.

She cursed. Instead of being outside the fortress as she hoped, she was inside an oval training ring attached to the temple behind it. Huge closed doors rose behind her, next to the grate. Dusty sand covered the ground, raked clear of snow. Across from her along the curving wall, a giant pen of some kind extended out past the ring, though no animals were visible. The gate hung open.

She saw all this in a flash, but it wasn't what captured her attention. In the arena, eggs the size of boulders lay nestled all around her.

And one of the eggs was hatching.

CHAPTER EIGHTEEN

No more than two strides away, the shell was mottled red and silver, speckled with black dots. It rocked back and forth, big as an oversized wine barrel. A sharp tapping came from inside.

Nell tensed her legs, ready to run. Anything coming out of an egg that size could eat her for dinner and have room for a late-night snack. She scanned the arena, and her heart sank. There were no other exits.

A split zigzagged down the side of the egg. The shell opened with a sharp crack and fell to the ground like the creature inside was throwing off a coat. A red baby dragon, a hatchling, stood among the remains of the shell, looking around as if a bit shocked by its sudden change in surroundings.

The hatchling was as big as a draft horse. It made

soft mewling sounds, and tiny sparks flew from its mouth. Leathery scarlet wings were tucked tight against its body. The scales along its back and face were scarlet but slid into orange near the belly. All of it shimmered with a soft iridescence. The hatchling was beautiful, majestic even in its first moments of life. It shivered and called a piercing lament, as if seeking its mother. Without conscious thought, Nell reached to console the dragon.

A full-grown dragon with blue scales stuck its head in the arena from the pen across from them, and Nell froze, hand near the baby. Mountaineers always warned never to stand between a mama and her baby, but her feet felt rooted to the ground.

The adult dragon was massive, far bigger even than the one Shane rode. It leaned into the ring, taking two steps in. Her belly was lumpy and low to the ground. She must be ready to lay eggs, but she also seemed to be this one's mother. She strained toward her baby but something held her back.

Noise rose from the doors behind Nell —men were coming, probably for the newborn hatchling.

The thought broke her paralysis. Shane was going to take the hatchling's magic, as he had the snow sprites', as he had the other dragons'. He would break its spirit and make it serve him, this beautiful, proud creature meant to soar free in the skies.

Not while I'm still alive, Nell thought. Her heart thudded, urgency pushing against the fierce poison surging through her. "We've got to get you out of here."

The sound of clanking metal and stomping feet grew louder.

The hatchling caught sight of the blue mother dragon and yowled, staggering toward her. The mother dragon mantled her wings and lifted her head into a miserable cry that broke Nell's heart. The huge dragon met her eyes, and for one moment Nell could see some semblance of thought inside the beast. And it wanted her baby freed.

Nell faced the mother dragon and said, "If you let me, I'll rescue your baby, or I'll die trying."

The doors slammed open. Two men ran through, brandishing swords.

The dragon closed her eyes and lowered her head. Then with a loud groan, it flew low across the open air. Nell dove and rolled out of the way, and the beast landed at the open doorway. Settling her huge body hard against the doors, the mother dragon effectively blocked the rest of the men from entering the ring, at least for now. It was the most rebellion she could achieve, Nell guessed. She sensed the same magical coercion working on the poor dragon as in her, sapping its will to rebel and fight.

She saluted the mother, who was doing her best to

resist the dark magic, just as Nell was. Whatever it took, she would free these dragons from Shane's power.

She turned to the two men who'd made it into the arena. Wounded hand or not, she could handle two regular fighters. She drew her dagger and pointed it at the opening of the grate. "Hello, gentlemen. You'd be smart to head down that tunnel right there."

The two men exchanged amused glances. The larger man had a gray beard, and neither wore a helm or shield. Their grins made it clear they thought this fight would be easy.

She grinned back.

Then she dove, shoulder connecting with the knees of the smaller one, knocking the feet out from under him. He landed with a thud and she rolled past him, snatching his sword from his loose hands. It settled against her cut palm, but she didn't flinch. She didn't like to fight with two weapons; that was true. Time to practice.

She sprang to her feet and laughed low, dagger at the ready, swinging the sword in lazy circles.

"Warned you."

The bearded man hollered and charged. So predictable.

Fierce joy poured down her sword arm into her swings, the lethargy from Shane's poison pushed back by the rush of battle. She'd pay for this hard work later, but for now, her blades blurred as the bearded man jabbed and slashed with no finesse or ingenuity. The smaller man staggered to his feet. Nell quickly parried the bearded man and clunked the other on the head with her dagger's pommel, returning him to the ground, unconscious this time. *I ought to kill him*, the thought came to her. It was persuasive. It coiled through her, snake-like. Her palm stung along the cut.

Backing up, she shook her head at the fallen man and his glaring colleague. "You're lucky I don't kill people anymore."

Saying it out loud made it more certain she wouldn't… forget.

"You're a fool then," a third man said from behind.

Nell whirled. A tall man had squeezed past the ridges of the dragon's back and had the bloody scratches to show for it. He charged, sword glinting in the last light of the sun.

Footsteps behind her warned of her other opponent's rapid approach. Keeping her eyes on the oncoming tall man, she jabbed her newly acquired sword at the man closing in behind her. She angled the sword hoping to hit his thigh, and he grunted. Without pausing, she yanked the blade free and brought it up over her head with her dagger, forming a cross to block the incoming blade of the tall man.

Sparks flew from the strike of their swords. The

ringing of the blades rose half an octave, and Nell feared her dagger might snap under the pressure.

The tall man glared. "Shane said he trained you, but I bet I can whip you. He might even promote me when I do."

She gave a hard shove and stepped around the bearded man groaning on the ground, keeping his body like a hurdle between them. She sheathed her dagger and snatched up his fallen sword. "Sorry, Shane only rewards people with skill," she replied.

The tall man jumped over the fighter's prone body and charged, as she intended.

She spun and kicked him in the back as he passed. His curse was muffled by the sand in his face.

The bearded man, blood still running down his thigh, grabbed her ankle and pulled a small hand-ax from his belt. "Give me back my sword, you stupid cow."

A quick flash of the blade in question—hers now—disarmed him. He wasn't worth her breath. She reversed her hold and knocked him harder to ensure he wouldn't be back in this fight. She didn't wait to watch his head hit the ground again before spinning to face her remaining opponent with a grin.

"You may fight well," he said, "but the Dragon don't hold with thieves. These here are his dragons."

The tall man flicked his blade lightly to one side before striking again. Nell didn't have to think about the movement that followed as she blocked him. She'd long ago learned to read the tiniest hints: a glance this way meant a feint; a wrist turned that way meant an overhead strike. She lunged, hoping to slice his sword arm and render him harmless, but her blade bounced off thick leather armor.

Nell shifted her feet and struck at the man again, ignoring her screaming muscles. If this fight stalled her too long, Shane would no doubt recover from whatever his own elixir had done to him, and she didn't think she could escape him again, not here, not now. She had to make this fight short.

Nearby, the hatchling staggered and cried out. The mother gave a heart-wrenching shriek. Her white eyes whirled like storm clouds.

Retreat wasn't an option. She yelled and charged. The startled man took two steps back. She kept running, using her momentum to strike with both swords one after the other, using the motion Shane had used against her when they first met again. *Clang, clang, clang,* like a windmill, until her left sword struck the man's wrist to numb it, and her right sword smacked his weapon hard, knocking it to the ground. The man stood gasping, hands trembling.

"What are you?" he asked with eyes wide.

A dozen answers flew through her mind—sword seeker, prophetess, healer, who knew? Nell shrugged. "I'm just a fighter, trying to make the world a better place." Before he could reply, she knocked him hard under the chin.

Three grown men were splayed unconscious on the dusty ground. This battle was over, but she had one left to go: She had to get the hatchling out of here.

The noises behind the mother dragon grew louder, and spears poked through the tiny spaces between the curve of her body and the doorway. The mother dragon shifted and growled but stayed put. Shane could arrive at any moment, though, and make the beast move. He could probably make her freeze Nell to death while he was at it.

The mother extended her wings and looked toward the sky. She looked at Nell and looked again to the sky, bugling once. Nell realized it was a message. The hatchling was born ready to fly and was big enough to carry her, if she could persuade it to let her on. The mother stared at Nell as if imploring for help. *Save my baby*, Nell could almost hear.

Somewhere under Shane's evil compulsion to serve, the wild dragon was drowning in fear and pain. Nell felt it inside, pulsing like a heartbeat. She gritted her teeth and touched the hatchling along the neck. "Hey there, little one, let me ride you, okay?"

The baby whipped its head around and bit her on the forearm with tiny needle-teeth.

"Ow!' Nell shouted as blood welled up under her sleeve.

The mother dragon screeched in fury. The hatchling screamed and roiled, tossing its head back and forth. Nell's heart pounded so hard it might burst through her chest. The baby's scales faded from red to blue, to red again. Blue inched along its wings. What was going on? Red mist shimmered around Nell and the hatchling, faint but unmistakable. Something rushed up her arm: fire, power… magic.

Nell stared at her arm in horror. Her blood. Her blood was contaminated by Shane's poison. Whatever was controlling the beasts must be in her blood, and now she'd infected the little one. His magic was drawing forth the newborn dragon's power, seeking the match to the blood that had touched it. The baby's scales bloomed with deep blue, replacing the fiery red in splotches across half its body.

"No!" she cried. She tried to refuse the magic, pushing back against the influx with the deep part of her that had awoken at the fairies' stings.

The bleeding of power slowed but still seeped sluggishly from the creature. She had to get the hatchling out of here before the transformation completed. Maybe Micah could help it fight the magic's compulsion.

At least one good thing came from this huge mistake: Nell sensed she could give the baby a command and it would follow. It wouldn't have a choice, not under the influence of Shane's icy magic. She didn't like forcing the creature, but it was necessary. "You will fly me out of here. I'll help heal you, but we've got to leave now."

More shouts came from behind the mother dragon, and she leaned harder against the door.

Nell took a deep breath, running her hands along the hatchling's shoulder. Alternating waves of heat and ice flowed along its slick scales. The ridges along its neck ended at the back of its shoulders, and it was there Nell aimed to sit.

The dragon was small enough for Nell to jump and sling one leg over, as if she were riding a big horse. She gripped the spiny dorsal ridges, ignoring the pain in her left hand.

"Let's go!" Nell said, trying to imagine lifting up into the sky. The beast wasn't intelligent like a fairy queen and was certainly no mermaid, but maybe it would understand the pressure of her legs.

The mother dragon roared at her baby, as if in demand. The baby shook out its wings.

They spanned longer than two grown men lying head to head. The wings flapped, up and down. A cyclone of air spun up from its motions. Nell's hair flew back, but instead of being terrified, she suddenly laughed. She, Nell Brennan, was about to fly on a dragon. She'd experienced a lot of amazing things in her life, but this one took top prize.

The little dragon jumped into the air, and Nell's stomach lurched, but everything steadied as the wings beat an even rhythm that lifted them higher and higher into the air. Down below, Shane's men had finally pried the big dragon away from the door with their spears and spilled into the arena. But it was too late for them and the archers that followed; she and the hatchling were already beyond their reach. She laughed and pressed her legs tightly to its sides.

The power of the dragon, even as a newborn, was a heady sensation. Heat from its belly kept her legs warm even in the freezing sky. She was thankful to feel the warmth, as it meant the fire of the little one still burned inside and she had a little time to find her friends, assuming she could. Hopefully she'd be able to spy them before she got too cold, though she bet she could fly to the highest mountain on the little dragon and stay warm.

At the thought, Nell gasped. A flying creature with strong wings and the ability to face any extreme of cold.

This dragon could fly her to the highest mountain peak. To the sword and the Tree. How had she not thought of this right away? She knew why, though: the hatchling's suffering and mother's fear had blotted out any long-term strategy.

But now safe in the air, she turned the idea over again, hands flexing against the tough dorsal ridge of the hatchling. She could go right away, be healed of the poison once and for all, grab the sword, and defeat her enemy.

Victory would be at hand, all because she'd contaminated this one little dragon and could force it to obey. She frowned. The poor thing would've been a servant to Shane anyway. And Nell would reward it greatly afterward, of course. Treat it right. Not like Shane, enslaving them like they were worthless. The pain in her palm stung, and she clenched her hand, hiding the fresh cut from sight.

She imagined the rush of flying dragonback whenever she chose. She could touch the sky. It felt like she belonged here. Excitement warmed her cheeks despite the cold wind.

On impulse, she leaned forward as far as she could and laid her hands gently along the beast as it flew higher. She touched a cold patch of deep-blue scales along its neck that had chased away the red.

Scales poisoned by her.

Nell pressed her lips tightly. She sat up straight, drawing back her hands.

Using this dragon to meet her own need was something Shane would do. Even if she got to the sword, she'd still lose if she became like him.

The blue coloring amid the red of the hatchling's scales hadn't gone away after they'd escaped. It had actually spread. The furnace inside the dragon would be snuffed out, along with its natural magic. There was no time for a trip to the mountain if the baby was to be saved. She couldn't—*wouldn't*—sacrifice the life of an innocent for her quest.

"Hang in there," she murmured. The air's coldness stung her eyes and her lungs, but it felt cleansing, as if she could breathe for the first time in ages. The wild scent of dragon musk, bitter and sweet, filled her nostrils. She begged Queenie and Grace to sense her, to find her. If there was any magic in her, surely they could seek her out.

A glitter of lights soon answered her hopes. Whether or not they felt her or the magic of the hatchling, tiny sparkles from the fairy queens and their entourage swept up and around her in a dancing cloud of lights and gold. Her eyes stung. The cold wind in her eyes, she told herself, and then followed the fairies down to camp with relief.

The tent was barely visible from above, blending in with the white terrain. She wouldn't have found it without the fairies, but that meant all the less likely that other beasts of Shane's would.

She leaned against the dorsal ridge and said, "Down!" and tried to send an image to the baby dragon of them landing. The magic in the hatchling tightened along its muscles until it responded. Forcing this magnificent beast to obey sickened her. She had to free it somehow.

They landed in a flurry of snow. Corbin stumbled out of the tent holding his boline knife, followed by Micah and Tristan. Sierra and Phoebe ran, too, Sierra armed with a bow, Phoebe with the little knife Sierra had given her.

"Nell!" Corbin ran out and stopped, dropping his knife in shock. "You're on a *dragon*?" His eyes lit up, with relief and curiosity. His scholarly mind never stopped.

She dismounted. "I'll explain later, but this hatchling might yet toast or freeze us all. It's been tainted by dark magic, and we've got to save it!"

Micah rushed over, examining the blue and red colors interwoven across the dragon's scales. He laid his hand on the baby and closed his eyes. When he opened them, tears shimmered. "This young one is indeed fighting for its soul. A dark power is trying to strip out its natural magic, leaving it twisted and enslaved. The poor creature has lost much already."

"It bit me, and I think the poison inside me began drawing out its magic," Nell explained urgently. "I felt it enter me, but I don't know how to give it back!"

"Lay your hands on the hatchling," he commanded, expression hardening. "Everyone."

They gathered around the baby dragon, whose head hung low as it shivered in pain. Phoebe cried silently, touching the dragon with shaking hands.

Nell wanted to cry, too. Shane would pay for this. The magic inside roiled, trying to reach the hatchling, but it couldn't pass through her fury. The creature's magic remained trapped inside.

Then Micah lifted his voice in song, the same song

he once used to calm a different young dragon four years ago. This dragon also relaxed, and Micah ran his hands along it. Sierra did too, closing her eyes. Nell could see the golden threads of their magic floating into the beast. Phoebe lifted her clear, sweet voice in song as well. Though she no longer had magic, her voice was soothing all on its own. Tristan reached up and sent blue tendrils spiraling around everyone, tying them into a unified group.

Nell's heart softened; her anger slipped away. As it did, the power of the hatchling rose back up, spinning out of her, red mist seeking its true home. She let it go with gratitude, feeling it pour back into the dragon to which it belonged.

The blue coloration along the scales receded, erased by vibrant red until not a single drop remained. The baby let out a deep sigh and stopped its piteous moans. It rubbed its head along Micah's hands as if giving thanks. Smoke puffed out of its nostrils.

"This little one was terribly unbalanced, but I believe she will be fine now." Micah patted the beast.

"She, huh? Of course she'll be fine." Nell ran her hands along the scales of the baby dragon. Smooth and stiff, but pliable, they now shone bright red in the dying light, as they should.

Sierra eyed the little trickles of fire now steaming from the dragon's nose. "Wait, Nell—you could ride her to the mountain peak, fast! It could be the answer we've been looking for!"

If only she could. Nell leaned her face against the warm neck of the creature, her unwounded hand resting where fire rumbled in the beast's belly. A similar fire burned in hers. She understood the beast's desire for freedom. For adventure. For flight.

Her palm throbbed, and she lifted her head. "Honestly, I thought about it, but dragons aren't for us to use. I felt its essence, and this is a creature that should never be tamed. We'll find another way."

Though she would miss the wild glory of flight.

"Be free," Nell told the hatchling, pointing to the sky. The beast arched its wings, looking skyward and back at her. It seemed uncertain of its ability to fly without her directing it, but Nell had no such doubts. Flying was what dragons were made to do.

Corbin looked at Nell with pride, his dark brown eyes glistening. He nodded at her.

"Go!" she shouted, slapping the hatchling's flank.

The little dragon reared and took off, red wings swooshing gusts of musky wind on them as it rose. It roared, high-pitched compared to an adult but enough to raise goose bumps on Nell's skin.

The healed hatchling flew off without looking back.

Corbin wiped tears from his cheeks. "But aren't you the one always talking about having to be practical?"

She flushed. "Yes, but not like this. I'm the one who tainted the poor thing. My blood is toxic now."

"You didn't do this. The Dragon's to blame," Corbin said.

"And I found out who he is." Her words sounded brittle to her own ears.

Everyone exclaimed, but Corbin cut them off. "First, we need to get away from here. Back toward to the highest mountain, to the sword. We'll set up camp and talk. The news can wait."

She replied, "Agreed. But you should know—there was a moment in there when he was making sense to me. His power pulled at me, made me want to give in."

She hung her head in shame.

Corbin ran his hand down her braid. "You're stronger than a dragon; you've kept him from breaking you all this time. Now that you know what his power feels like, you'll be able to resist it. No one can hold the line like you can. Now let's go."

She didn't know what to say. She stole a glance at her palm; a deep red spread from the skin like decay. The voice inside her was doing the real guarding, and she feared they were both losing this battle.

Nell didn't want to steal Corbin's hope, though, so she kept the words to herself and closed her hand into a fist. If they knew he'd cut her again, Micah and Tristan would no doubt offer a healing, but they'd already given all they could spare to the hatchling.

Queenie, Grace, and a flurry of their agitated wee fairies surrounded Nell just then, squealing and dancing as they had in the sky. A sensation of deep love covered her, and she leaned into the hope that came with it. Shane's magic might have left a stain, but she'd been marked by another magic long before his.

ell's burst of positive emotions faded as they hurried along. She kept shuffling through her memories of Shane, searching for an explanation of why he'd turn evil. How could this madman be the same person who had taught her so well those years ago? Her very soul ached, draining her already worn-out body.

They finished setting up their new camp, as far from the lair as they could travel until the darkness was too thick to see through. The fairies helped light the camp enough for them to tie down the tent and unroll the sleeping bags. Nell missed their second tent, just to have some room to think alone, but she had a report to make.

They huddled inside. Corbin leaned forward. "First of all, I'm so glad you are okay. We all are. We never doubted you for a moment, but let's just say, please don't do that to us again, okay?" He squeezed her hand.

"Trust me—being snatched is definitely not on my list of things to do. And I was just as worried about all of you."

"Okay. Now. How did you know him? Who is the Dragon?"

"He showed me his face. The Dragon is the sword master who taught me in Port Iona when I was fourteen. Shane McConnell."

Sierra and Corbin gasped. "I thought he was dead," Sierra said.

"Who is this Shane?" Micah asked.

Tristan and Phoebe also looked blank.

Sierra bit her lip, glancing at Nell before continuing. "Shane was with Bentwood's crew, but trained Jack's advanced crew members in weaponry."

"Like Nell?" Phoebe asked.

Nell answered, "He worked with me when I was fourteen, yes. For a few months."

"So it's personal," Micah said.

"You could say that. I saw him as a role model." Nell mashed her lips into a line. For a lone female in a rough all-male crew, the chance to work with someone so talented who treated her as a true peer had been empowering. *That's my girl,* he'd said when they'd last fought at Port Iona. The comment made a lot more sense now.

Sierra explained further, "He was smarter than Jack, stronger than Bentwood, and they all knew it. They bragged they'd gotten rid of the upstart before he could cause any problems, but I guess they lied to keep people from getting any ideas about escaping."

Shivering, Nell said, "Shane's smart, all right. A genius, and he's got a dozen dragon eggs ready to hatch."

She ignored the oaths and gasps. "Not only that, he's turning poor little snow sprites into monsters, robbing them of their magic in the most perverse form of dark alchemy. That's what sent the storm to us, those were the faces I saw in the storm and that Micah and Tristan sensed. As air elementals, they can spy for Shane anywhere, slipping past doors and through windows like thieves. He's got other creatures in there, too, firebirds and a griffin he's drained and changed."

"So this Dragon is a stronger foe than we feared," Tristan noted.

The memory of the promising young man made her heart hurt, not with smoldering anger, but with a pulling loss. Such a waste. "Don't call him the Dragon. The name's part of his delusion. Shane's just a man, though a really powerful one."

"You're lucky to have escaped," Micah said.

She nodded. The thin slice along her palm was already scabbing over, but the deep redness spreading from the cut was darker and wider. His contamination was moving faster.

"I know it's a long shot, but is there any chance you could still convince him to stop?" Phoebe paused. "You said you had a good relationship once, yes?"

"He's nothing like the man he was. I don't even understand how he changed so much."

The words weren't quite true. In the cold place inside her, she was beginning to understand how such a change could happen. After all, she'd been caught up in the rush of riding the dragon, too. She'd been tempted to use the hatchling for her own purposes, if only for a brief moment. She'd even relished the thought of Shane's defeat and imagined a host of ways to kill him. The similarities scared her more than anything yet.

"People change for lots of reasons, some they don't understand for themselves," Corbin said.

She couldn't share her deepest fears, but anger, a long habit, easily leapt off her tongue. "It's not like he's just changed cloaks. He's taken over the home of the guardians. His stronghold used to be another temple like the one in Port Iona. That's why it's on their map. He's twisted their knowledge and power into a perversion. As sad as I used to be when I thought he had died, I wish he had. Now, I have to kill him."

"Nell, you don't have to kill anyone," Corbin said, gently.

"You didn't see what he's doing. I have to try."

Sierra shook her head. "You said when we left Port

Iona you couldn't defeat him without the sword. Has anything changed since then?"

Nell cursed. Nothing had changed, and everyone knew it. She gritted her teeth and rubbed her hand along her ribcage, hunching as another pang raced from her heart to her fingertips.

"More to the point," Corbin said, eyebrows lowering, "why are you in pain? And don't lie—I can see it written all over your face. Is it the poison from Shane? Has it grown worse?"

"I don't know," Nell replied. It was most certainly his toxic touch spreading through her, but they'd either get to the Tree and sword in time, or they wouldn't.

"It looks like he cut you again today," Tristan said, jerking his chin toward her wounded left hand. The mottled skin around the cut looked like a shadow in the light of the fairies.

She clenched her hand tighter. She should have put her gloves back on. This news would only distract them.

"He cut you again?" Corbin's voice spiraled up.

"Just a little," Nell muttered.

Everyone stared, but she didn't open her hand.

Corbin asked, "What if his sword was contaminated not with just poison, but a different kind of magic? You said he had all kinds of vials in there."

"Even if it is," Phoebe said in a soothing tone, "if the sword can free those poor snow sprites, the dragons, and all the others, it'll heal you, too, Nell. That's what the voice said, right?"

Nell nodded. "But in the meantime, those creatures are having their life energy stolen from them."

"We do not have the right kind of magic to counter Shane's. We cannot even heal Nell fully and only could heal the hatchling because it had not been poisoned by him directly. In a fight for the creatures' souls, we will lose every time," Micah said.

Nell wished she could pace. "Before it disappeared, the voice told me his magic was the same as mine, but his was twisted, dark. The red and silver light that came out of the sprite—Shane absorbed it, almost like drinking it in. And the magic of the little dragon sought me out the same way, even without me doing anything on purpose. Isn't that too much of a coincidence?"

"Let me see the book," Corbin said urgently. He dug through Sierra's bag until he found the ancient codex he'd been reading and rereading. He flipped to the back page with the map and stared hard at the hand-scribbled message. Grace flitted to his shoulder and landed.

"Corbin?" Sierra asked.

"I'm thinking. We know there's magic of the earth and sea. Maybe Shane isn't corrupting either of those into something unrecognizable, but he's twisting a new and different magic altogether. One of the air and sky? That would explain Shane's obsession with flying creatures. I'm so close to figuring out the code to translate these words, they've got to hold the key..." His voice drifted to a mutter as he ran his fingers along the page, eyes trained only on the words.

Sierra said to Nell, "That makes sense. And maybe holding the voice inside you allows you to control this other magic, too."

Micah added, "Or maybe they shared their magic with you, like wet ink pressing from one page into another. A permanent change."

Nell shuddered. She'd hoped for freedom from this life of magic when things settled down, away from the eyes of the public. If she couldn't be a warrior, she'd at least have a quiet, honest life that helped others. A life with the boy she loved.

Corbin.

He stared at her, shocked. "Do you think that's true?"

"I don't know. The voice had said Shane was trying to take *my* magic. Mine, not theirs. But I don't feel like I have magic of my own," she replied, confused.

Micah said, "We must consider that the fairies could have begun a change in you as the voice's vessel that's only reaching completion now, like wind wearing away a stone until the gem inside is revealed."

She couldn't tell if Corbin was thrilled or jealous.

"Maybe," she said, though discomfort curled in her belly like a snake. "I don't know."

"That's okay. The answer can wait," Phoebe broke in,

dissipating the rising stress. "The sword will hopefully explain everything."

"And we know the sword is up there." Micah pointed in the direction of the mountains marked on the map.

Nell said, "Then we'd better move fast. We leave at first light."

The next morning, they marched through snowfall. Faint sunlight streamed through the clouds now and then, but the thin beams didn't offer any warmth.

They'd passed through the lower mountains, and the stretch of blue-white rising into the foothills of the taller mountains went on forever. The highest peak was somewhere among the tallest range but was hidden by clouds and seemed to be running away from them out of spite.

The spot under Nell's heart throbbed, a steady discordant note now.

I don't know what to do! Help us! She felt no hesitancy about begging the guardians anymore. Searching out a disembodied voice inside herself was the least of her worries. Her palm burned far worse than it did when she was first cut. The red stain was marbled with indigo, like a bone-deep bruise.

Nell grumbled and gritted her teeth so hard they should have exploded into dust, but she could only trust and follow the last directions she'd been given. Use the map. Go to the summit. Seek the sword and the Tree.

She pushed them hard, making fast progress, but by sunset, they were still too far from the mountains, much less the peak. They all knew it, but no one wanted to say it. Furthermore, the mountain was so sheer and high that getting to the top looked impossible anyway. Shane would beat them to it, easily, him with his flying beasts. And his icy wasteland would spread to all of Aluvia, sucking it dry of all its hard-won magic.

Nell's moment of conscience may well have cost the world its freedom when she set the baby dragon free.

"Let's get some sleep," Nell grunted. She didn't want to talk. She didn't want to hear the light banter between Tristan and Phoebe, or see the loving glances between Sierra and Micah. She purposefully ignored the miserable expression on Corbin's face as he stared at the ancient book, trying to puzzle out the scrawled message.

An hour later, Nell remained awake in her bedroll. She missed home. Would she ever see it again? Her little sisters? Her mother? Tears pricked her eyes. For her family, for her friends, she'd do anything. Give up every chance at being normal. Serve this strange magic for the rest of her life, in some forsaken land like this. *Just save them,* she begged. She received no response.

She stepped outside to the smoldering remains of the fire, hoping the icy coldness might help her breathe easier.

A figure sat by the fire. Corbin.

"I thought I was the only one who couldn't sleep around here." She sat beside him.

He gazed at the swirling red and silver lights in the sky, glancing at her once before returning his attention to their mysterious dance. "I was thinking about yesterday."

"A lot to think about."

"Yes. And while I'm so proud of you for escaping and saving that dragon... when you drew your weapon against the griffin like that, you took too big a gamble with yourself, the one and only prophetess Aluvia has." His voice steadily rose from calm to sharp.

She pulled back. "What, you wanted me to let the griffin kill someone else? You do realize that I was right, don't you? It was under Shane's influence." And not only had she been right, but listening to his fears had compromised her fighting. Fury bubbled up at the thought.

He lightly touched her hand. "Nell, answer me this: When you first drew on the griffin, did you know it was under Shane's control?"

Nell was silent. She wrapped her arms around her waist and tucked her chin down. If he hadn't gotten in her way, she could have shot the griffin, she knew it. It would be unfortunate, as it was a slave as much as the blue dragons, but she wouldn't have been taken. She wouldn't have had to feel this part of her that found Shane's words… enticing, not even for a moment.

"Forget the griffin. It's not about just that, or the wolf, or your insistence on keeping up with your swordwork." Corbin's voice cut through her racing thoughts. "You're a wonderful, beautiful person, Nell. I think that when he cut you, he did more than silence the voice inside you. I think he's influencing you. Making you more like him, faster to anger, quicker to reach for your sword. And let's face it, it's not like you had a tight rein on your temper before."

She sucked in her breath. "So, you think I'm bad now? Evil?"

Corbin's jaw dropped. "No! How could you think—No." He blew out a hard breath. "What I mean is that you're amazingly strong. You can take care of yourself, and no one doubts it. But by the stars, Nell, you stood in front of a griffin out to get your blood—did you ever think how that makes me feel? To watch you risk your life like that in front of my eyes?"

"It's not like that. Besides, you risked yourself, too." But she was a fighter—he wasn't.

"I know," he said, voice calm as ever. "And I don't want to argue. I just want you to be safe."

She suddenly felt a great wave of tiredness. "I understand. It was scary, does that make you happy to know? I was terrified. I don't want to die, and I didn't want to lose you, either. But I escaped, didn't I? Took three men down on my way, too."

"What?" His voice went deeper with shock.

"Don't worry. I only knocked them out." She'd skipped over the skirmish in her retelling, knowing it would bother him and it hadn't mattered anyway. But it did matter. It mattered that he was so upset.

"That's my point," Corbin said. "The sword can be necessary—and is sometimes, don't misunderstand me—but it doesn't need to be your first choice. In fact, I'd say drawing your weapon should never be a first choice, *especially* for a warrior."

Her chest squeezed tight. Her throat ached, making her angrier. She wouldn't cry because her beloved thought she was a monster. "Maybe what you're really saying is fighters are just less than you? Barbarians. I thought you understood me better than that, but maybe you're just jealous because I have more magic and don't need you to save me."

He looked like she'd just slapped him, eyes wide, jaw loose. Even under his dark skin, he grew waxy with shock.

She'd gone too far. Nell wanted to apologize but couldn't squeeze the words past her own hurt. So she sat there, stubborn, awkwardly angry and confused. Part of her knew she was being irrational and unfair, but she just kept picturing Corbin's disappointed face. Would he ever understand what drove her?

In the silence, she longed for the guardians to give her insight into his heart again. But even if the voice had been able to speak, Nell doubted it would have. Love seemed to be beyond its expertise. It was obviously beyond hers.

Maybe the voice was already gone forever, destroyed by the second slice of Shane's poison. She hadn't heard a thing from it since then. Without the voice, she'd be truly alone if Corbin left.

Or if he died.

Finally, though, he spoke.

"I'd marry you."

Nell gaped at him. "Excuse me?"

"You think I don't love you. You think I look down on you because I disagree with your methods sometimes. I don't know how to make you hear me on this—I believe in you. I'm worried for you, because you're not acting like yourself lately, at least in some ways. But I'd still marry you tomorrow if you'd let me, because I love you and always will."

She wanted to shout it to the heavens: *I love you, too!* Because she did love him, and had for years. But the words felt trapped, stuck behind the pain in her chest, the hurt that still thrummed sharply at his hard words.

When she said nothing, he sighed and said, "It's too late, and we're both upset. Let's talk tomorrow."

She nodded, and they headed in. She stepped carefully, as if she were made of glass. And when she lay down in the tiny tent, she listened to his steady breathing. He fell asleep quickly—that was Corbin for you. Nothing could put him off food or sleep.

Nell, on the other hand, relived every word of their conversation. Her hope clashed with her fears, fighting a war in her mind that kept her awake far, far into the night.

CHAPTER TWENTY

ind screamed against the tent, sounding like the shrill cries of the sprites from the storm. Nell sat up with a gasp. She'd fallen asleep at some point, but it was still dark out.

Snow hissed against the slick fabric of the tent; the scent of it was thick in the air. Sweat dripped from her brow though the temperature was dropping fast. If this tent was destroyed, they'd all be dead within hours, and even if the tent survived, a bad storm could keep them trapped here for a week.

The fabric beat back and forth against the willow poles. Beside her, Phoebe thrashed. It was too dark to see much, but the younger girl let out a low moan of pain that had Nell shooting out of her bedroll. Phoebe's hand was cold and unresponsive.

"Sierra! Something's wrong with Phoebe! Tristan!"

Tristan was at her side in an instant. Queenie and her fairies spun up like a small tornado around the tent, and Nell squinted against the golden light of their magic. Phoebe's shadow writhed against the tent wall.

Then came another cry from within the tent. Corbin. Red light bloomed, radiating from Grace in a rage. The fairy and her wee ones darted around, screeching. Micah, sitting in his bedroll, restrained Corbin as he screamed. Leaving Phoebe in Sierra's capable hands, Nell scrambled to Corbin's side.

A ghostly form roiled around him. She stared hard and made out the faint features of a snow sprite, one of Shane's with shriveled skin.

Her heart stuttered in her chest. Unlike the last storm, she was sure the wraithlike creature wasn't her imagination. She really wished it was. Another sprite flowed around Phoebe.

"Snow sprites, changed ones! Do you see them this time? Shane sent them after us!"

Phoebe moaned, and Sierra screamed, "I'll kill him!"

"There's two of them. I see them now. They're more powerful than before." Tristan reached for Phoebe with arms that glowed with magic, casting its blue light into the red and gold of the fairies.

Corbin cried out again, sweat slicking his skin. Nell reached toward him, uncaring if the sprite hurt her, but her hands touched nothing, moving right through the transparent air elemental. Corbin kept thrashing, eyes squeezed closed.

"What's it doing to him?" Nell yelled. She squinted and caught a clearer glimpse of the white-eyed ghoulish sprite. It seemed to be feeding on something, eyes narrowed, jaw working. When the sprite grew clearer, she shouted, "It's biting him!"

The creature's long teeth were buried deeply in Corbin's shoulder, and its empty eyes met hers with a snarl. She snarled back at it. "Stop it!"

"The sprites' magic is hungry, warped by the Dragon to bring death to any he chooses," Micah said, eyes closed, hand outstretched toward the sprites.

Sierra shouted, "Get off her!"

She sounded furious, which meant she was terrified. Queenie and her fairies had turned a blazing red as well.

Corbin's fairy queen's cries of distress were high enough to break glass. Every time she tried to land on Corbin, the snow sprite swiped a hideous claw at her. The fairy danced back and hissed, but her stinger could find no purchase in a creature made of air. She couldn't save Corbin.

Nell glanced over to see Tristan and Sierra holding Phoebe. The red lights of the fairies were like a kaleidoscope inside the tent, spinning in their agitation.

"You will not take her." Tristan thundered at the sprite and placed his hands on Phoebe's shoulders. He whispered in his ancient language, and blue light flared bright. The light seeped from his hands into her, settling into her body as the magic recognized her. Her tattoos glowed blue, and the snow sprite flung itself from her and flew away, straight through the tent's walls.

Her tattoos slowly faded back to black, and Phoebe drew in a deep, quivering breath. A hint of color returned to her cheeks, and she fell into a heavy sleep.

"You saved her!" Sierra hugged Tristan hard.

"We've shared magic so closely as to be almost one. The sea knows her as one of us, and its magic will always protect her even if it cannot reside in her as it once did."

Looking hopeful, Micah tried to send his magic to defend Corbin, but the faun's golden power was simply blown back by the air elemental. Tristan's magic was blocked as well. "Corbin isn't tied closely enough to either one of us," Micah said. "Perhaps if his fairy stung him—"

"No!" Nell interrupted. "He could die. You know he could."

"He will most certainly die if we don't stop this madness," Micah said.

Corbin cried out again. Hopelessness boiled up in Nell like a toxic elixir.

"Why them? Why not attack me?" She ran her hands along Corbin's clammy arms, her stomach in knots.

Micah said. "They have the fewest defenses of all of

us, and the Dragon knew well whose pain would hurt you the most."

"What can I do?" she begged. "Tell me and I'll do it. Anything but having Grace sting him."

Tristan said, "I fear a third type of magic is at work, as Corbin thought. Magic of the air, maybe, given the sprite belongs to the sky. If that's the case, Nell, you are the only one who can defeat it, if you do indeed have magic like Shane's. It is the only possibility."

She couldn't think clearly. Fancy talk about magic meant nothing to her. How could she have believed all those horrible things about him last night? How could she have said those hateful things? He said he'd marry her—and she'd sat there, silent.

He was *Corbin*; he loved her. Tears were ready to fall, but she refused to let them spill. Not now. They served no purpose, and she had to stop this attack.

"Can I make it let go?" She thought of the way she'd made the hatchling obey. But she had no more idea of how to save Corbin from the sprite than she did of how to defeat Shane.

She placed her hands on Corbin too. She tried to imagine her power radiating into him, as Tristan's had into Phoebe. *Come on, come on!*

But her hands remained powerless. Human. And if she couldn't give Corbin magic, she couldn't save him.

Ignoring the white misty shape wrapping around

him, Nell leaned down close and whispered in his ear, "Corbin, hang on! We're going to figure this out! Don't die! I'll kill you if you die on me!"

A rough chuckle mixed with a moan of pain. "Nell." Corbin opened his eyes.

"I'm here!" She gripped his hands.

"Nell!" His voice grew urgent. "I figured out the translation from the book!" He coughed, and blood welled on his lips.

"Not now, Corbin! Save your strength!"

"But it's the way to reach the sword! To heal us all! You've got to fly… up… and claim the sword. Use the windsteeds! You saw one; you can find one!"

Another corrupted snow sprite blew through the tent walls. It latched onto Corbin, next to the other, its transparent body merging with his in places. The creatures' coldness seemed to sink right into Corbin's body, turning his face paler, shading his lips blue. He screamed.

Nell couldn't even think about Corbin's gasped message—only his suffering.

"Go! Go to the sword!" Corbin yelled again, eyes opened wide but unseeing. "Only you can do this! It's for you to finish!"

"If you know where to go, do it!" Micah urged. "We will care for him." The other two young men wrapped Corbin in a thicker swath of blankets. They firmly ignored the snapping teeth of the snow sprites, which couldn't reach through the faun's and merman's own magic to wound them.

Corbin's eyes drifted closed, and his teeth clanked in the cold. The color of the fairies made him look coated in blood.

Shane had done this. Someone she'd once admired, even trusted. His disgusting magic sent this threat right into her camp, and sweet, peace-loving Corbin was the one to suffer. It should be her.

"Come get me, then," Nell yelled to the screaming sprites.

"No…" Corbin murmured.

"I've got a lot of magic for you, don't I? More than even a fairy keeper," she taunted. Those milky white dead eyes rolled back in their heads as they fed on Corbin's strength.

Corbin arched his back on a silent scream. Something stabbed her heart, and she winced. Shane's magic was burning deeper. Not now. She didn't have time to collapse.

Micah whispered, "We must stop his suffering soon. This coldness is directed at the heart and will rapidly steal his life. Does not the voice have any words for you? Perhaps the guardians can use your desperation to reach you?"

In her panic, she'd forgotten to even try. If she could just hear the voice, even faintly, she felt sure they could save Corbin from Shane's magic. Nell turned her attention inward, focused as hard as she ever had. *Please!* she pleaded. *Anything!*

Silence echoed.

"Here," Micah said. "You'll need the strength to reach them."

She nodded. He put his hands on her and sent a burst of magic into her, a flood of strength. The world was tinged with gold and silver.

The voice rose immediately, though faint and muffled as if it spoke through a thick wall.

Listen carefully, Nell…

Relief flooded through Nell, as well as a joy so powerful it almost hurt from hearing the long-silenced voice call her by name. She never knew how much it had become a part of her until she thought it might be gone forever.

We will try to help. But you must give us more yet. We have nearly lost our battle for your heart. If that happens, we will die along with you.

Nell said, *What more can I give? I've given you my life! I've given you my body!*

We need your soul.

Well. Of course they did.

How?

Find a space to sit in solitude. Still your mind. Then we will show you. Quickly!

Nell said to her friends, "I've got to go outside. The

voice can barely reach me. There's an answer, but I can't focus seeing him like *that*." She gestured with her hands. "Will you stay with him, Micah? Sierra and Tristan need to watch Phoebe and keep her safe."

"Yes, I'll watch him until you are able to return. The sprites cannot harm me and do not frighten me." He asked no further questions. His dark eyes seemed to see more than Nell could even imagine.

"Do what you have to do, Nell. We've got your back," Sierra declared, arms tight around her sleeping sister. Tristan nodded solemnly, reaching one hand to Corbin's shoulder.

Nell left the tent, wishing the morning sun was up already, but the night was still cold and dark. And she was so alone.

It had always come down to this. No normal, happy life for Nell. She'd lost so much already. *At least let all the sacrifice and hard work be worth something*, she thought to herself. *Let Corbin live.*

She walked until she came to a frozen lake over the rise. Two rocks sat along the edge. It wasn't snowing, at least. She settled carefully on one of the rocks, legs crossed, back straight.

Corbin's mother had taught Nell to meditate, or tried to. It was supposed to bring the magic to the surface, allow the voice to speak more clearly. Nell had never worked at it. Her mind was already full of too many voices, as far as she had been concerned. But now, she needed unobstructed communication, the clearest she'd ever had.

Nell let the darkness wrap around her like a cloak. She noted the solidness of the rocks below, the chill of the wind against her cheeks, the taste of winter in the air. The stinging of her heart interfered, but she ignored it. The pains of the body faded in time, she knew from experience. She pushed all sensations to a small corner of her mind.

Fears for Corbin brushed against her, but she trusted her friends to care for him. Her best gift to him was to do as the guardians had asked.

How to give her soul like a gift?

She closed her eyes. Taking a long breath, she focused on the frigid air flowing deep in her lungs. The cold filled her until the shivering stopped. Such chill could be a danger, she knew, but even as her fingers grew numb, she sat still. She tried to be calm and open her mind to any message from the magic within, but her thoughts still whirled like a cyclone.

What did Corbin mean, to use the windsteeds? Writhing in mortal pain, he'd still managed to throw a message of hope to her. He still believed in her despite all her hatefulness earlier.

Concern for Corbin led to thoughts of all her friends and family. Memories of each of them crowded her mind, so many people she loved, and yet, no one else could carry this frightening burden but her, this magic she'd never asked for. She was alone after all.

But you aren't truly alone… We will help you… the voice whispered, a mere hint of sound in her mind. But the message warmed her, enough to push aside her remaining fear. The ache of her heart receded further.

I'm not alone, she told herself, embracing the statement instead of fighting it.

Images flashed as she focused on the truth of it.

Corbin and Nell laughing by the fairy field.

Nell and Sierra talking by firelight as they journeyed to the ports.

Nell holding her sisters tightly before and after every trip.

Phoebe laughing and running to Nell.

The quiet knowing of Micah's and Tristan's expressions when the voice spoke from her.

They weren't like her—no one was—but they loved her.

Peace flowed through her. Time lost its meaning. There was no pain at all. It seemed clear to her that even those who'd left this life were somehow with her still. She drifted into a quiet place in her mind, a place where her friends and family were safe and happy.

If she were to offer her soul, surely this is where it would be—in her happiest memories.

Great swells of calm and tranquility rose inside, making her gasp though her eyes stayed closed. Something lifted within her, something that seemed to want to stretch to the sky.

She'd always avoided it, this power, this feeling. It made her separate, made her *other*, but if the guardians were correct, there was a reason she'd lived through what her father hadn't. It wasn't her fault. She'd been chosen.

The air was silky smooth across her skin. The sky itself felt fluffy and soft, as if a warm blanket were laid across her to keep her safe. A new-felt joy covered Shane's poison and held it steady. His toxin couldn't hurt her through this rippling wave of power.

Quietness followed the peace until she was overflowing with *yes*, content to hand over her deepest essence to the voice that had been dwelling within her. It seemed she could touch the stars and, for once, her ever-present anger and resentment were gone. She'd had a good life, after all. If she could keep Corbin and her family alive, she'd consider her life a worthy gift. But she still didn't know how to hand over the soul demanded as payment.

A whicker broke the silence of her mind, and Nell's eyes flashed open. Dawn had broken while she'd waited. Light streamed over the land. She staggered to her feet, facing yet another impossible moment.

She knew if she had a mirror, her eyes would be dark pools from the magic rising, but flames would be dancing in them, reflected from the creature before her. A creature of legend—a windsteed.

CHAPTER TWENTY-ONE

*N*ell had never seen anything so beautiful. The windsteed had the body of a pure white horse, down to its long flowing mane, but with eyes never seen on any horse, eyes the color of fire, orange encircled with deep burgundy. They actually flickered as if with flames, but Nell barely noticed. She was too busy staring at the huge wings curving up from the steed's body, covered in countless flames of orange, red, yellow, and silver. Once again, a beast of myth unseen for generations was staring her in the face. Literally.

Soft warm breath puffed across her as the mare—for it was a mare—whickered and leaned closely, touching her velvet nose to Nell's cheek.

A flurry of images raced across Nell's mind, and she

steadied herself without thinking by placing her hand on the beast. The images became even clearer.

She saw a throng of windsteeds, locked-away without enough magic of the sky to fully manifest themselves, unseen now but always there, trapped above the Tree of Life. This free-roaming magic had been long lost, with the small amounts remaining taken by the waking dragons and other creatures of the sky. Only the queen mare was strong enough to have escaped their prison, using all the magic of the combined herd in order to appear to Nell.

Corbin's agonized plea came to her mind: Fly to the sword. She thought he'd been out of his mind with pain, but maybe he meant exactly what he'd said. He'd told her windsteeds were formed of the wind itself and could travel anywhere in an instant. Was he right?

The steed gazed into her eyes and nodded once. Nell blinked. She patted the creature's neck instinctively, and again, images flowed between them, though not words. Images of Nell leaping on the mare's back, flying to the mountain summit, just the two of them. The bars along her heart opened wider.

I thought you wanted my soul? Nell asked the voice within. Being with the windsteed was like being given a new soul instead.

At the end of your life, a piece of your soul will remain in the fiery sword, with us, as guardians and mentors to the next leader of the guardians. That is only if you accept the role as the first guardian of a new generation. The windsteeds were sworn to serve us, to take us across the world in a heartbeat, as needed. Their magic, as with all air magic, is capricious but powerful. Even dragons obey the windsteeds. Do you dare lead them?

Nell licked her lips. The windsteed stood steady, her long legs stock still. She blew out a breath that pushed Nell's hair from her face and made her laugh.

"That's what you think, huh? That I'm some kind of coward?"

She wanted nothing more than to jump on this creature and fly away to the sword and finish this battle to save Corbin and their world. But if she went alone without an explanation, the others would worry. Or worse. Corbin's anger from their fight at the campfire haunted her.

The others long to serve with you, but in this, you are right: No one else can take on this mantle of responsibility. You are uniquely gifted for it. Will you do it, Nell? Will you serve Aluvia the rest of your life, leading others into service as guardians to restore Aluvia's magic to its proper balance, ensuring it is not lost again? Answer quickly, before the darkness inside locks us from you once more. It's spreading, Nell. You don't have much time.

Nell stared into the flaming eyes of the steed before her. In those eyes, she imagined herself in this new possible future. Flying through the skies, wearing the red cloak from her memories, leading others with assurance, not reluctance. Healing the world, one small part at a time, the bearer of a glorious sword fit for any warrior. Keeping magic safe for the creatures that needed it and guarding it from those who would abuse it.

She might not be left alone in a quiet cabin in the woods or fighting as a hired swordswinger for her coin, but she'd be protecting others, an honorable mission. She'd be healing Aluvia in a new way. It was a life she could be proud of.

"I will," she said, to the voice, the steed, and herself.

The windsteed gave a triumphant whinny and tossed her head, a clear invitation to climb on her back.

"But what is your name, beautiful one?" Nell asked, one hand pressed to the animal's neck.

Brigid, came the combined voice of the guardian leaders, spoken with long-held affection and love. And Nell knew—these women spent their lives with the windsteed queen in service to Aluvia's magic. They loved her still.

Which suggested this mare was very, very old. The mare whickered a sound suspiciously like a laugh. Nell eyed her, and then broke into a smile.

A warrior horse for a warrior. The whisper in her mind could have been her own, though it wasn't. For once, Nell was in full agreement with the guardians.

She leaped lightly onto the back of the animal despite

having never spent much time atop a horse. Brigid was reassuringly solid and warm, though her body seemed to contain the surging power of the wind itself. Now the memories of the many guardians before Nell guided her, making it easy for her to weave her hands into the silken mane. The windsteed's flames did not hurt as Nell brushed against the wings, though she had no doubt they could hurt others if the steed so chose.

"Let's go to my friends. I can't leave them without a word," Nell whispered.

The steed rose into the air, its wings sending huge gusts of fire on either side of her. Nell hadn't traveled far—Brigid only soared the length of a lark's tune before they landed at camp.

Sierra staggered out of the tent, and her jaw dropped. "What have you done this time?"

"I've found an answer, and you won't like it. Corbin was right about the windsteeds, but only one is strong enough to come to us. I have to go to the mountaintop with her. With Brigid. She knew the guardians and will know where to take me." Nell patted the beast's neck with a loving familiarity, as though she had done so a thousand times before. And in a way, she had. With the rush from the windsteed connecting them, she and the other guardians were woven too tightly right now to discern which memory was whose.

"You can't go alone! Are you crazy?"

"Maybe," Nell said. "Take care of Corbin. He'll be cured once I reach the Tree."

"There has to be another way! Can't the windsteed scare off the sprite?"

Nell laid her hand on the windsteed in question, but then shook her head.

"She barely has enough magic to get me where I need to go. I've got to get the sword to defeat Shane and his creatures. Sierra, the truth is, the poison he used on me is growing out of control. The voice says his magic has almost reached my heart. I couldn't tell you before. I didn't want Corbin to know I was being corrupted, but the guardians have warned me. If I fail, and if Shane turns me like the dragons and sprites, don't let me hurt anyone. Kill me if you have to, and tell Corbin I'm so sorry, but I had to go."

"You won't give in." Sierra jerked her chin as if daring Nell to say otherwise. "You're the most stubborn person I've ever met."

"I'll do my best, but I'll feel better if I know you'll be keeping an eye on me to make sure."

Sierra lowered her head in agreement. "I'll be on watch. But Corbin's going to kill me if anything happens to you."

"I can't promise anything, but you know I'll never go down without a fight."

"That's what I'm afraid of," Sierra muttered. But she

took two steps back and promised, "I'll explain where you are."

That was all the confirmation Nell needed. If she saw Corbin's pain-filled face again, she wouldn't have the courage to do what needed to be done. And she always did what was needed.

"To the summit!" she cried out before she could think too carefully about her choice. The answer she'd needed had arrived with wings of fire.

Together, Nell and Brigid rose straight into the air, the giant wings fanning gusts of hot wind, creating summertime in the middle of winter. The steed gave another triumphant whicker, and suddenly the sky and the icy world around them disappeared. The windsteed and Nell winked out of existence.

The whole world stood still. Nell was in utter blackness. Her breath was loud in her ears, and her pulse stormed through her veins. She had a second to wonder if they'd somehow gotten lost in nothingness before the world reappeared without a sound. For the span of a heartbeat, reality stretched languidly and then snapped back into focus.

She shook back her coat's hood to look around and lost her breath. Surely she was on the edge of the entire world. Dotted clouds clung to snowy mountain peaks behind them. Before her, the summit ended at the sharp edge of a cliff.

A salty tinge wove through the air courtesy of the sea beyond the cliff. A steady wind kept the cliff clear of clouds, leaving the ocean visible to the horizon, dotted with icebergs.

But another shock awaited her. Near the cliff soared a tree that had been cloaked from their view during their journey, hiding above the clouds. It had to be the Tree of Life. As thick around as Nell's healing cabin and taller than the tenements in Port Ostara, its knobby roots dipped up and out of the ground like burrowing snakes. The Tree—surely a better name existed for such a thing—reached needle-thin dark-brown branches into the blue sky, piercing the brightness with spiny fingers. Not a single leaf clung to the branches, and the limbs did not wave in the gusting wind. A large rock formation sat off to one side.

The windsteed landed softly, folding its wings along its flanks, but Nell remained astride. Something wasn't right with the picture before her. The wind blew hard again, here at the top of the world, but the Tree stood frozen in place.

Frozen. That was it. It was truly frozen. The branches didn't move because a layer of ice encrusted every part of the tree, down to the base. And then Nell's eyes widened. At the base, deep in thick ice and snow, a sword handle stuck out at an angle. The handle was gold, and the blade was half-hidden within the frozen snow mound.

The blade.

"That's the sword we've been searching for?" she asked the guardians, speaking aloud to help keep her mind separate from theirs. But silence had descended, the curtains closing between her and the voice.

The sword didn't look fiery. It looked drab, cold, hidden away. Perhaps its magic was extinguished.

But maybe she could change that, if she truly had magic inside her like the guardians seemed to believe.

She took a deep breath. With a world as vast as this, anything seemed possible. Then a nearby pile of snowy boulders shifted with a loud creak, and her muscles tensed without thought. A rockslide would crush them.

Without having to be asked, Brigid jumped into the air, leaving Nell's stomach momentarily behind. The rocks continued to expand, stretch, reach into the sky, until suddenly the strange shapes resolved themselves into their true form.

An ice giant.

Corbin had spoken of them, and she'd heard stories of them growing up, much like dragons. *Be good or the ice giants will come for you.* She'd always assumed people had been exaggerating the horrors of the creature, but for once, the stories had it right.

The ice giant looked like a moving, connected pile of rocks, with hunks of ice and hoar frost rimming its rough-hewn face. Mist from its gaping maw left a vapor trail around its head like smoke. Blue glacier eyes burned brighter than a smith's forge. Chest plates of ice armor covered a torso that looked to be made of steel-gray boulders. The giant's thick legs were like tree trunks, wrapped in animal skins.

It roared as loud as a dragon. The sharp teeth left no doubt this was a hunter. Right now, she was its intended prey.

"You have invaded my home." Its voice held the rumbling sounds of an approaching blizzard.

A cold wind gusted sharp against her face. The flames of her windsteed wavered but kept burning. Nell was glad. She had a feeling they would need them.

"Who are you?" Nell reached for her bow and arrows. Corbin said ice giants weren't supposed to be evil, but this one sure looked it.

"I am your death," the giant said with a snarl.

"I don't think so. I'm just here for the sword."

"The tree is mine, and the sword is my treasure. You cannot have it. I am a giant. You are but a tiny pebble on my mountain."

The creature didn't know how stubborn Nell could be. He was about to learn.

Nell scrutinized him as he swung a tree trunk like a quarterstaff. Her fingers slid along her bow, mentally picking her target. An eye, most likely. Its skin looked as thick as a manticore's.

She eased the bow into position. The giant didn't appear to be the smartest or fastest creature in the world. Her windsteed held steady, wings barely moving.

The ice giant growled. "There are so few creatures left here. I need more to sustain me. Your magic will feed me for months, young human. I will try to make your death fast, though."

"Nice of you." Nell smirked, nocking an arrow.

She took aim, hoping the wind wouldn't gust at the wrong moment. She got lucky, and the arrow sank deep into one of the giant's eyes. The creature bellowed in pain and stomped around the ground, turning the snow into churned mud.

Nell quickly sent two more arrows soaring. One missed entirely—she clenched her jaw in frustration—but the other stuck into its elbow. A snaking crack ran from the arrow down its forearm, and the giant screamed in rage. Hope rose in her. This thing wasn't invincible. Even icy stone could be destroyed.

She slid her bow onto her back and pulled her sword. Her mind blanked as it did during a fight, leaving only enough space for noticing the opponent's move and countering. He swung a club that would have taken off her head, but she and Brigid dropped fast to duck. Nell jabbed at him, but the sword bounced off his hard skin. He swung again, and she and Brigid flickered out of range before diving in again.

Her world narrowed to a quiet place, of counter and

attack. Though she battled, she was at peace. Unlike in times past, she had no need to use anger, fear, or revenge to keep her strong.

Appearing in the air right next to the giant, she swung her sword hard and was rewarded with a small slice along his neck on his blind side as the windsteed flew past him quickly and kept going. With the size of the giant, the only way to win was to move fast.

Dart in, attack, get out.

But the monster was stronger than she'd given it credit for, and it was wising up to their tactics. It waited for her and Brigid to appear, stabbing wildly at the first sign of them. Even their fastest dive couldn't keep it off-balance for long, and this sword just wasn't the right tool for the job here. She needed the fiery sword, but who knew how long it would take to hack it out of the ice? She had to get rid of the giant first.

Brigid responded to Nell's every thought, swerving, diving, and flickering away as Nell plotted out her attack. The warmth of the windsteed pressed into her legs but also into her heart, driving the icy darkness back further.

The steed was fast and strong, but Nell could tell she was tiring. Her magic was growing thin already, limited by the short supply of sky magic available. Nell sensed tremendous amounts of it looming close, though, like a swelling thunderstorm not yet spilling a single drop of rain on a parched, dry land. She squeezed her lips together. She needed a new plan, fast.

The giant sent a fist the size of a cauldron flying and managed to hit them. A tearing sound filled her ears. Her left sleeve and glove ripped away, leaving her skin exposed to the bitter cold air. Pain radiated through Nell's ribs, and her left arm felt like a hot poker was sticking her. It might be broken, from one hit of the giant's fist.

Nell blanched, and Brigid whinnied a challenge. Nell leaned over the steed's neck.

"We have to retreat!" Her arm throbbed. Winning felt impossible.

The horse-like creature made a sound Nell swore was scoffing. Brigid looked back over her broad shoulder at Nell, eyes like twin suns. Her wings swished heat across Nell's freezing skin and brought a surge of calmness. If ever an ice giant could be defeated, it could be done with a windsteed.

Nell tracked the lay of the land, the size of the creature's club. She didn't know yet how fast the windsteed could fly, but she had a feeling the answer was fast.

"Taunt him. Let's see how mad we can make him," she whispered to Brigid. "Anger makes people do stupid things. I bet giants aren't any different." Nell held her sword high with her good arm and yelled a taunting shout.

They dove like a griffin, sleek and fast and sharp. The monster needed to see her coming this time, to be infuriated by her broad grin and shining sword. She sliced his ear as they soared past, and Brigid's wings burst into brighter fire to singe him.

The giant howled in pain. The cut was deep enough that her sword came away heavy with blue blood. Ice giants bled blue. No nursery rhymes had ever mentioned that part.

They charged again. This time, though, the giant was ready and swung his club with surprising speed. The windsteed spun and dove between his legs. Nell clung like an oak spur to keep from falling off, knees aching with the pressure held against the steed's ribs.

As the two of them twisted back above the giant in a wrenchingly tight arc, Brigid's wings flared again. The ice giant bellowed with rage, and clumps of snow fell from his shoulders and legs.

Nell gave thanks she seemed to be immune to the fire. The steed shrieked in defiance.

"The cliff," Nell yelled, sending the windsteed a mental image of what she wanted and hoping the steed would see it.

Brigid responded immediately, the perfect mount, charging past the giant, tantalizingly close, drawing the lumbering giant to the edge of the cliff.

They circled around so fast Nell's braid streamed

straight back from her head, and as they darted toward the giant this time, she threw her sword straight at him.

The sword did little damage, merely sticking into his rocky thigh, but it made him stumble. The creature was huge, but thinking was not his strong suit, especially when half-blinded and wounded. He just wasn't fast enough and tripped over a root as thick as his leg. While his arms flailed, Nell and Brigid flew right at him. The windsteed curved her wings, twisted midair, and lashed out at his chest with a vicious kick of her back legs. Sparks flew.

The giant spun hard and slid over the edge of the cliff. He caught the ledge with one hand, but his weight worked against him. He let go with a yell that faded as he plummeted. The fall likely wouldn't kill a creature like him, but he wouldn't be back for a while.

They landed in front of the sword. Nell dismounted, gaze sharp, watching for another trap. This simple sword was supposed to hold a piece of each guardian's soul who had wielded it. When she took the sword, would it pull her soul out right away? Would it hurt? She swallowed hard. She had no idea what would happen, but it was time to trust the voice with all of her heart. And her soul.

CHAPTER TWENTY-TWO

he sword was such a small object to hold so many hopes. Brigid stood at Nell's back, nose barely touching her shoulder. The animal whuffled, and warmth slid across Nell's neck. Heat radiated from Brigid, as well as acceptance. This steed would ride with Nell always, she knew. She didn't need to fear losing anyone or anything.

A shrill cry from beyond the cliff yanked her attention from the sword. Nell's eyes widened. A horde of twisted snow sprites sped over the water. They were tiny specks now but were closing in fast. They'd taken on a more solid form in the wind as they flew, and she could see they were starving. Furious. They'd swarm her, take her magic.

She flashed back to the memory of Shane stealing

the essence of the snow sprite, shriveling it into a ghoulish creature. Compassion filled her, and strengthened her resolve.

The snow sprites weren't the ones at fault. Nor were the dragons. Shane was the threat, and he was the one who would pay. Not because she wanted to kill him or seek revenge, no, but because justice needed to be served and his wrongs set right. The world's magic needed protection from his greedy reach.

She gripped the sword's hilt with the hand of her unwounded arm. Before she could pull it from the ice, light burst from the blade. Nell's hand felt melded to the sword, as if it had always been hers. She struggled to keep her footing through the shock, while the hilt heated against her palm, blade still deep in the frozen earth at the base of the Tree.

The sword seemed to sing, a concert of harps filling her mind, a joy like the dawn after a long, hard night cascading through her. Flame burst out from it, evaporating the ice encasing it. The blaze flared all around the sword, flashing orange and yellow.

Inside her, a different heat kind of heat burned, mixing with the joy, the music, the light. It healed her arm and chased away the worst of the darkness that had taken up residence in her. The bruised-looking stain on her left palm disappeared, and the red cut tingled before fading to a thin silvery line. Her heart opened wide.

The voice broke free and spoke clearly into her mind. Instead of sounding like a single woman's rich voice, it sounded like many women speaking in complete harmony, unified. Amplified.

The guardians said, *The Tree of Life was frozen when we hid away the fiery sword. Thus, the first of our magic was lost through our fear and doubts, followed by the rest of our world's magic over time. Sierra brought the land's magic to the world again. Phoebe helped set free the magic of the sea. And you, Nell, you must free the magic of the sky so our world can be complete and balanced. The fairies gave you sufficient magic to allow us to speak through you, but your true gift is with the sky.*

"What do I do?" Nell's voice was hoarse. The sprites had almost reached her. It all came down to this.

When you claim the sword, you will become the first guardian of Aluvia in time beyond counting.

"Then what? Corbin needs healing! You said you'd help me beat back Shane's power!"

And so we will. Defending life is not the same as taking it, and the sword has power to heal, power only you can free as its wielder. You'll know what to do.

The power of the sword buffeted her. Could she actually control it? She tightened her grip and wrapped her left hand around the hilt as well.

She was a warrior, by all of Aluvia. A good one. She was born to hold this sword in her hand. More, she was destined to wield the magic of the sky, something she never believed was possible.

Until now.

Now she was a warrior with a purpose, one who would bring healing to their lands. She could live with that. She only hoped Corbin could.

"Then so be it!" she shouted. "This sword is *mine!*"

With one smooth, easy movement, Nell lifted the sword before her, hilt gripped tight with both hands, the flaming blade level with her eyes. New light burst from it, a nimbus of radiance, dazzling her. A fiery sting traced over her left hand and arm, leaving behind a silver marking that glittered in the light of the flames above her. She fixated on it: the shape of a tree tattooed on her arm, its branches along her fingers, the heart of it on the back of her hand, the trunk of it stretching along her arm toward her elbow.

The Tree of Life.

A ripping sensation staggered Nell as the guardians poured down her arm and hands, into the sword itself. An echoing silence filled her mind. The voice, as she'd known it for so long, had left her.

Unexpected grief stung, but there was no time to dwell on it. Flames of the sword grew until they surrounded her, running up along the frozen tree with a shower of sparks, flaming up the limbs and lighting up the sky. Ice shattered from the tree in an explosion of light and mist. Green leaves unfurled along the branches in a wild burst of life. Fire flashed across the blue bowl of the sky, a bright orange and red tinged with shining silver. Like lightning, the flames roared with speed, straight into the air. Out and up… and then down.

Fire fell from the sky like streaks of falling stars. The very air itself shimmered with the silver-edged red of magic—the magic of the sky. It drenched Nell, singing through her sword and into her soul. The flames didn't reach the ground but instead spread farther and wider. Some slowly disappeared into the air like rain water soaking into a desert. Others kept rushing outward.

The snow sprites that had nearly reached her shrieked as the fires flowed over them. They covered their faces against the brightness of the blaze, and when the fire moved beyond them, they were merely mischievous snow sprites once more, eyes black with their special magic of the snowy air. No longer hungry. No longer miserable. The ties binding them to Shane had burned away. The magic of the air still blew through the sky, a hurricane of power spiraling outward, and Nell was the eye of the storm.

Thank you! the snow sprites cried, then disappeared, leaving behind only a blue sky rich with magic of the air, available in a way it hadn't been in centuries.

Bracing her legs, Nell raised the sword high, opening herself to its calling as fully as she could. Its power thundered through her like a thousand windsteeds, carrying her into a place of perfect peace. The flames still surrounded her, now raging higher. The last lingering icy taint of Shane's magic evaporated. Her anger at Shane, Jasper, Jack's old crew... they were nothing. There was no room for hatred when the universe unfurled at your feet.

All that was left inside her was a purity of purpose. She would teach others about keeping the magic of Aluvia balanced—earth, sea, sky. She would guard the Tree of Life with her sword and lead others to do the same.

The magic wasn't done yet. As the glow of the fire faded from her and expanded farther out, silver-hued ribbons of red swirled among the flames. The colorful strips unfurled as they rolled across the sky and reformed into a herd of windsteeds with fiery wings, neighing their triumph, then racing across the deep blue above them. They disappeared, blinking out one by one.

Brigid pranced beside Nell while the herd thundered past in a wave of silver and red. Elation filled the mare, and Nell realized that the dancing lights in the night sky had been the windsteeds, trapped and waiting for freedom. The most powerful creatures of the sky were no longer penned by their missing magic. Like a joint snapping back into place, Nell could feel the stability now across the land, sea, and air.

Then a voice spoke to her, the voice she feared she had lost forever. Her heart leapt at the familiar whisper.

So the sword has opened the sky with fire as we foretold. You are our sword, Nell. Do you not see yet? You, yourself, not the steel in your hand. Now go and be our champion.

"I felt you leave me, but how is it you're talking to me now?"

We're connected through the weapon you now bear and its fiery magic, daughter. Each leader of the guardians has wisdom to preserve. After we shed our mortal bodies, the sword keeps a small piece of each of our souls, not our whole being. We are memories; we are hopes. Many pieces making a whole. You were our vessel for a time, and for your service, we thank you, but this is our rightful dwelling.

"But you'll stay with me? Guide me?"

"Yes, but rather than being our vessel, you will be our prophet, our champion, the sky's redeemer. You've lived with the land's magic within you; you've been touched and recognized by the sea's. Now you've been filled with the sky's magic, which few have the discipline to control. But you do. You are the world's protector. You will be Aluvia's guardian.

Her heart swelled with joy. The sword opened the sky with fire.

And she was the sword.

Fire still burned inside her, a flame she knew now would never die. When she passed on from this world, her flame would join the other guardians. Though the fire in the sky had faded from sight, she'd never feel its loss again.

You need not fear anymore. The voice was a caress, like a mother's comfort to her child after a long, hard day. *You will never be alone.*

She wouldn't either. Because unlike those women, she wouldn't retreat to a hidden place to tend and mend the world. They'd tried to protect Aluvia's magic by keeping knowledge of it secret and sacred, fearful of magic's power in irresponsible hands. But everyone needed to be a part in Aluvia's healing journey, not just a chosen few. And Nell would be the one to tell them.

Nell tipped back her head to the sky and let tears streak down her face. They were badges of victory, hard won. They were tears of joy as much as loss, and for once in her life, she didn't begrudge the sign of weakness. She wasn't weak. She'd been chosen for her strength.

The wind whipped against her, still freezing, but the land around the Tree of Life, she realized with awe, was now green and covered with tiny yellow blossoms, despite the ice and snow around them. The entire Tree, from its highest branches to the deepest roots, was revived and healed.

Like her. Healed and whole at last.

"The sword can't save you now, Nellwyn."

The voice had Nell spinning on her feet, dashing tears from her cheeks. Brigid stiffened beside her.

Shane appeared, not behind Nell on the mountain top, but in the air above the cliff edge on the back of his dragon with a sword in each hand. A dozen other men rode dragons behind him. His dragon snarled and puffed icy mist.

Shane said, "The fight ends here. I've given you enough chances to come to your senses. More than you deserved."

Behind him, the other dragons dipped and wove among each other like a dizzying nest of snakes. Arching blue necks, whipping tails, mantling wings. One after another flung back its head and gave a defiant shriek. The men tightened the reins, yelled at their mounts, and the dragons obediently soared as one to line up in a half-circle, all facing Nell. The heavy scent of jasmine and musk and winter storms surrounded her.

The dragons held their heads downward, docile, but radiating rage. Their white eyes and blue scales marked them still as servants of Shane. Why hadn't they been freed when the snow sprites were? Shane's magic must be extremely powerful. The dragons needed to be cleansed from his toxic touch just as she had been.

She laid a hand on her quivering mount. "The sword's chosen me. You're the one who's on his last chance."

The men hovered near the Tree, waiting on Shane's

command. She recognized Jasper and Carrick, the old alchemist. Jasper sneered at her, and Carrick looked away, pale and drawn. There was Donovan, too. The others were unfamiliar. Shane had been recruiting men from all over Aluvia.

He lifted his voice so it echoed across the mountain peak. "I control the magic of the air and need no sword to do so. Nothing rises higher than the sky. Not even the tallest tree."

Shane's dragon breathed a plume of ice at the Tree of Life, the cold flurry coiling through the air. But as the white mist touched the highest branches, a flare of fire rose up in a column from the Tree, flashing and hissing against the ice of the beast's breath, evaporating it. Steam and heat saturated the air. The dragons backed away from the unexpected flame, and the red glow diminished, withdrawing into the branches as if it had never been.

She couldn't see beyond Shane's mask, but his dropped jaw betrayed his shock. Nell smirked. Apparently the Tree of Life wasn't going down again without a fight.

Neither was she.

She leapt onto Brigid's back, taking advantage of their surprise. Nell might not be truly alone, but one woman, even with a windsteed and a flaming sword, against a dozen skilled men on dragons with icy breath? She narrowed her eyes. Those weren't good odds, but she wouldn't give Shane the sword. He couldn't touch the souls of the guardians inside it, desecrate them with his evil magic like he did their home. No matter what. The Shane she'd known had died years ago. She'd just be finishing the job.

He sneered. "So you healed the Tree, but does it matter? I'll still win and be king. Why die for a world that doesn't even want you, Nellwyn?"

"You'll never understand," she answered. "And the name's Nell."

Then she charged.

Nell clamped her legs tight to her steed as Brigid pounded across the green land and jumped off the cliff, snapping her wings open. The wind caught them, and they soared straight into the sky, Nell's sword drawn. The only way to win was to free the dragons first. Their Master Dragon needed his wings clipped.

The dragons mantled their wings and snarled icy mist. Nell and Brigid disappeared and reappeared above them in a flash. Tingling ran across her skin from the sky's magic. She breathed it in, let it build inside her. She focused on the sword, pushing the power through it.

"The sky and its magic will heal its children!" Nell shouted, and flames burst from her sword. She pointed the blade's tip at the flight of dragons below her. Magic billowed out from it, a glowing cloud of red, covering the dragons, sinking into their bodies.

Twelve of the dragons glowed with a silver hue that pushed the blue from their scales, first from their heads, then their necks, until red and orange shined across their entire bodies. Blackness filled those empty white eyes. Fire curled from their noses, and the men on their backs shouted as the dragons bucked and spun, dipping and diving above the mountain peak. The men fell from their dragons like coins falling from an upturned purse, landing hard on the ground. The dragons trumpeted and flew off.

But Shane's scaled beast remained solidly blue.

"You might have freed those dragons—for now—but you'll never defeat this one. He and I are bonded more closely than you can imagine," Shane said.

Nell compressed her lips and pulled her dagger with her left hand, swinging the fiery sword with her right. Flames roared along the blade. The steed needed no other instruction. They blinked in and out of space, arriving directly above him. They charged, the windsteed spiraling over and over in a plunging descent. If Nell could just get her sword on him once…

She lunged and aimed a jab at him, but he blocked her with a hard smack of his sword. The flames along her blade sputtered. She tried again, this time with an overhand swing. Their blades clashed, and her sword's fire went out completely. He laughed.

She pressed her attack anyway, Brigid flashing in and out of space to keep them safe. Nell sent them higher and higher into the sky to draw the fight beyond the reach of the recovering men below. Shane was just so fast, though, almost neutralizing the advantage of moving through space in a blink of an eye. He had his own magic in this fight.

He twirled his swords like a spinning wheel, knocking her blades aside one after another. She fought back, though her arms trembled with the force of each blow. Their weapons crashed and sparks flew. A line of fire zipped up the edge of her sword before fizzling out beneath the hiss of Shane's icy magic.

The thwack of his blade sent sheer agony running along her hands and up her arms. She held her sword and dagger tighter, and the windsteed shouldered closer to the icy blue skin of the changed dragon.

The dragon swiped its claws at Brigid, but she simply flickered in and out of the air in a heartbeat, letting the claws pass harmlessly through empty space. They reappeared on the other side of the blue beast, but the dragon turned to meet them without missing a beat, as if it could sense the windsteed before it appeared. Maybe it could. The dragon's anticipation of the windsteed's location was improving by the second.

The ring of their swords chimed like metal on a rock. Something more was necessary to free this dragon, to defeat Shane. A sword wasn't enough. The windsteed wasn't enough. She needed the power only this sword could muster.

Nell called to the guardians. *Help me find the magic!*

The answer was immediate. *The Tree has the power to heighten ours! It holds near limitless magic within.*

Brigid flashed to the Tree. Nothing happened.

The green leaves fluttered in the fiery huffs of wind from the windsteed's wings, but Nell's sword remained fireless.

"Come on!" she screamed.

Shane laughed. "Already abandoned by your benefactor?"

His dragon swung lazily in front of the Tree. An arrow flew past Nell's head from below, and Shane raised one hand to his men indulgently to halt the others from following suit.

"What, afraid to fight me, Shane?" she goaded him.

"You know what they say. Fool me once. You won't have my help to set that Tree ablaze again."

He was too clever by half. This was no Jasper, no Bentwood. Shane was smarter even than Jack. She'd have to trust the magic she'd always feared.

She met the furious eyes of the enslaved dragon who carried her enemy. Focusing on every ounce of magic in her heart and mind, she commanded the beast, "Breathe your frost! Now!"

"No!" Shane yelled, but it was too late.

The blue dragon sent a freezing blast at Nell. When it hit the branches below her, the flames flew up from the Tree, even higher than before. Nell and Brigid were completely engulfed in its fire.

The flames danced across her, like soft caresses, turning the world into a shimmering maze of red and orange. Sounds outside the roar were muted, but her own laughter rang in her ears.

The Tree's fire dissipated, but Nell's did not. As the branches withdrew their fire, Nell sat tall and straight on Brigid's back. Flames remained dancing over her entire body, coated her without consuming. Her sword blazed like a bonfire, though no heat touched her skin.

Shane drew back, jaw dropping, and then smiled. "I have power of my own."

He blew out a breath, and ice shot forth from his body like an expanding bubble, slamming against her flames and pushing her back. The two forces met and were immovable. Fire and ice, ice and fire. Sparks flew and the flames hissed. Nell concentrated harder, letting the power of the flames ride through her body. The ice crackled and exploded but simply reformed.

With a wild yell, she dove and swung her flaming sword again and again, moving too fast for his ice to reform. She swept her blade in a blazing arc, a perfect strike, but he blocked her with a chime of steel, his double swords forcing hers back above their heads. Ice reformed around him, pushing away her fire.

Sweat poured from her brow. The world beyond her was awash in wavering shades of red, orange, and white.

Her arms trembled, but still she pushed. The guardians had said the sword could defeat him. She had to do this.

But she was running out of energy. Fighting this way was like being consumed by the fire itself. Magic had a price. Magic always had a price. Her heart was sealed against his poison now, safe forever, but she could die by a sword as easily as anyone.

"Goodbye, Nellwyn," Shane said.

She felt him gathering his muscles and magic. She could flicker away to safety, but she wouldn't run from Shane anymore. She dug her knees harder and pushed back, increasing the flames along her skin, trusting the guardians and hoping for a miracle.

"Nell's not going anywhere," a familiar voice called.

Shane spun to see who had spoken, breaking contact and winging back a dragon-length.

Nell gasped. "Corbin!"

Hovering above the Tree of Life, Corbin rode on the back of a windsteed with wings glowing with fire. Without any direction from Nell, Brigid flashed out of space and reappeared next to Corbin before anyone else could move. The flames coating her had been banked by the jump, so her vision was perfectly clear.

The last she'd seen Corbin, he'd been writhing in pain. Now, his back was straight and his face was flushed with health. He looked different. Truly different.

The guardians whispered, *Magic healed his snow sprite attackers, but he healed his own heart by accepting he needs nothing more in life for happiness, not even more magic. He could then accept that you have your own vital role to fill. The fears he banished were just as toxic in their own way as Shane's touch.*

Corbin held a bow and looked ready to use it. Grace floated next to him.

Nell's knees went weak, and she clutched Brigid's mane. Corbin could die here, but she was still fiercely glad to see him.

Shane drew closer. "So, it's the fairy fanatic. You only escaped my sprites because of Nellwyn. This is a fight between real warriors."

Corbin ignored the taunt and spoke right to Nell. "It's hard to lie to yourself when you're staring death in the face. And there are some things worth fighting for. This is the right time and place."

He leaned forward across the space between their steeds and pressed something into her hand. An arrow. She immediately recognized the unicorn-horn-tipped arrow with its distinctive fletching, one of the last of its kind: Jack's magically powerful arrow she'd tucked away, never intending to use again. She stared at him, eyes wide.

"I thought you might need it. I'm sure Old Sam would be glad to be of service here," Corbin whispered with a small smile, squeezing her hand before he backed away.

He'd known, somehow, it might come to this. He'd

packed that arrow before they'd come on this trip, before he'd been attacked by the icy magic, before he'd wrestled with death. He'd understood and was willing to stand by her, even in a fight such as this.

Her heart beat so fast she feared it might explode.

Shane jeered, "Touching, but you've only flown to your death, Fairy Lover. My men below have their arrows ready."

His words were a punch in the stomach for Nell. It was her worst fear come to pass.

"Look again," Corbin smirked.

Grace and her fairies swirled around him then darted down near the men below with their bows, causing them to flinch and duck, dropping their weapons in fear for their lives.

Shane glared at the scene below. When he looked back at Nell, his black eyes were malevolent, wild with fury. "No matter. I'll still win. I'll kill you all, one by one."

His dragon spouted a curl of ice.

"I don't think so," Corbin said. And then he raised his hand and shouted, "For Aluvia!"

Over the mountainside rushed a herd of windsteeds in numbers impossible to count, a sea of beating wings of fire. Four of them in the lead carried Tristan, Phoebe, Sierra, and Micah, armed and ready for battle.

Nell's mouth went dry. Shane seemed just as shocked. Queenie and her host of little fairies flew off the mane of Sierra's steed and in circles around their keeper.

Corbin said to Nell, "We'll help you bear the power you've been given and will stay with you always. I promise."

For the first time, she believed it with her whole heart. Her friends had come. It was as magical a feeling as the flaming sword in her hands. The riderless windsteeds circled around the men below, blinking in and out like the lights of fireflies in the summer fields.

The men on the cliff didn't know what the windsteeds were but cursed the arrival of more fairies. Dragons were immune to their stings, but men were not. Retreat would be the smart strategy in this situation, but Nell doubted Shane would call for it. He couldn't leave a challenge like this unmet. His ego wouldn't allow it.

Shane scowled. "My own magic will protect me from theirs. Neither those old nags nor the little fairies can hurt me. I'm indestructible, Nellwyn. I can always create more dragons and take the ports one by one. But you can't hide forever, dashing away on your winged donkey like a pesky fly."

She told Sierra and Corbin, "Tell your fairies not to sting anyone if they can help it. He brings death, not us." She slid the unicorn-tipped arrow into her quiver, saved for a last resort.

They nodded, and Corbin looked heartened.

Compromise. Nell felt it was possible now.

"Well? Still want to try to take me?" she goaded Shane. Her friends' arrival had given her new strength. All they had to do was free his dragon and take down the man who'd enslaved it. Then this fight would be over.

The riderless windsteeds fenced in the men below, creating a barrier of fiery wings they could not push past. Corbin flew behind Nell so that he was guarding her back with a short sword he must have hidden in his bag. Phoebe and Tristan took a spot high above to keep an eye on the entire attack, and Sierra and Micah covered the danger from below. In the air, an attacker could come from any and all angles—and Nell's friends had all of them covered.

Shane's dragon came in fast, spiraling like a tornado. It blew a frozen breath that crackled. Flames rose from her, flowing along her skin, but her friends had no such protection. The dragon's breath could kill a human in a heartbeat, but her friends blinked out of space before they were hit, reappearing with the magical transporting ability of the windsteeds. Nell let out a breath of relief.

Shane lifted his hands up and shot an icy blast from his palms. It moved much faster than the dragon's breath. Screams came from the riderless windsteeds who weren't fast enough to get out of the way. Her friends' mounts spread their wings wider, encasing their riders within their flames. The wintery blast shattered against their fire.

Shane growled. He drew his swords and charged again, aiming straight for Nell. She wanted him to. This was between her and him.

His blades glowed a white-edged blue, but Nell met his with her own fiery one. The windsteeds screamed challenges, and his dragon roared back in answer. The wind rose like a fury, with wings buffeting the air into a bubbling cauldron. The fire of the windsteeds couldn't reach past the icy shield of Shane's magic to free the dragon. It was completely enslaved.

Behind his mask, Shane's eyes seemed to glow with rage and power. Her blade protected her but couldn't get past his defenses. Still, without it, she'd be dead already. The magic had already healed her heart. The rest of the promise would come to pass; she believed it. Today, peace would return to Aluvia.

Corbin was yelling at someone below them… Jasper, by the sounds of it.

"Him you can kill!" Nell shouted over her shoulder.

Corbin's sputtered laugh lifted her spirits.

Phoebe began to sing, and Micah joined her. They sang a song of peace and joy while Tristan sent his magic to unite with Micah's, and Sierra guarded them all with steel. Nell could see the magic of land and sea weaving together to form a shield that pulsed around her friends, their voices directing the magic where to go as the merfolk learned to do to protect their cities.

What a team they make, Nell thought with pride. Fighters and peace keepers, held together in the bonds of love, fighting back in a way that wouldn't leave a wake of destruction across their path.

Shane's tainted sky magic could not break through their shield. But perhaps the power of their combined magic could destroy his tie to the dragon, setting the poor beast free at last.

"Give me some room," she murmured to Brigid. The windsteed flickered in and out of space, appearing a dragon's-length away from Shane.

Nell slid the blade of Aluvia into the empty sheath on her back, patting the hilt once in thanks. She whipped out her bow. Her hand hesitated over which arrow to grab.

Corbin called from behind her, "Do it, Nell. Use the arrow. Take our magic and send it all. It's the only way."

She looked over her shoulder to him. He nodded once, hard, and she pulled the arrow he'd given her.

Shane sheathed his swords along his back. Raising

his fists above his head, he chanted, words Nell didn't understand, and an icy wind swirled around him, widening and growing darker.

Nell took careful aim, the windsteed staying as steady as possible in air churning from repeated icy attacks from Shane's dragon. A few fairies had apparently decided they were done with waiting and flew at him with their stingers ready, but they were pushed back by Shane's magic.

He smirked. "A flaming sword can't stop me, but you think that pathetic arrow will?"

Shane was a hard enemy, and it wasn't the arrow or sword that would stop him. She would. *She* was the sword. And she would be an instrument of justice today

Corbin yelled, "Now, Nell!"

In one quick movement, Nell drew back the string and sighted down her arm. The quietness that always guided her in battle stole over her. She no longer heard the screams of the windsteeds or the song of her friends. Everything faded to silence. Letting her breath out slowly, she saw it: colors dancing around the air, silvered swirls of red, burnished gold, and the deepest blue. Magic of Aluvia—land, sea, and sky—flowed into one powerful stream like a current around her.

The tree tattoo along her left arm flared silver, and she released the arrow with a twang that reverberated in her heart. She had just enough time to call all that swirling power to work together. And with that thought, the magic flew to the arrow and surrounded it in an incandescent rainbow glow. Sparkles of light trailed after it like a comet's tail.

The arrow, strengthened with three forms of magic, soared through the air in a heartbeat and crashed through the icy maelstrom brewing around Shane. The sharp point plunged into his chest. Red bloomed against him like a flower in winter.

Corbin shouted, and triumph surged through Nell. Then Shane laughed.

Grabbing the arrow by the fletching, he said, "That's the best you can do? Too bad. You had so much potential."

Shane yanked the arrow from his body, and blood seeped down his chest. The wound gaped open, and wisps of smoke lifted from blackening edges of the hole.

The sword could defeat the enemy and his frozen wasteland, the voice had said. But if she herself was the sword, then she would have to take his magic back directly. The arrow could only do so much.

The choice remaining wasn't one that Corbin would like, not at all.

She sent an image to her windsteed of what they needed to do. The steed shook her head and stamped her foot mid-air but did as Nell asked.

Nell winked out of existence before appearing directly next to Shane. She reached over and snagged him right off the back of his dragon and disappeared again before his dragon could respond.

Take us far away, Nell thought to the windsteed. The blackness was as dark as ever, and she shivered at the thought of being lost inside it with a madman.

Before she could take one full breath, they reappeared in a blue sky, above a remote island in the middle of the sea. An unfamiliar single mountain peak edged by cliffs stood alone in the icy water. The sun dazzled the sky above them, not hidden by a single cloud.

The land was high in the air, surrounded by water. Nell had no idea where they were, but Shane wouldn't be able to leave this place without her. She landed and pushed him to the ground.

"If you wanted to duel with just the two of us, you had only to ask," Shane said, climbing back to his feet and drawing one sword. He laughed, but under that laugh Nell could hear it—he was finally afraid.

"Why don't you give up?"

"I've defeated you without my dragon before. Come down off that horse, and I'll do it again."

The battle rage she'd once leaned on for strength had disappeared, and she was glad. She didn't need it. It was just about the mission now.

Nell eyed the black smoke seeping from Shane's chest. The arrow wound seemed to be weakening him.

She patted Brigid in thanks and slid to the ground. "I'll offer mercy if you lay down your swords."

"I don't need your mercy." One corner of his mouth lifted in a sneer.

Who was this man, really? The brilliant weapons instructor she'd known seemed to have been swallowed up entirely by hate.

"Let's try this again. Will you give yourself up? Set your dragon free? The other dragons are free now, but yours remains bound, and your wound will weaken you enough for me to win."

"I couldn't set my dragon free if I wanted to. He's a part of me and has been since he bit me. I didn't ask for that, but I've lived with it." Shane reached up slowly with his free hand, and Nell backed away, drawing the sword she'd come so far for.

He pulled his mask from his face.

Shane was handsome many years ago, she remembered. He could still be so today. The thick white scar marred his cheek and neck, but the fierce scar didn't make him frightening. His eyes did. She swallowed hard.

His eyes were black, full of magic, even darker than the last time they'd fought. Her long-ago sword master had also become a master of magic, but the kind that had slowly destroyed his soul.

"You never told me what happened, Shane. All this time, I thought you were dead."

"Aye, I was a potential threat to their little thrones. They thought they'd kill me off with poison, since none could touch me with a blade. Of course, I'd known that day was coming and had built up a tolerance to Jack's poisons over the years. I escaped but knew there'd be no rest for me while they hunted for me, so I left for the wilderness to make my fortune and show Bentwood his mistake in tossing me aside. I found myself attacked by a dragon instead, and when he bit me, he set something free in me that must have been waiting. I had magic, like none I'd ever heard of."

Nell didn't lower her sword, but she listened.

"I bided my time, here in the Ice-Locked Land, gathering strength, and then I heard stories of you. How well I remembered you, Nellwyn. Such a fighter, working for that gutter snake Jack."

"Jack respected you."

"Jack respected no one. But he knew how to use people, like he used you and me. You had more talent in one sword arm than he had in his whole body. I was pleased to see you come into power, until you started convincing people they were second-class citizens to magical creatures." He scowled, tossed the mask aside, and drew his other blade with the ringing of metal on metal.

She took a step back. "That's not our message. We say only we're all equal."

He could attack at any second, but she didn't want to

fight him if she didn't have to. Not now. She couldn't leave him here—he could call another dragon and escape—but she'd rather give him a chance to change his mind, out of respect for the man he'd once been, the mentor she'd needed as a fatherless girl fighting for her family.

Shane said, "You've taken our dignity."

"Equality only feels like a loss of freedom when you've had all the privilege and power."

She studied his expression to discern if he understood at all. He would have, once upon a time. But now his eyes weren't quite right, even beyond the magic.

The voice from the sword whispered, *You did well, Guardian. But now do what you must. You are free of reprisal.*

"So, trading human dignity for magic, is it worth all you've suffered, Nellwyn? Having a responsibility no one else can fathom as the so-called prophetess? You'll never be normal. Is it worth being alone?" He gave her a slow, horrible smile.

"I'm never alone," she replied without thinking, and the windsteed billowed its wings. Flame surrounded them both, spread to cover Shane as well.

Shane stumbled back, dropping his swords as the handles glowed bright red from the heat. He raised his hands, and ice formed around him like a shield, but Nell aimed her sword at him, and flames shattered the ice. He collapsed with a roar, palms up, burn marks clear.

She walked toward him, and he scrambled back to the edge of the cliff.

Can I take his magic? Leave him without fangs? Heal him? she asked the voice through the sword.

Possibly. He'd have to want the healing.

It was worth a try. His magic had been wrongfully taken all these years, and Nell was a creature of the air now too. She could end it.

Nell reached out her empty hand to him and concentrated. She envisioned the magic lifting from him, pouring out from the arrow wound. Red mist rose slowly like steam from the wound, coiling and twisting.

"What are you…What are you doing?" Shane cried out, frantically grabbing at his chest, trying to hold the magic in.

"I'm taking back what you stole," Nell replied softly. The red mist floated to her in a delicately curling line and disappeared into her hand in a steady stream, tying the two of them together.

She felt no hatred. No anger. This was simply justice, calmly administered. Shane wasn't safe with this much power. Their world would be safer because of her choice right now.

"Nooo!" he cried.

She felt his hold on the power, but it wasn't enough anymore. The magic continued to drain from him, his eyes fading from black to a dark brown, then to a deep green. They were lovely eyes, or would have been, if it wasn't for the grief and fury in them.

As the last red ribbon of magic was pulled from his body, her new tattoo flared red before fading back to silver. She would give back this magic to his dragon and hope it healed the beast.

Blood shined deep red on Shane's chest. He blinked and groaned, pulling himself to a kneeling position, hands pressed hard against the ground near his dropped blades.

She readied her sword, but she heard one whispered word.

"Free..."

She froze. "Shane?"

"To be... finally... free of the madness that came with the bite." He looked all around, no longer glaring. Relief filled his face instead of rage.

He continued, shaking his head, "It's... incredible. A glimpse of the sky after years in a dark dungeon. But my dragon is still captive to me from our binding. My power over him is too complete for him to be freed while I yet live. I never intended it, nor did he, but we've lived with what the magic wrought between us."

This man sounded like the one she remembered from years past—tough, but fair. Honest. Respectable. Perhaps without the dragon's magic in him, he'd returned to sanity. She'd seen stranger things.

Compassion and hope softened her heart. He had not asked for the burden of power, just as she hadn't.

"We can do a lot of things to help you—"

"You've done enough. Thank you, Nellwyn… Nell. I know what needs to be done."

Shane straightened his shoulders, his eyes bright with a new light. "My dragon has earned its freedom. And this way, I will always fly!" With those words, he jumped to his feet and dashed away from her outstretched hand.

"No, wait!" Nell shouted.

Shane leapt off the cliff and extended his arms as if they were wings. He seemed to hover for a moment, as if he could truly soar through the air through sheer determination. But then he fell. He fell far and fast, landing in the icy water at such speed not even a true dragon would have survived.

Nell breathed hard, staring down at the dark spot in the ocean. The sea would claim his body and use it to nourish life. She picked up his mask, tracing the wooden carving.

She imagined him as he had been years ago, laughing, strong, arrogant, determined. He'd helped her believe in herself, gave her skills she'd needed to survive and thrive.

With a sigh of regret, she shook her head. She'd always feared losing everyone she loved like she'd lost her father. Being left completely alone. But Shane really had been alone all these years, alone in his power and strength in the Ice-Locked Lands. Power and strength weren't enough to keep you warm.

That's what friends were for.

She slid onto the back of Brigid, caressing her neck. "Thank you," Nell whispered to her beautiful mount. The beast whinnied, and the two of them disappeared.

Back at the tree, Nell found mass chaos.

The windsteeds and fairies had penned in Shane's dragon, keeping its icy mist from reaching anyone. The fairies lined the windsteeds' manes, so the manes appeared to be entwined with tiny lights.

The beast was screaming, tossing its head. Its connection to Shane had been destroyed, but it still lacked its own magic. Windsteeds, as agents of the air, had authority the dragon would obey, once the corruption of Shane could be healed and the dragon's magic restored.

"Nell! It's Nell!" cried out someone, Sierra from the sound of it. And then Nell was lifted off the back of Brigid and engulfed in a tight hug against a familiar chest. Corbin's sweet scent of honey and cinnamon wafted around her. She laid her head against him.

"I ought to kill you!" he said into her hair.

"If Shane couldn't kill me, you sure can't," Nell countered.

He stiffened. "Where's he now?"

"Dead," she replied, meeting his eyes. "After I took away the magic that drove him mad, he jumped to his death to free his dragon. He sacrificed his life for this poor creature, but I suspect Shane didn't want to live without his magic, either. It was all he'd known for so long."

"What a sad decision," Phoebe said, who'd chosen life without magic herself for the sake of merfolk.

"Not everyone is as fortunate as we are," Nell said. "We're together. We'll never be alone. And I, for one, intend to make sure it stays that way!"

She paced to Shane's dragon through the windsteeds and fairies without fear. None of their magic could hurt her. The dragon paced with agitation, roaring every few steps. It looked at her with eyes made ancient from years of servitude. Nell's heart cramped with pity, and she called her magic to surround her with its flames. Her own light reflected in the beast's white eyes. Then Nell touched its cold flank and let the magic she'd taken from Shane flow back into the beast.

Without Shane's connection keeping the power locked away from it, the magic knew its home and rushed into the dragon with relief. The beast's scales warmed to the touch, and when she opened her eyes, the dragon was bright red. It bugled and a plume of flame rocketed into the sky. It touched her head with its snout, perhaps in thanks, then shook off her touch and rose to the sky, flying off, Nell presumed, to its home. Dragons should be free, like all creatures of Aluvia, magical or otherwise. But the windsteeds would watch over them now to keep them from destroying what they shouldn't.

Nell lifted her palm and concentrated. Red and silver mist lifted from her hand, and the rest of Shane's stolen magic dissipated into the sky, where it belonged. She didn't feel empty. She knew the magic of the air would come to her call whenever she needed it. It belonged to her, and she belonged to it in a way Shane had not.

Without the presence of their master, many of Shane's men had revolted and escaped. But, happily, Jasper hadn't. He was tied against the Tree, crying like a baby.

Nell aimed her sword at him, allowing a few tendrils of fire to lick down the blade and curl right under his nose.

"Well, Jasper. Do I need to remove you permanently from our world, or can you agree to stop making trouble?"

He shook, gazing up at Nell. She let the fire engulf her once more and stood before him, shrouded in red and silver flames, sword extended.

He wept harder. "I promise, Nell. I promise!"

Corbin said, "You're gonna trust that weasel?"

She glanced at him. He was smiling at her, awe and love shining clearly from his eyes.

"I know where he lives if he ever changes his mind."

Carrick sat on a rock nearby, head clasped in his hands. The older alchemist had turned himself in after Nell had taken off with Shane. Carrick's boney shoulders slumped; his scarred hands trembled.

Pursing her lips, Nell moved to his side. "So, you survived."

"I'm sorry, Nell. I should've been brave enough to stand up to Jasper, not get all caught up in my elixirs, but I was a coward."

She'd walked the same path he did, for much the same reasons. He used to have a family. By the time they died, he was trapped in the Flight crew. For a crew member, he was as honorable as he could be and still live.

"You know, Carrick, if you want to make it right, we could use someone with skills like yours." The words fell from her mouth before she could consider them. Apparently, mercy was easier for her than it once had been. She offered him her hand. His eyes widened at the tattooed tree along her arm. Her palm still held a silver scar line, a reminder that it was never too late for redemption, not for anyone.

"I'll teach you the ways of balancing and healing without abusing our world's magic. Treasures we've barely touched and centuries of knowledge are stored in their ancient temples."

The voice spoke to her sharply. *The guardians have always been women.*

Nell thought back to them through the sword: *Didn't you say it was time for a change? If I can have a second chance, so should he. I'll take on this job, but I'm doing it* my *way. We'll live among others, too, including as many who wish to learn, so we never forget what we once knew.*

A feeling of surprise came from the presence of the guardian voice, which sounded again like the single deep, rich voice of the last four years.

And so the newest of us teaches the oldest, the voice whispered, with a feeling of quiet acceptance... and pride.

Nell stood taller as joy pressed inside her like a bubble expanding outward. Her eyes stung at the stunned hope on the man's weathered face.

"Me? But, Nell—"

"You can choose a new path now, Carrick." Her windsteed whickered behind her and touched her soft nose to Nell's cheek.

He wept, this jaded man still broken inside, but Nell knew he could be healed.

She had been, after all.

And the Tree of Life stood tall and vibrant, healed and made new, tying together all of Aluvia's magic, balancing the ebb and flow of the three strands.

Magic could heal them all.

Corbin stood alone, a short distance away. Nell couldn't stop thinking of how he'd looked rising into the air on his windsteed, eyes bright with determination. He'd risked his life for her. For all of Aluvia.

She walked to him and simply wrapped him in a tight hug. "I'm sorry for the things I said to you, before. I might have been right that time, but you were right to be worried about me. Thank you for telling me the hard things I needed to hear."

"You'd do the same for me. We all watch out for each other. Everything's going to be fine. In fact, do you want to go check on your family? I imagine you'd like to make sure all is well with them." He stepped back with one last squeeze, and motioned toward Brigid, who could take them back to Covenstead in the blink of an eye.

"Soon," Nell promised. She couldn't wait to invite her sisters to join her as guardians, but there was something she needed to do first, something long overdue.

Taking a deep breath, she reached into her pocket and pulled out the dried steel thistle flower. Holding it out to him, she said, "Corbin Lannon, you've wanted me to lay down my sword for the longest time. Now that I've picked one up that will stay with me always, are you willing to accept me, steel and all? Because I love you more than words can say and would be honored to spend my life with you."

She could barely choke the words out. Being vulnerable wasn't easy, but there was a time for armor and a time to set it aside. She left her heart open and exposed there on that cliff, with magic at her fingertips and hope thrumming like rising music in her soul.

He took the flower with a hand that shook just a little. "I fought to stay with you through the pain of his dark magic. I see things I couldn't before, but I've always loved you as you are. You're like your own weapons—strong, beautiful, and dangerous if needed."

Tears trickled down from her cheeks, and she let them. Twice in one day. It was a record.

Corbin smiled. "Will you marry me, Nell Brennan? If we need to live here, or travel the whole world, I'll follow you anywhere."

"If you mean that, I'll say yes," she warned. She laid her hand over his, covering the flower, uniting them both.

"You'll never be alone," he said again, joy lighting his face.

"Nor will you," she replied. Her heart would break if she lost him, but she'd no longer keep her heart safely locked behind walls. She wouldn't live a life of fear.

We are, all of us, never alone even in our darkest moments, the voice whispered clearly through the sword.

Her life would be shared with that voice because of her calling, and she was glad for it.

Nell swallowed the lump in her throat and smiled at all the friends who had gathered around, including them in the special moment. Corbin kissed her lightly and then held her tight.

"About time!" Phoebe whooped, and everyone clapped and cheered.

"The mark of the guardians," Corbin murmured with a smile, running his fingers along the silver tree on her arm, tracing down to her fingertips where the branches reached. "It suits you."

"You know they'll be calling you a goddess now, Nell. Lighting yourself on fire? Nice trick. Makes my fairies look like child's play," Sierra teased.

"Oh, I think we all know I'm no goddess." Nell smirked, and everyone laughed.

"What are you then, Nell?" Micah asked, his voice low, gently challenging.

She held Corbin's hand but raised her sword. Her windsteed stood behind her. Her power gathered within, rising to his question, demanding an answer. This was the magic that would lead her, give her purpose, and bring her joy all the rest of her life and beyond.

Her voice was strong and completely her own when she answered, "I'm the one who'll stand between the magic of Aluvia and its enemies. I'm the one who'll train others to heal and protect our world. I'm a warrior, the sky's champion. But at the heart of it all, I'm Aluvia's guardian."

Her proclamation and Corbin's answering, proud smile healed any last kernel of doubts she had about the path her future would take. She laughed out loud. Flames flew up the sword and into the clouds, but they weren't nearly as bright as the fire burning inside her.

The End

ACKNOWLEDGMENTS

Many thanks to Snowy Wings Publishing for this second edition of DRAGON REDEEMER. I'm grateful to several author friends who helped me find this new home for my books, especially Clare Dugmore, Matthew Cox, and Lyssa Chiavari.

The first edition was published by Curiosity Quills Press.Thank you to my editor, Krystal Wade, who worked on the whole series. The lovely map is courtesy of Ricky Gunawan, and the beautiful cover is by Amalia Chitulescu.

Heartfelt thanks also goes to: Lara Barrett, Ann Miller, Jeannine Johnson Maia, Christina Nelson, Stacy Webb, Heidi Boyd, Valerie Collins, and Elizabeth Arroyo. Special thanks to Carol Pavliska, friend and author.

To my family, both immediate and extended. I love you!

Finally, thank you so much to those who read the first two books and told me how much you loved Nell and wanted to hear her story. I actually drafted *Dragon Redeemer* in 2015, so it's taken a long time to reach this final point. I hope you enjoy it!

Thank you for reading!

ABOUT THE AUTHOR

Amy writes fantasy and light science fiction for young readers and the young at heart. She is the author of the World of Aluvia series and SHORTCUTS (CBAY Books, 2019), for ages ten and up. She is also a former reading teacher and school librarian.

As an Army kid, she moved eight times before she was eighteen, so she feels especially fortunate to be married to her high school sweetheart. Together they're raising two daughters in Texas.

A perfect day for Amy involves rain pattering on the windows, popcorn, and every member of her family curled up in one cozy room reading a good book.

You can find Amy online at www.amybearce.com and at:

Other Books by Amy Bearce

SHORTCUTS (CBAY Books, 2019)

When psychic powers and secrets collide, no one is safe.

Parker is a fun-loving girl with a secret supernatural gift of psychic empathy who tries to turn heartbreak to happiness when a new student arrives with a mysterious, tragic past. But her psychic power goes haywire, threatening to expose dangerous secrets… starting with her own.

World of Aluvia Series

Fairy Keeper

Sierra hates being a fairy keeper, but unfortunately, it's her destiny. In the world of Aluvia, little fairies aren't cute or friendly—more like irritable and dangerous. But when the fairy queens mysteriously vanish, the consequences threaten everything Sierra loves. She will stop at nothing to find the missing fairies, but the journey will risk even more than she thought possible.

Mer-Charmer

To save her beloved merfolk from an ancient sea beast, 14-year-old Phoebe dives into the ocean and discovers her own magic. But when the beast decides she is the tastiest prey in the ocean, she must learn to control her wayward sea magic, earned at a shocking cost, or lose the very people she loves the most.

The Falling, by T. Damon

In the mystical first volume of The Forest Spirit series, an entire enchanted Forest is swept into a drastic upheaval when a protective Higher Spirit falls from grace and succumbs to his negative Spirit's counterpart. Now it's up to a group of the smallest and most oblivious of creatures, the nymphs, to save their Forest and reinstate the spiritual balance of good and evil. Narena, her brother Nyxen, and debonair warrior Kellen join forces with a sassy faery, a wise salamander, and three human witches to discover that even the tiniest of beings can have an enormous impact on the world around them. Available now!

Trial by Song (Book One of the Faery Trials Series)

by Alicia Gaile

As the youngest of seven brothers born with magical gifts, Jack's often felt he has something to prove. But revealing their powers makes them targets of the fae, who will stop at nothing to hide their existence from mankind.

In spite of the danger, Jack sneaks out on Halloween to compete in the Battle of the Bands, shattering his family's rule to guard their secret at all costs. When Jack gets dragged through a portal and winds up in Faerie, he finds an ancient relic he simply can't leave behind. But escaping from Faerie is only the beginning as the harp's former owner is determined to see Jack pay for his crime.

With old enemies returned new enemies awaken, revealing the Sorleys aren't the only family in Straifield with ties to the fae. Available now!

www.snowywingspublishing.com